"Although thoroughly modern in content, Alan Brennert's fiction has an old-fashioned quality to it, old-fashioned in the best sense of the word. The author of *Time and Chance* demonstrates in his new collection of short stories, *Her Pilgrim Soul*, that he knows how to write about love, loss and sacrifice . . .

"The stories mix classical with popular mythology, and their settings range from pre-Aztec Mexico to Disneyland, from modern Greece to a dead Manhattan of the distant future. Almost all work exceedingly well, and the title story is especially memorable, a tender tale of an unhappy scientist who conjures a woman's soul in a hologram."

— *San Francisco Chronicle*

"Perhaps the best and most effective story in the book is 'The Third Sex' . . . searingly honest . . . this piece is damned close to being the sort of humane masterpiece that [Theodore] Sturgeon would have given a finger or two to write."

— *Locus*

"Brennert's stories are character-driven and touched with romanticism. It's to his credit that the romantic streak never slips over the line into bathos; sentiment runs deeply through his prose, but the rough edge of reality is always present as well. . . . Brennert proves himself, time and again, to be one of the best contemporary fantasists we have working in the field today."

— Charles de Lint

Tor Books by Alan Brennert

Her Pilgrim Soul and Other Stories
Kindred Spirits
Time and Chance

HER PILGRIM SOUL

ALAN BRENNERT

TOR ®

A TOM DOHERTY ASSOCIATES BOOK
NEW YORK

HER PILGRIM SOUL AND OTHER STORIES

Copyright © 1990 by Alan Brennert

A Tor Book
Published by Tom Doherty Associates, Inc.
175 Fifth Avenue
New York, N.Y. 10010

TOR® is a registered trademark of Tom Doherty Associates, Inc.

Cover art by Boris Vallejo

ISBN: 0-812-53195-7

First edition: December 1990
First mass market printing: April 1992

Printed in the United States of America

0 9 8 7 6 5 4 3 2 1

ACKNOWLEDGMENTS

"Her Pilgrim Soul," "Healer," and "Voices in the Earth" first appeared on the CBS-TV series *The Twilight Zone*. "Voices in the Earth" also appeared in *Rod Serling's Twilight Zone Magazine*, and "Healer" in *The Magazine of Fantasy and Science Fiction*. "Queen of the Magic Kingdom" first appeared in *New Voices III* (Berkley Books), "Jamie's Smile" in *The Ides of Tomorrow* (Little, Brown), "The Third Sex" in *Pulphouse*, "Steel" in *Cobblestone*, and "Sea Change" in *The Magazine of Fantasy and Science Fiction*. Copyright © 1976, 1977, 1980, 1987, 1988, 1989 by Alan Brennert.

For Asha, who inspired it,
and Anne Twomey, who embodied it;
And for Phil, Jim, Rock, and Harlan,
who helped me say goodbye.

AUTHOR'S NOTE

It's far easier to dedicate a novel than it is a book of short stories; a novel usually has one set of emotional associations, one or two people who are linked in the author's mind with that particular work. A collection, on the other hand, spans years, and each story is a remembrance, of sorts, of a time and a place and a person, or several people. (This may be why writers so love short story collections; they are, in a way, a journal of the author's life, often decipherable to no one but himself.) An extended dedication and thanks, then, to: Carter Scholz, Asenath Hammond, Daniel P. Dern, Terry Caldwell, Candy Mishler Fresacher, Richard Kyle, Phoebe Jackson, Cheryl Cuttineau, Pat Murphy, Greg Bear, Michael D. Toman, and Nicole Ballard; Kristoffer Tabori, Wendy Girard, Gary Cole, Wes Craven, Bruno George, and William Goldstein; and to the memories of Leonard N. Isaacs—a good and gentle man who meant a great deal to more writers than he might ever have imagined—and Terry Carr, who gave Jamie a home, and first introduced me to Charity Payne.

CONTENTS

Sea
Change

A violet dusk was descending on Mykonos town, a brief
moment of color on an island usually dominated by the
white of its cubist buildings and the dun brown of the surrounding hillsides; residents whitewash these walls twice every day,
and only in their trim—the pastel blue of a doorway, the pale
green of a balcony or banister, the vivid red of a church
cupola—were brighter hues permitted. Yet that was exactly what
made Mykonos so beautiful: during the day, the bleached white
buildings blazing in the sun made the deep red of window
shutters all the more striking; a small dinghy—its hull a dark red,
its gunwale and interior a bright aqua—seemed all the lovelier
for sitting on a tan stretch of beach, sand the same color as the
rocky hillsides, or the wooden trim of shops and restaurants.

Tonight I sat at a small table in one of the larger tavérnas
along the harborfront, nursing an oúzo and staring out at the
fishing boats rocking back and forth along the crescent-shaped

bay, lights atop their masts snapping on about the same time as those in buildings all over the town. Blue-black waves slapped soundlessly against the docks; in the distance, a motorboat put out from one of two huge cruise liners anchored in the bay, but there was no roar of engines, no rush of water as its bow cut through the foam. Gulls swooped silently across the surface of the water; tourists by the dozens hurried past the open-air café, seeming to glide noiselessly over the cobbled walks, their mouths opening in pantomimed laughter and wordless chatter.

I suddenly became aware of a waiter standing close by, stepping into my field of vision; I imagine he'd been trying to get my attention for some time. I looked up, catching him in mid-sentence.

—vradinó, kírie?

I don't lip-read Greek all that well, but I gathered he was asking if I wanted to order dinner. I was on my third oúzo and any thought of food was still remote. I shook my head, the waiter nodded, looking annoyed, and I decided it was probably time to move on. I left two hundred drachmas on the table and joined the hundreds of tourists crowding Akti Kambáni, the esplanade fronting the tiny harbor. It felt even stranger, here, in their midst, than it had watching them; I couldn't even delude myself, however briefly, that the three oúzos were responsible. I still hadn't gotten used to this damned silence; I kept expecting to hear words emerging from the mouths of those around me, kept expecting to hear the shuffle of feet as they—as I—walked past the boutiques and bazaars along the waterfront. Even now, six months later.

I should never have agreed to the stand in Rome. I should have listened to my manager, to my friends; but it had been so long since I'd been on tour, so long since I'd released an album that *justified* a tour . . . I'd never been a Top 40 singer, my voice was competent but unexceptional; my strength was in my writing. People bought my songs, not me, but for ten years it had been enough to sustain a modest career and a comfortable income. I cut three albums, had one single that hovered around No. 85 on the charts for a week or two back in '78, toured much of the States and most of Europe (where I'd always been more popular than in my own country) . . . until it all went away.

Not all at once, of course. You don't wake up one day and discover you can't write anymore; there are a lot of dead ends and aborted attempts along the way, dreadful songs that your own label won't release, half-started efforts not worth the time. It took me maybe two years to realize that I'd run dry. I still toured, but without new material I simply recycled past successes, and slowly but surely the audiences dwindled and the bookings grew fewer and further between. At the end of those two years, I gave up; better, I thought, to be remembered as a flash-in-the-pan than propped up every few years as a nostalgia item. I had enough money to live comfortably: I finally had reason to thank the naive young twit who'd bought outright his house in Sonoma upon the sale of his first major album, because with no mortgage payments to worry about I had sufficient savings to live, modestly, for some years. Even my ex-wife had remarried: good-bye, alimony. And so I retreated, secluding myself, losing myself, in dope, and women, and—when I'd tired of both—fitful attempts at writing a novel. For, oh, the next eight years.

Then, suddenly—just a little over a year ago—it came back. I'd put aside the novel, nagged by a fragment of melody that refused to leave my head; in an attempt at exorcism I scribbled down a few bars . . . and in three hours had a completed lead sheet—chorus, bridge, and coda. Along the way I took some of the words I'd been fruitlessly trying to stitch together into a book, and inside of a day had both lyric and music. Six weeks later, in a recording studio in Marin County, I was cutting a single for the first time in ten years.

Others followed; the dam had broken. I tried out a few on local engagements, and the reaction was enthusiastic enough to kick me into overdrive. Soon I had an album, and my label was talking a tour of Europe, my old reliable audience: Amsterdam, Salzburg, Munich, Brussels . . . and Rome. God damn it.

The meltémi was blowing hot and dry, as it always did in August, but far from sweating and complaining about it, as most tourists did, I welcomed it; in the absence of sound, I'd learned to appreciate other sensations. I loved the hot brush of the wind on my face as I window-shopped along the harborfront; I savored the warm afterglow of the oúzo; I lit a cigarette and took in a deep pull of smoke, exhaling it slowly. I smelled the fresh salt air, I watched the sun set behind a slowly turning windmill, I fed the pelicans at water's edge and smiled at their boldness in coming up to take the bits of bread I offered them.

I bought a watercolor in an art shop and had it mailed back to my niece in San Francisco, then, as night fell over Mykonos town, turning the violet sky as black as the waters slapping against the fishing boats, I decided I was ready for dinner. I found another tavérna, near the town square, across from a piano club; this time, thankfully, the waiter spoke English and I was able to read his lips without difficulty.

—What can I get for you? he asked, smiling. —Some oúzo, perhaps?

I knew when I'd reached my limit. I ordered moussaka and a Greek salad sprinkled with black olives and feta cheese, relishing the meal as I did the wind, the sea air, the smell of food from adjacent restaurants. I concentrated on those sensations with such intensity that I almost forgot about the other, missing, sense. At least until halfway through my meal, when I saw musicians with instruments and amplifiers starting to warm up, and I felt a knot forming in my stomach, tension coiling in my chest. For an instant I wanted to bolt and run, but common sense prevailed: I hadn't even finished dinner. And besides, was this what I was going to do the rest of my life—run away every time I saw a goddamned woodwind? No. I had to start learning to live with it sometime; might as well be now. I looked down, took a forkful of moussaka, and tried to focus all my attention on the food, the wind, the briny air.

I didn't have to look up to know that the band had begun their first set; I felt it. I felt the big amplifier pounding out a heavy bass, resonating in the pit of my stomach; I felt the beat—a fast rock number—like a blind man reads braille. Except that braille is closer to the actual experience of reading—gives you the same information, more or less—than this. I felt the beat, but the melody was lost to me; I knew the meter, but not the measure. It was a tantalizing, frustrating kind of half-vision, and despite myself I started eating more quickly, hoping to finish before the band began its next number. There was a short pause after they finished—I applauded, politely, with the rest of the diners, then returned to my meal, only to look up when I felt the music begin again.

It was different, this time; no hard percussion and aggressive stings of the synthesizer, but the distinctive 7/4 meter of traditional Greek music. I looked up and saw that only the keyboard man and guitarist were playing, and it wasn't an instrumental, but a vocal; a young woman stood before them, microphone in hand, singing to what seemed to be rapt attention all round.

She was extraordinarily beautiful: long, shining black hair, piercing olive-green eyes, rose-petal lips that opened and closed silently as she sang. She sang mostly in Greek, only a few words here and there in English; I could make out only a few snatches of lyric. It didn't matter. For the first time since the accident, I found myself watching a singer without pain, frustration, anger, or envy; not just because she was beautiful, but because I *couldn't* hear her sing, and, stripped of voice and melody, I could see the *way* she sang. There was pain and sadness in her eyes, and in her face; her body swayed like a reed in a wind, and that was how I began to see her—fragile, vulnerable, sad. I felt an instant empathy for her, whether the result of her own expressiveness or my own melancholy, I don't know; but for the first time it didn't bother me that I could no longer hear, because I *understood*, nonetheless.

She finished to what appeared to be tumultuous applause from the largely male audience; most looked like locals, not tourists, and by their manner seemed familiar with the tavérna staff. They had obviously been here, and heard her, before. She accepted their applause with a small bow and a short nod, but there was something odd in both—I knew what it was like to hear applause, and even though I might never hear it again, I knew what should have been on her face, and it wasn't there. She seemed to take no pleasure in the approbation; her smile was pleasant, gracious, but somehow artificial. She quickly launched into a second song, more expansive, her head tilting back as she hit her high notes. This, like the first, was a traditional Greek bouzouki number—Greek love songs always seem to be mournful, or bittersweet, but it was more than just tradition I saw in her face. I saw again the pain, and—was it loneliness, or did I just *want* it to be loneliness?—in her eyes. Assuming it was there . . . assuming I wasn't just projecting my own isolation and hurt . . . what, I wondered, could such a young, beautiful woman have experienced to evoke such terrible sorrow?

I found her attractive, but by the end of the third song the reaction of the audience—more animated and appreciative with each succeeding song—was beginning to depress me. What were they hearing that so transfixed them? What kind of voice elicited such enthusiasm? I didn't know. I could never know. And so rather than torment myself, I paid my check and slipped quietly out of the café between songs.

Was it my imagination, or did the young woman cast an odd, puzzled look at me? I couldn't tell, and I didn't linger. I went back to window-shopping along the esplanade; it was a little after eleven and I didn't much feel like returning to my room at the Petassos Hotel.

Eventually, though, the memory of those olive-green eyes and shining black hair, that haunted face and pained smile, drew me back to the tavérna just as the band was packing up its equipment and the café was starting to close. Toward the rear of the restaurant I saw a crowd of perhaps a dozen people—mostly men, ranging in age from early twenties to late sixties—clustered around something or someone; as I drew closer one of the men moved, allowing me to see that the nucleus around which they were all orbiting was, in fact, the singer I had seen earlier.

A more motley assortment of stage-door Johnnies would have been hard to find. Most seemed to be tourists, Americans, Frenchmen, Brits; one middle-aged man in a loud shirt and white slacks was getting his cocktail napkin autographed, gazing at the singer with schoolboy infatuation. His frumpy wife didn't look terribly pleased, and the moment the singer finished signing her name, the wife looped an arm through her husband's and practically dragged him away.

It was the same with the others—some wanted autographs, some were smiling and nodding and moving their lips in a manner I recognized from my own concerts, doubtless telling her how much they enjoyed her performance, et cetera et cetera. And there were the younger men I'd tagged earlier as locals, for whom this was not their first visit. But what struck me most about these fans—returnees and first-timers alike—was the almost universal enchantment in their eyes; the kind of ardor one usually expects to find in fans of rock singers and movie stars. Clearly, they were all smitten by her, and she, for her part—

She accepted the attention graciously enough, but . . . maybe it's just because I've been on that side of the footlights myself, but I thought I could detect something just a bit forced about her smile . . . something infinitely weary in the way she took each napkin or brochure or slip of paper and signed it, smiling and nodding politely at the man who'd presented it. She was used to this, this kind of admiration; maybe it had been a long day, maybe she wasn't feeling well, but she was clearly weary of it all. My empathy as a fellow performer—or ex-performer—won out over my hormones; I turned and headed out the door, not wishing to add to her entourage, though not without noting her name on the small poster announcing that night's performance: Leucosia. Leucosia Polodori.

I started wending my way through the narrow, twisting streets of the village—or Chora, as these tiny towns were called here—up the steep inclines, under balconies on which fresh laundry hung to dry, around people laughing and shouting, silently, at one another. I was diverted for a little while by a serious-looking chess game being played out in front of someone's whitewashed home: two old men solemnly contemplating the board, seeming almost to be living at a slower rate of time than the rest of us; there were neighbors gathered around, and every time one of the old men would make a move the crowd would nod and talk among themselves, debating, perhaps, which man held the upper hand. Obviously a grudge match of some proportions, and one on which not a few bets were placed. Amused, I watched for five or ten minutes, until it became apparent that they—and I—might be here all night, and I moved along.

I was walking up a street with the impressive name of

Ayion Tessarákonda when I caught my first glimpse of them: two people standing in the middle of a narrow, intersecting street, arguing. You didn't need ears to recognize a Greek altercation: their bodies did most of the arguing. An intense young Greek man wearing a polo shirt and Americans jeans, and a beautiful young woman—with shining black hair and olive-green eyes— trying to fend off his unwelcome advances . . .

At first I just stood there, not knowing if I was perhaps watching a lovers' spat, something I should steer well clear of; but the longer I watched the more I detected genuine anger and resentment in her face, and, perhaps more importantly, that same starry-eyed adulation in his. She tried to walk away, but he grabbed her by the arm, half threateningly, half imploringly. She tried to wrest loose, to no effect, and I found myself hurrying toward them. They looked up at my approach, irritation flashing in the man's eyes at what I suppose he perceived as competition.

—Miss? I said. —Are you all right?

At least that's what I heard myself say in my mind. I spoke in English, since she'd spoken it in the café; but before she could respond the young man turned to her, a look of rage on his face, and shook her arm violently. He was speaking in Greek, so I could only make out a word here and there; in lip-reading you only catch about a third of the words anyway, so most of the time you rely on "speech-reading"—interpreting someone's meaning not just by the way they move their lips or tongue, but their body posture, hand motions, and general demeanor.

Frankly, I didn't give a shit *what* he was saying. The minute he shook her with that savage jealousy, I stepped in, clamped a hand on his wrist, and pulled his hand away from her. She shrank back, rubbing the red marks left by his fingers.

—Do you know this man? I asked her.

She shook her head.

The young man broke my grip on his hand and regarded me with disgust. —Is this what you go for? he said to her, purposely, I suppose, in English. —*Turistés?*

She snapped something back, as did he, but most of it was lost on me; either their heads were turned away or they were talking too quickly. But then he lurched forward again, making another grab for her, and this time I didn't just clamp down on his wrist, I twisted. Hard. His mouth widened in a soundless cry, and before the pain could turn to anger I stepped in front of him and gave him a hard, sudden push to the chest. He staggered backward, nearly slipping and falling on the cobblestones.

—Leave her be, I said, not knowing if I was raising my voice too loudly or not loudly enough.

He regained his balance, and for a moment I thought he might just sail into me; for a moment, to be honest, I hoped he would—he'd have made a convenient and justifiable object for the rage and bitterness within me. But maybe he was smarter than he looked; maybe he saw that pent-up anger inside, because he abruptly backed off, though not without a few parting epithets. He called me a son of a bitch, and the woman a whore. He retreated, muttering to himself, turning a corner and vanishing into the cloistered night.

I turned to face the woman, expecting—what did I expect? Gratitude? Attraction? An offer to buy me a drink? All three, probably. But what I got—

What I got was a weary, jaded look—the same world-worn expression I'd glimpsed in the café, but up close I could see how genuine it truly was. There was a touch of grudging gratitude there as well, but for the most part she seemed to see in me just another variation on what I'd just driven away.

—Thank you, she said with a small nod and a tired smile. —I appreciate what you did. But please . . .

I lost the rest of it because she'd already turned and was hurrying up the steeply inclined street. In moments she was gone, and I stood there feeling confused and not a little stupid. Strange. A singer I'd never heard of before, performing in some small tavérna for doubtless smaller money . . . and yet she was so inundated by groupies that she was practically assaulted on the street. And expected—not unreasonably, I suppose—that even her rescuers had the same thing in mind. An odd woman, I thought, returning to the hotel, an odd evening, all round.

Three days later I was having breakfast in a small outdoor café, looking out at the fishing boats putting out to sea in the early morning breeze. The meltémi was still blowing hot and fierce and I was growing tired of Mykonos, ready to move on to some other island. I didn't have to check back in with the Portmann Institute until mid-September for my follow-up exam, so I had four or five weeks to play with and any number of places I could wander. I could've gone back home, of course, but that was no more a consideration now than it had been when I'd checked out of the hospital in Paris. The thought of going back to Sonoma, surrounded by my instruments, my albums, my music, but not being able to hear any of it—of standing in a backyard stripped of the sound of crickets, birds, a deer standing in a clearing, bolting skittishly into the woods at my approach—all the large and small sounds I had come to know so intimately during my long seclusion . . . It might have been home, but it would have been home with an entire layer of feeling, of memory, subtracted; I wasn't up to facing that yet. Better to stay in strange surroundings, the silence no stranger than the environs. Perhaps Delos next . . . or one of the distant islands, Youra with its goats and its fir trees, far from tourists and souvenir shops. Perhaps—

A shadow fell over me, blocking the bright Aegean sun,

and I looked up to find the woman I'd "rescued" a few nights before standing in front of me, mouth open in mid-sentence. She looked puzzled, as people often do when I don't respond to their calls from behind or out of my line of sight; I stood and smiled apologetically.

—Sorry, I said. —I'm afraid I have to see you before I can . . . "hear" . . . you. Could you repeat that, please? Slowly?

She started, taken totally off-guard. For a moment she didn't say anything; then:

—I was asking if I could . . . join you for a moment?

—Of course, I said, gesturing to her to sit. —Would you like some coffee?

She shook her head. She was staring at me with more than the usual amount of disbelief; as though she could not quite accept what I was implying.

—You have an . . . exotic . . . accent, she said slowly. —New Zealand?

I laughed, shook my head. —American. When you can't hear yourself speak, your pronunciation becomes a little . . . eccentric. I like "exotic" better, though. Makes me feel like a man of mystery. You think I should start wearing a black eye-patch?

She laughed, and I extended a hand. —John Ridley.

She took my hand, smiled. —Leucosia Polodori.

I held up both hands in mock-surrender. —You're going to have to give me a phonetic on that one, I'm afraid. Just reading your lips it's impossible to tell where the accents fall.

She took a pen from her purse and on a paper napkin wrote: *loo-koh-SEE-a*. God. It was bad enough trying to pronounce these names if you could hear, but when you *couldn't* . . . —Do you mind if I just call you Sia, for short? I asked sheepishly.

She stared, blinking, at me a long moment. She was

wearing a white cotton dress, a sun hat, and a white enamel bracelet on one wrist. Why did she look so bewildered? Most people adjusted to my condition fairly quickly, but this—this was something almost approaching wonder.

—Yes, she said, at length. —That would be fine.

She hesitated a moment before asking: —Have you been . . . deaf . . . since birth?

I shook my head. —An accident. About six months ago.

—I'm sorry.

—Not your fault. Blame the Red Guard.

Her eyes now showed more compassion than surprise, though that look of wonder still lingered. —A terrorist bomb?

I nodded.

—Not the hotel, in Rome?

I nodded again, not liking the direction the conversation was headed in but knowing I'd pointed it there myself. —My tragic flaw, I said, trying to be flip. —I'm always late checking out. If I'd left that lobby just five minutes sooner . . .

Shit. Enough of this. I signaled a waiter. —Garsón? Kafé evropaikó, parakaló?

I turned back to her. —Sure you don't want something?

She shook her head. —No. I just saw you sitting here, and I wanted to apologize if I seemed . . . brusque . . . the other night. I *was* grateful for what you did. The man you chased off . . . he's not dangerous, but he is persistent. He's followed me from Hydra to Santorini to here. I thought you . . . that is, I imagined . . .

—I understand, I told her. —I used to be a performer myself.

She looked as though she immediately understood all that that implied. —A performer?

—A songwriter. A singer, like yourself.

—And you cannot hear at all now?

—It's not that bad, I lied. —I only wish I could have heard your performance last night.

—You . . . didn't actually hear me, then?

Either this woman was uncommonly thick or uncommonly strange. —'Fraid not. I could make out some of the words, but not your voice.

My coffee with milk arrived; Leucosia changed her mind and ordered one, as well. I lit a cigarette, mindful of the unusual way she seemed to be studying me; I'm not sure if I was flattered or embarrassed. She asked me about my career, and I told her about my albums, the one or two semi-hits, the places I'd toured. I asked her if she'd ever toured the States; she shook her head. —Europe, Africa, Southeast Asia . . . I was in Japan a few years ago, then the Philippines . . . I did stop over in Hawaii for a day or so, but that's as close as I've come. I've always wanted to visit New Orleans, though, to see—what is it called?—the Missis-sippi?

—You must be very popular.

She laughed uneasily. —Not really. I make a living, that's all. I'm fortunate that people are willing to pay me for doing what I have to do.

That struck me a little odd—what I "have" to do, not "like" or "love" to do?—but I dismissed it as we chatted on about favorite places in Europe, cities we'd both visited. —But you were born here? I asked. —In Greece?

Was it my imagination or did she hesitate just a fraction of an instant? —Yes. In Athens.

She looked at her watch then, suddenly impatient. —I really must go. Again, I apologize if I offended you the other—

—Wait, I said, standing. —Would you . . . I mean, I don't want to sound like your roadie friend, but . . . would you be interested in having supper with me, tonight?

She stopped, looked at me with an expression part surprise, part confusion, part . . . pleasure?

—I . . . work very late. It would have to be a late supper.

—That's fine. I'll meet you at the tavérna when you're done.

For the first time she allowed herself a full, open smile. —That would be . . . very nice, she said, almost as though no one had ever asked her before. —I'll see you tonight.

I watched her perform again that evening; there were maybe half a dozen faces I recognized from the night before, but though by and large the audience was new—tourists fresh off the *Stella Solaris* for their six-hour stopover on the island—the reaction was very much the same as last night's. Wild enthusiasm, spontaneous applause, even, at the end, something of a standing ovation—with once more the men more avid in their attentions than the women. It was interesting the way women looked at Leucosia: many were puzzled at her popularity—envious, maybe a little threatened. But others seemed drawn to her, as well: an elderly woman seemed rather motherly in the way she smiled at her; a young girl gazed up as though at an older sister; and at least one woman in her twenties looked as smitten with her as any of the men in the audience.

Halfway through her second set Leucosia did something quite peculiar. By now I was watching her more than I was the audience, but I couldn't help but notice as everyone around me suddenly flinched at something I couldn't hear—hands went to ears, faces screwed up in annoyance. I looked around, puzzled, and when my gaze returned to Sia, I saw that she was staring at me—studying, scrutinizing me even as she continued to sing. When our eyes met she looked away quickly, as quickly as her hand, the hand holding the microphone, pivoted.

I realized, with a start, that she had been pointing the mike directly at the monitor speakers—the small speakers turned away from the audience, toward the band—a sure way to create feedback. She'd done it on purpose, and I had the crazy suspicion she'd done it—God knew why—to test me. To see if I was, indeed, deaf.

Whatever her reasons, she seemed more relaxed now, and in those times when her eyes met mine while she was singing, there was a warmth and an openness I'd not seen before. Afterward, we dodged her hordes of admirers and sought out the sanctuary of the Lotus, an intimate little restaurant on the town's main street.

For a woman with so many admirers, she seemed uncommonly surprised when I made a first, tentative pass at her; surprised and pleased. We went for a walk along the harborfront, arms around one another's waists, lights glittering along the bay like stars tossed along the curve of a crescent moon. At the far end of the harbor, past the boats and the quays and the souvenir shops, I kissed her tentatively; she returned it with an eagerness and a . . . I don't know how else to describe it . . . a *relief* I couldn't explain and didn't understand. Later, in my hotel room, we made love in much the same way: slowly, tenderly, with an edge of desperation and redemption to it. For my part, this was the first intimate contact I'd had with a woman since the accident, and I held her and kissed her and caressed her olive skin with the gratitude of a man who had felt utterly alone, until now. But I saw the same gratitude in her eyes; I felt the same relief in the way she exhaled a breath, long and slow, against me. We held one another as though onto lifelines of some sort, and though I knew why *I* was holding on so desperately, I couldn't begin to guess why she was.

Later, I tried to find out, but she remained oblique as ever about her past.

—Were you ever married? I asked.

She hesitated. —A long time ago, she said, though she looked to be only twenty-nine or thirty at the most.

—You married young?

She laughed, as though at some secret joke. —When all the world was young.

She studied me, then, a long moment, running her long fingers along the curve of my face; I did the same, smiling at her odd look. —You're so beautiful, I said in what I hoped was a whisper. —So lovely.

For a moment I thought that she was going to burst into tears; but instead she said, with a look of wonder on her face: —Really?

—I can't have been the first to say so.

She smiled sadly, kissed me lightly on the lips, and then the smile became a happy one—happy and warm and content.

—But you are, she said, and embraced me again. —You are.

We remained together for the rest of her engagement on Mykonos, then, when she moved on, I moved with her. She had four- and five-night gigs at tavérnas and nightclubs throughout the Aegean: Delos, Santorini, Corfu, Crete . . . Sia showed me the islands by day, knowing each one of them, each ruin and excavation and museum and café as though she'd been there a hundred times before; and by night I watched her sing. She discouraged me from it—told me to go off by myself and we'd meet afterward—but I didn't. I wish now that I had—that I'd just taken things as they were and not begun to question—but—

It was always the same: every island, every club, every audience, the same cheers and approbation and stage-door Johnnies. It didn't matter if they were a French tour group or American; local Greek audiences or exotic-looking blacks from

Mozambique. They loved her. They adored her. And more and more I wondered what they could possibly be hearing to evoke such spontaneous affection; how any singer, even the best of singers, could have such universal appeal no matter where she went.

But even more puzzling than that: why would a singer capable of evoking such a response remain largely unknown? Why wasn't she an international star? More than once I asked Sia about her management, offered to introduce her to heavyweights at ICM or CAA, but she always dismissed the idea with a laugh, as though it were preposterous. Yet somehow I knew that she was being merely disingenuous; behind that self-deprecating smile lay a mystery. It wasn't enough that I was in love, that that love helped blunt the pain I'd felt these past six months; I loved the woman, but had to solve the mystery of her.

My first clue came in Athens, where she was playing—again—at a small club in the Plaka. I met her booking agent, a pleasant, aging gentleman named Karlovassi; he told me, not without a sigh of frustration, that he'd been trying to get Sia to take bigger engagements for as long as he'd represented her—almost ten years—but she seemed to have no desire to be a Star, no urge to escape into any larger venues. She had a devoted following in many countries, and derived a comfortable income from her tours; she liked to travel, though much of it, oddly, was coastal travel—if not islands, then cities like Athens or Salerno, relatively close to the sea, or rivers. —I like the water, she told me later, unruffled. —I've always found it calming, peaceful.

Why didn't I believe her? —But there's a whole world out there you haven't even touched! And you're still only—what—twenty-eight, twenty-nine . . .?

—Ah, she said. —So that's it. A clever ploy to get me to reveal my age. Well, we'll have none of *that*.

And as she said it she began nibbling at my neck, I began

caressing her shoulders, and the subject was expertly turned aside, as usual. Our lovemaking had become more playful, more joyous, as though our love were taking a burden of sorrows off both of us; when she sang, I thought I detected a more upbeat demeanor in her, no longer all sad bouzouki songs, but a few happy ones as well. As though it mattered. Happy or sad, her audiences remained vocal and loyal.

One morning, as Sia slept in after the previous night's performance, I slipped out, leaving a note saying I was going to the library to catch up on some American newspapers. I went to the library, true, but not for the papers. Damn mysteries, and damn the men who love to solve them. I accessed an entertainment database—in French, which I read passably well—and searched for any biograph cal material on a Leucosia Polodori; not too surprisingly, I suppose, nothing turned up. I narrowed the field to singers of Greek origin with last names of Polodori, wondering if she might have assumed a different forename for the stage, but the twenty-odd women whose names came up on the screen weren't Sia. Finally—out of frustration more than inspiration—I cross-indexed by first name. *Leucosia*. Singer. Greek origin. And, to my surprise, came up with:

Trahos, Leucosia. b. 1897, Katerini, Greece; d. 1941. Greek Soprano, debuting in 1922 with the Athens Opera, best known for her role as Mimi in La Bohème, *which she performed in 1926 at La Grand Théâtre, Bordeaux. She was soon singing such roles as Musetta, Hansel, and Sophie in* Werther. *Her astonishing range in roles also included Marguerite, Thäis, Salome in* Hérodiade, *Cio-Cio-San, and Louise. Toscanini heard her in Paris when she sang Antonia, Giuletta, and Olympia in* Les Contes d'Hoffmann *and entreated her to perform at La Scala in Milan, and though she did sing at Il Teatro La Fenice, in Venice, she never did appear, oddly, in*

Italy's most renowned opera house. She sang at Das Nationaltheater, Munich; Die Staatsoper, Vienna; El Gran Teatro Liceo, Barcelona; El Teatro Colón, Buenos Aires; L'Opera, Monte Carlo; as well as at the Salzburg and Florence festivals. She won great acclaim and popularity in the following decade, but her performances became increasingly rare as the 1930s came to a close, until her eventual disappearance and apparent death during the Second World War; she was last seen in Hamburg, Germany, in 1941.

Interesting. At first glance, the antithesis of my Leucosia: this one sought, not shied from, the limelight. But the same popularity; the same ardent following. And the closer I examined the locales of her performances, the more uneasy I became: all either coastal cities, or, like Vienna and Munich, situated on a river—the Danube, the Würmsee. And Milan—Milan was some distance away from its nearest rivers, wasn't it? With a growing, yet nameless, sense of disquiet, I decided to look up a newspaper review of this Leucosia's 1922 Athens debut. In the microfilm library I threaded a spool of film through a viewer, searching for the day and date of the debut; finally, after several minutes, I slowed the machine, stopped, backed it up . . . and found the review. In Greek, of course, so I could barely make out a single sentence, but I didn't need to; as soon as the page had settled into place on the screen, all need to translate the review vanished.

Above the review dated November 12, 1922 was a photo that, even given the poor reproduction of the time and the quality of the microfilm, I immediately recognized as Leucosia. My Leucosia.

In Greece it is easy to believe in legends. You stand amid the ruins of the Minoan palace at Knossós, on a marble floor in what once; perhaps, was a bedchamber, or a servant's quarters, and you look out at a brown hillside dotted with contemporary farmhouses—not so modern that they seem unnatural beside the ancient ruins; in fact, just the opposite. Stands of trees border the palace, softening its jagged edges; a few steps down a road, horses graze in a farmer's pasture. The ruins, the farmhouses, the horses indifferent to the history beyond their fence, all of it seems connected, and seamless—you can imagine that these pale skies and rolling hills are the same skies and hills that residents of Knossós woke to, each morning, before fiery Thera extinguished the city and its people.

You stand, as I stood, in an inner chamber supported by cobalt-blue pillars, gazing at a reddish-brown mural depicting some strange hybrid beast—half peacock, half lion—and you wonder if such creatures once stalked the hills just outside. You see a bas-relief of a raging bull, vivid and realistic, and you wonder: If the Minoans were capable of such literal and precise replication of life, might not that strange hybrid creature also be taken from life? Some rare species of animal wiped out, along with Knossós, in the volcanic eruption?

I made my way through dim, narrow passageways that frequently led to dead ends, finally ascending up crumbling steps to daylight; the brightness of the Aegean sun made me blink, made me shut my eyes for a few seconds, and when I opened them and turned around—

Sia stood in front of me, as vivid and frightening as the beast in the mural. I jumped, reflexively, and her smile dimmed quickly.

—John? she said. —Are you all right?

I laughed, but still it took me a moment to loop my arm through hers. —Fine. You just startled me.

She looked dubious. —Are you sure? Perhaps all this sightseeing is catching up with you.

Perhaps; but not in the way she meant.

—Maybe so, I lied. —Let's get back to town.

That night, back in Iráklion, I sat as Sia captivated, as usual, the diners in the Ta Psaria restaurant; I was drinking perhaps too much of the potent local oúzo, called *tsikoudiá*, but even that wasn't enough to blunt the new edge of fear I felt when gazing at my lover. Back in Athens I'd looked up the mythological origins of her name, and though I failed to find any other renowned Greek singers named Leucosia—it was a mark of my obsession that I actually searched the microfiche and other files for as far back as two hundred years—I did find several disturbing parallels in other singers . . . other women, scattered in time from the seventeenth to the nineteenth centuries, with careers similar to the one I'd discovered in the 1920s: a rapid rise to fame, a public fervor and adulation remarkable in its intensity, engagements in coastal or river cities, then sudden death or disappearance. Their names weren't Leucosia, but for all purposes they might as well have been.

With the help of a young reference librarian, I had all the newspaper articles I could find on Leucosia Trahos translated into English. Most noteworthy was a brief mention of the fact that Miss Trahos, like other opera singers before and after her, disdained and forbade any recording of her voice—claiming that the recording could not capture the full scope of her high soprano tones.

I remembered Sia's manager, Karlovassi, telling me how Sia had steadfastly refused to cut an album, even a single; how she went to great pains to arrange, with the management of the clubs she performed in, that no tourists be allowed in with tape recorders.

It was then, I think, that I truly became afraid, for the first time.

From Crete we took a late-night cruise ship to Rhodes, where we would arrive the next day; we walked alone on the upper deck of the ship, the meltémi barely cooled from the day, a bright canopy of stars above us. Out here, so far from the lights of any city, I saw more stars than I'd ever known existed; I saw the Milky Way in its full glory for the first time. It was easy to see the gods in the constellations above me; easy to believe what I now believed. We walked silently for some minutes, and then, emboldened no doubt by the effects of the tsikoudiá:

—When did you decide to go back to using your real name? I asked, as casually as I could manage. —Did you suppose that by 1922, people would have forgotten?

She stopped dead and looked at me—first with surprise, then shock, then an anguish that made me regret ever having said the words; that made me wish I could take them back, put things back as they had been before. As though anything could do that, now.

She turned away, careful to keep in profile so that I could read her lips all the better, though at first I wondered if she would say anything at all—make any kind of acknowledgment of what I'd implied. After almost a full minute, she looked down and said, simply, —I missed it. It was the name I was born with, and after so long, I missed it.

She looked up at me, sharply. —Obviously a stupid, sentimental error on my part.

There was anger in her eyes, anger at herself, anger at me for having found out. The breeze blew her hair around her neck and a spray of salt was carried on the night wind. —How long? I asked, terrified that she would tell me.

She looked at me, and I saw that there was fear in her eyes as well. —Are you frightened? she said. —Is that why you've been acting so strangely this past week?

I hesitated. —Yes, I admitted. —I guess I am. But . . .

I put my hand to her cheek, gently, a gesture that seemed to surprise her. —The more I know, the less frightened I'll be.

She considered that a long moment; turned away, staring into the darkness of the Aegean at night, toward unseen islands black against black; and, slowly, she nodded.

—All right, she said. —I'll try.

She took a deep breath and began:

—I lied when I said I was born in Athens . . . I don't know where I was born, really; but I was raised, along with my sisters, Parthenope and Ligea, in the town of Halos, on what became known as the Halian coast. We were brought up by a middle-aged spinster who doted on us as though she were our own mother; who told us, when we were old enough, that we had been placed in her care shortly after our births.

—She told her neighbors that a messenger from the gods had delivered us to her; that we were the offspring of two muses and a god—the river god, Achelous, having taken both Melpomene and Terpsichore as lovers, and from that union of nature and inspiration came three daughters, three golden children with great beauty and voices to match. She told them that we had been placed in her care because of our lineage from Achelous; that though our souls belonged on Olympus with our mothers', our bodies were, like our father's spirit, bound to the earth—to its rivers and oceans and seas. We would never be able to wander far from the water, but by the same token the divine beauty of our song could grace the earth.

—The townspeople thought her mad, of course, but as we grew older, their doubts paled. Because almost from the day we were able to utter sound, we sang: nonsense-songs at first, the high fluting singsong of babes, but as we learned to talk we added words, and learned to memorize rhymes with astonishing speed. The townspeople, enchanted by the beauty of our voices, began to accept that we were who our guardian said we were. We could have been . . . we should have been . . . a source of light and joy, as our celestial parents intended. Terpsichore was the muse of song and dance, and it was from her we inherited our voices; but Melpomene, in addition to being the muse of lyric poetry, was the muse of tragedy . . . something we came to realize only too late.

—Our voices began as the beguiling laugh of children whom adults fawn over, then, as we matured, turned into the seductive giggles of adolescents who could have their pick of any of the boys in the village. I liked it. I was very different, then, from what I am today; you would not have liked me much, I'm afraid. I was vain and fickle and quite taken with myself; I enjoyed the attention, and began to think of it as my due. If a boy showed less than total interest in me, I was affronted, and went after him with all my wiles and skill until he was utterly smitten. Then, once I'd conquered him, once I'd grown bored with him, I cast him aside. He kept on loving me, but I ignored him, wouldn't even speak to him; I'd moved on to other quarry by then. My sisters and I even developed a competition, to see which of us could lure a particular boy away from one of the others . . . a game, a sibling rivalry.

—Other girls worked to achieve *charis*, or grace; we were above such things. And the older we grew, the more powerful our voices became; it was an involuntary effect, though none of us, at the time, complained about it. We didn't have to sing, you see, to enthrall our listeners . . . just the sound of our voices were enough to charm any man, and, if she were to listen long enough, any woman . . . but we discovered as we entered adolescence that we *had* to sing—we were *compelled* to sing—each day. Sometimes in choirs or recitals, sometimes just sitting on the porch of our home, Ligea playing the lyre, Parthenope and I joining in in song. Each time we would be besieged by young boys and older men, some of the latter wealthy merchants enticing us to marriage with promises of security and luxury. Parthenope took one such man as a husband, only to have him killed by another, jealous, suitor less than a year after their wedding. She remarried just days later, shocking the entire village; though not half as much as Ligea. Ligea cared not for wealth and, after she'd sated herself with all the men she desired, grew bored with such easy conquests and set her sights on women. Women, as I say, were more difficult to entice—but not, as Ligea proved, impossible. She seduced a poor young peasant girl and had the little waif following her around constantly; when she tired of her, she cast her aside as I'd cast my share of boys aside, and the young girl, disowned by her family and ostracized by the village, left Halos in shame. In many places, back then, young boys were routinely "initiated" into manhood by older men called *erastai*, but outside the few female communities, or *thiasoi*, like Sappho's, love between women was by no means as tolerated as that between men.

—As for me, I was as entranced with my own power as were my victims; I delighted in the lure, the hunt, the capture, and became quickly bored once I'd won the heart of the hapless prey. A fistfight between would-be suitors excited me, back then; I even encouraged them. After all, I told myself, I was the daughter of a muse and a god; was I not a prize worth fighting for? Ultimately, would not some proud Jason claim me as his due treasure?

—But it never came to that. Our vanity undid us even before we had reached our twenties. Parthenope, now married to a third wealthy husband, had so enraptured a visiting merchant that he demanded she run away with him to Athens, promising gold and glory. When she demurred—not out of morality, but simply because she didn't believe him half as wealthy as he claimed—he killed himself, leaving behind a note pledging his eternal devotion, promising to wait for her in Elysium.

—Ligea, meanwhile, had seduced the wife of a village magistrate—a patrician woman some ten years older than she. This proper, elegant woman fell so wildly in love with Ligea that she attempted to kill her own husband, to be free to be with Ligea; Ligea, far from horrified, was flattered that her charms had turned this courtly, gentle lady into a cunning, would-be murderess, unrepentant even when captured.

—It was then I began to realize what our mixed heritage had done to us, but by then, it was far too late to do anything about it.

—Divine or not, we were clearly a threat to Halos. In the end it was the women—the wives—of the town who came for us, dragging us from our homes, gagging first Ligea, then all three of us, before we had the opportunity to entrance them. They bound our hands behind our backs and paid a fisherman to take us to an uninhabited but fertile island, Anthemoessa, many miles offshore. We were marooned there with enough provisions to live for a year, and seeds to sow a crop for the following season. There was a fresh-water spring on the island, and an abandoned house belonging to a long-dead goat-herder; that became our new home. The waters were too deep, the land too distant, for us to swim ashore, and none of us had the slightest idea of how to go about building a boat—everything had always come so easily to us, and now that was to be our undoing.

—We sang each day as we always did, and in the first month we realized that the louder we sang, the farther the north wind carried it across the sea; one day a fishing boat veered toward our island, and we rejoiced at the thought of rescue . . . until it wrecked itself on the jagged rocks of the shoals surrounding us. I watched men drown in the foaming surf, and I felt sick. Yet we were compelled by our lineage to sing, and so we did, standing for hours at the edge of a high steep cliff, our song carried on the dry meltémi. Men aboard ships heard the song and changed course to follow it; all of them—so horribly many of them—perished on the same rocks that had claimed the first boat. I grew sick with each wreck, horrified as the ships splintered on the shoals, spilling their fragile cargo of men into the sea.

—But Parthenope and Ligea . . . perhaps it was the passing of years, the isolation, the hopelessness . . . or perhaps it was simply the way they were, the way they would have been in any case. Parthenope and Ligea went a little mad, and came to relish each shipwreck—competing with each other to lure boats to their dooms, laughing with delight as the sailors were slammed by the surf onto the reef. Bitter and angry and increasingly insane, they gazed with unfocused eyes and crazed smiles at the bleached skeletons of sailors strung like necklaces of bone on the rocks below.

—Years passed, but we grew no older. Once, a sailor survived the wreck of his ship; I nursed him back to health, and he, of course, fell in love with me. It was the first time, I think, that I valued a man's love, appreciated it as something more than balm to my own vanity; I loved him, as well, and for a short while . . . a handful of months . . . we were happy. Until . . .

—Until Parthenope and Ligea, out of jealousy and spite, trained their voices on him . . . sang to him, in a vicious duet that I could hardly compete with. Slowly his affections changed . . . he came to worship my sisters, and they turned him against me, forcing him to shun me if he wanted their affections. They took him to bed together, and I could hear the guttural laughter from the next room, could imagine the perversions they were performing on him. He scorned me to the end;

and I finally discovered what it felt like to be on the other side of things . . . finally realized how hollow and unreal the "love" I instilled in men truly was. I couldn't bear being near him, seeing what their songs had turned him into; I preferred to die. And so, one gray and cloudy morning, I dove off the highest cliff on the island, into the rocky shoals below.

—I hurt, but I did not die. My arms, my legs, virtually every bone in my body was broken . . . but they healed. I *couldn't* die. Heaven knows I tried, then and later, but I was paying the price for my misuse of the gods' gifts; this was our damnation, to walk the earth and sing and never know true love. Even Parthenope and Ligea would come to realize that, some-day.

—As the decades passed, fewer and fewer ships strayed anywhere near our island. But once the sailor was in their thrall, Parthenope and Ligea had him build a boat for us, from the wood of a myrtle tree; and nearly a century after our initial imprison-ment, we escaped the rocky shores of Anthemoessa. We went our separate ways, only meeting once again, hundreds of years later. I'd been performing as a singer all those years—even allowed myself the indulgence of a few soaring, triumphant careers, always cut short before my eternal youth became evident—and it was perhaps fifty years ago that I saw Parthenope again. It was as though she were a different woman. Watching centuries of human misery and war go by had made her, finally, aware of her own cruelty and shame, and the blood on her hands. When I saw her she was living in self-imposed exile on an island off the Cyprian coast, tormented by her guilt and loneliness. Ligea, when I'd seen her a decade before, was in Paris; she'd gone mad in a different way. The guilt had finally gotten to her, as well, and her solution was a different kind of exile. Every day for a month she had stood in her tiny room near the Seine, stared into a mirror . . . and *sung to herself.* Like Narcissus, she fell in love with her own reflection, and now her penance for her many sins was to love an image in a glass . . . to pine away, as Narcissus had, for the one thing she could never have.

—And I, she said, —I paid penance, as well. I took lovers . . . many lovers . . . over the years; I couldn't live without affection, even unearned affection. Because that was my particular damnation: I knew no man would ever truly love me, for the mere sound of my voice, let alone my song, made all love false and hollow. And then . . .

She hesitated. —And then you. And for the first time, someone loved me for *myself* . . . someone who couldn't even hear my voice. And now, I see, my penance is not complete. Now I have to live with the knowledge of having truly been loved . . . and having lost it.

She turned away from me, abruptly, fatalistically, and hurried into the night breeze; I followed her, called out her name, finally caught up with her on the foredeck and grabbed her by the arm, forcing her to turn around and face me, so I could read her lips. I was trembling, no longer with fear, but with anger; anger for what she had endured, for the purgatory to which she had been so randomly—or at least unjustly—condemned.

—No, I said, hoping my voice was soft. —You haven't lost anything.

Her eyes widened in astonishment; I took her by the shoulders, drew her to me, and, as tenderly as I could manage, kissed her. She wrapped her arms around me as though grasping at life itself; I returned the embrace, kissed her again, and as I stood there, stroking her, reassuring her, I felt something wet on my neck. I had not heard her weeping, but I'd felt her tears. I wiped them off her cheeks, took her to bed, and in the silence hoped to show her how much she was loved.

That summer we came to cherish our relationship as never before. Knowing the truth about Sia freed me; I felt as though I'd been entrusted with a rare, fragile gift. Being able to offset, in some measure, all those years of her pain and loneliness made me almost giddy with pleasure; more and more I saw the happiness in her eyes when she sang, the melancholy now an undertone in a richer, more resonant song. I was pleased to be the catalyst for the sea change in her mood and in her smile. We—she—continued to tour the Mediterranean, from Majorca to Cyprus, Sia acting as my tour guide in each new city or country, for she'd visited each so many times in her long lifetime. I asked her if she wasn't bored by the sightseeing, but she looked genuinely surprised and laughed an easy, don't-be-silly kind of laugh. —Of course not, she said, smiling. —It's different when you have someone to share it with.

—But you have. You said yourself you had other lovers.

—I had . . . liaisons, she said carefully. —It isn't love when they have no choice but to love you. And even then I couldn't share all this as I do with you . . . couldn't tell them that I stood over there, on that road, five hundred years before, when it was just a dirt path; that I saw Rome rise and fall, watched kings ascend thrones and revolutions topple them. There's so much I've never been able to tell anyone . . . not even my sisters.

I took her in my arms, kissed her gently. —I'm honored, I said.

—Honored? she said playfully. —Or just horny?

I laughed. —Maybe a little bit of both.

We kissed again, then continued walking along the wind-blown path. We'd driven up from Bari, an Italian port on the Adriatic Sea, and she told me how she had stood on this very spot, unimaginable years before—on the banks of the River Aufidfus, watching Hannibal's armies in their march to Cannae, two hundred years before the birth of Christ. It was like that everywhere we went—Palermo, Valencia, Dubrovnik—as her past, so long concealed behind false identities and forged birth certificates, was opened up to me . . . to me and, I believe, to her as well. In a way I think she was reclaiming her past, coming to terms with it as she revealed it to me, place by place, memory by memory, over the next two months.

The change in her was slow but profound; she laughed more and more, her smiles no longer forced but gracious and open. It was like watching a garden bloom after a long winter.

And yet, every once in a while, there was still a stab of doubt and worry. Like the night we lay in bed in a hotel room in Marseilles, having made love, she nestled in my arms, I tracing a line around her jaw as she listened to the call of a foghorn somewhere outside . . . when suddenly, without moving, without showing any physical trace of tension or fear, she said:

—It'll be all right, you know, when the time comes. When you have to leave.

I started. —*What?* I said.

She shifted position. —If a time comes when you decide you have to go, I'll understand. Really.

—What the hell brought this on? I asked, baffled. —What makes you think I want to go anywhere?

—Not now, she said, and that shadow of melancholy appeared again in her eyes, —but twenty . . . thirty . . . forty years from now . . . you may feel different. As you grow old, and I remain . . . the same.

I considered a moment before replying. —Has that happened before, to you?

—No . . . no, I was always careful to break it off in time . . . ten years, fifteen . . . but . . .

—If anyone's likely to get cold feet, it won't be me, I said, trying to sound offhanded about it. —Are you sure *you'll* want to stick with the doddering old fart *I'll* be in thirty years?

She looked panicky. —Don't say that! she said so quickly I almost couldn't make out the words. —I *love* you, I'll love you when you're forty or fifty or seventy. If anyone is used to seeing the ravages of time, it's me.

—Then what *are* you afraid of? I asked gently. —A *real* relationship . . . a lifetime relationship? Does that frighten you?

She hesitated. —No, she said, very seriously at first; then she looked up and I saw the beginnings of a smile on her lips, turning into a broad grin. —It *terrifies* me! she said, collapsing into laughter.

I joined in the laughter, even though I couldn't hear it, and drew her closer to me.

—It terrifies everyone, I said as I gently stroked her back. —Welcome to the worries of the everyday world.

She was half turned away from me, smiling as she gazed out the window at the foggy night, but I think I read two words on her lips. "Yes" was one. "Welcome . . ."

In September I returned to the Portmann Institute outside Paris, as scheduled, for my four-month exam. It had been here, in these pleasant but impersonal rooms some six months before, that I had learned how to lip-read, and, even more importantly, how to speak. When you can't hear your own voice, even conducted through the bones in your head, you speak too loudly, you begin to enunciate oddly; audiogenic dyslalia, it's called. In many ways the lip-reading was the easiest part to learn: I walked past rooms in which I'd spent hours watching videotapes —some instructional, some plain old movies and TV shows— learning to interpret speech through careful study of a person's face, or body language. Learning to glean as much from the visual as I could, to compensate for the dialog I couldn't hear. In movies you start to study the way an actor stands, or walks, or what bits of business he does with his hands; at first I was allowed the luxury of remote playback, slow-motion, and stop-frame, but after I'd been taught the fundamentals they took my remote away from me, on the reasonable assumption that in real life you can't back up the action for a second look.

My auditory trainer, Renata, greeted me with a warm hug and a kiss on the cheek. She was a skilled, compassionate woman in her late forties, blonde hair going gray, with bright blue eyes. —John, she said, smiling. —How have you been getting on these past months?

—Fine, I said. —Traveling quite a bit. The Mediterranean mostly.

Her nose wrinkled a bit as I spoke; when I'd finished, she frowned thoughtfully. —Your vowels are becoming rather . . . baroque, shall we say? And when you said "mostly," there was the hint of an *h* after the *s*. I think you need a little brush-up.

—That's what I'm here for, I said. And for the next several days, while the doctors took follow-up X-rays and examinations, I went back into speech-correction therapy with Renata, back to the visible speech devices and the videotapes: they used video to tape me pronouncing certain vowels and consonants, then showed me, side by side, someone pronouncing the same syllables the correct way. It was irritating to think I could so easily forget the basics of something I'd taken for granted most of my life, but I put aside my embarrassment and tried to emulate the people on screen. By the end of that week I was up to speed again, and ready—impatient—to leave, and return to Sia; but on the last day Dr. Peyrot and Dr. Bousquet sat me down for an unexpected chat, and I wasn't sure what to make of the guarded, sober expressions on their faces.

—Now we don't want to get your hopes up, Dr. Peyrot

began cautiously. —But the new X-rays seem somewhat promising.

I started. This was the last thing I expected to hear; I'd assumed the exam was routine, that the primary purpose of this visit was for speech correction. The prospects for any improvement in my condition had been made very clear to me months before. —What the hell is that supposed to mean? I said sharply. —I thought you told me nerve deafness couldn't be corrected by anything.

—That's true, Dr. Bousquet admitted. —And you *are* totally nerve-deaf, in your left ear, the one that was closest to the explosion. But as we also told you, you only suffered a partial nerve loss in your right ear—perhaps 50 percent—and the remaining hearing loss was the result of ossicular discontinuity.

—The small bones in my middle ear?

—The explosion separated several bones in the ossicular chain, Peyrot explained. —Most severely, the malleus and incus. Frankly, we'd feared further deterioration with time, but happily, that's not the case . . . which makes tympanoplasty a viable option, now.

I felt numb, stunned. —Surgery? I asked dully.

Dr. Peyrot nodded. —We can't promise a total hearing recovery in the right ear . . . not just because of the neural damage, but because the repair to the ossicles themselves will probably only be seventy to eighty percent effective. You should, however, end up with something approaching 50 percent of normal . . . enough to perceive the higher tones, such as the human voice.

They looked at me expectantly, clearly pleased that they were able to break this news to me . . . waiting for me to say something. Except I didn't know what *to* say. The numbness was starting to wear off, as it finally began to sink in: I'd be able to *hear* again. Maybe not well, but enough to hear music, enough to hear my own voice again, *other* people's voices, Sia's voice—

And then I realized.

Oh, Jesus. Oh, Jesus, no . . .

Peyrot and Bousquet were looking at me with concern. —John? Are you all right?

I fought back the cold fear in my chest, the chill starting in my heart and growing, metastasizing, throughout my body. I looked up. —You're sure? I said. —You're sure this will work?

—As I said, Peyrot assured me, —it looks promising. Almost certainly you'll regain enough of your hearing to resume songwriting, though performing might not be advisable . . . at least not around large amplifiers with high decibel counts. You play guitar, don't you?

I was barely paying attention to him. —Yes, I said distantly.

—You could probably perform in smaller situations . . . small clubs, with just your guitar as accompaniment, but larger concerts . . . well, I'm afraid not. Nothing to stop you from recording albums, however, if you—what do you call it?—"mix" in the accompaniment later.

How could they know that that was the furthest thing from my mind just now? I stood, and I must have looked very pale and shaky, because both men moved almost as though to catch me.

—I'll have to think about it, I found myself saying, and even though I couldn't hear it, I knew my tone was flat, dull.

The two doctors exchanged startled looks. —The procedure is quite safe, Bousquet assured me. —The prognosis is excellent. You needn't—

—I have to think about it! I repeated, louder I hoped, even as part of me knew that if I said yes, I wouldn't have to worry about such things anymore. Oh, Christ. Why the hell did I come here? Why the hell had they done this to me?

I started for the door; Peyrot and Bousquet hurried after me. —John! Please. Where can we reach you?

—You can't, I said, opening the door. —I'll reach *you*.

—But the procedure is . . .

I was gone before I caught the rest; out the building, before I could turn back. I caught the next flight back to Athens, a late flight; I dozed during the trip, and dreamt that I could hear again. When Sia greeted me at the airport, she saw immediately the stress in my face; I chalked it up to the travel and told her I'd be fine after a good night's sleep. Except I barely slept all night, and in those moments when I did, I dreamt I heard Sia's voice, high and fluting, raised in song, and I woke, frightened and afraid.

If Sia had any inkling of what I was going through, she never let on; and in fact I don't think she did. We spent the next two weeks completing her Mediterranean tour, and through it all I became increasingly tense and irritable. For the first time I began to feel uncomfortable—began to feel like a groupie, an appendage, remembering the days when *I* was the focus of attention, when it was I who sang for the crowd, I who the audience came up to, afterward, and asked for autographs. When Sia asked me what was wrong, however, I merely attributed the irritation to the traveling—we had, after all, been on tour for the better part of three months, and it *was* beginning to wear on me, though not in the ways I let on. We decided to go back to Mykonos, where Sia could perform at her old clubs for a few months, and where we could enjoy more stability and relaxation than we could on the road.

We rented a small villa near the Paraportian Church,

settling into a more domestic relationship. And despite my conflicting emotions, the one thing that did not change was the depth of my love for Sia. Perhaps it was because now I, too, had a glimpse of a life that *could* be, and could appreciate all the more Sia's centuries of longing and loneliness, and then, sudden fulfillment; but she became dearer to me with every day, apace with the frustration inside me at not being able to hear, knowing that I could change that, knowing too that I could *not*.

Well, hell, I told myself; Beethoven composed his Ninth Symphony while he was totally deaf—if I was truly the artist I fancied myself, I should be able to compose, if not to perform, new material. Unlike many pop musicians these days, I can actually read music—I was never at the mercy of computers and sequencers to create my songs—and so I set about writing some, as I always had, in longhand on sheets of music paper. I could still remember the sound of a dominant seventh chord or a suspended fourth, and with those in mind I spent the better part of a week composing a song which had begun forming in my mind from the moment I'd been told I might be able to hear again. It was a bittersweet melody, and while I was writing it my mood improved greatly; Sia was happy to see me at work again, and I could even go to her performances without feeling useless, or frustrated.

But once the music had been written, there was no way for me to play it and see if it worked. I'd wired my business manager back in L.A. to send me money for a synthesizer—God knows what he must have made of that request—and though I tried playing it for Sia, I couldn't finish: I had to *hear* the music, had to know whether it was working, where to polish, what to omit. Desperate now, I remembered the vibrations I'd felt from the amplifiers in that taverna months before, and embarked on a long, arduous process of compensation: I placed the amp close by as I slowly and laboriously depressed each key on the keyboard, trying to memorize the particular vibration I felt with the note I knew I was playing. It was slow, frustrating, and virtually impossible to discern the minute differences in pitch between, say, bass notes; and I couldn't even be sure if the timbres I "felt" were the differences between actual tone-colors or simply indicative of the particular "voice" I'd chosen for the synthesizer. Finally, after another month, I gave it up in an angry shove to the synthesizer; the keyboard flew off the stand, soundlessly crashing into the amplifier, falling facedown onto the stone floor.

It was impossible. Perhaps Beethoven was able to compose things of beauty without being able to perceive them as anything but notations on a sheet; but I wasn't Beethoven, by a long shot. I needed to hear the work, whether out of genuine artistic technique or simple unadorned ego: the thought of creating something beautiful, something that could touch people's hearts, and not be able to appreciate it myself was something I could scarcely imagine.

So I quit. Sold the synthesizer, got rid of my computer (I already knew I wasn't a novelist; little point in going over that tired terrain again), and asked myself which was more important: my art, or my love for Sia?

It was too close to call. In the end what swayed me was what I have already said: Trapped in this private hell, I could, ironically, appreciate all the more the purgatory to which Sia had been condemned. If she could stand it for as long as she had, I could stand it for the few decades remaining to me.

And that would have been the end of it, but for the vagaries of fate. Or, as I'm sure Sia would maintain, the legacy of Melpomene.

The only person who knew where I was living was, of necessity, my business manager; he continued to collect the royalties on my various recordings, deposit them in the appropriate accounts, make payments on my credit cards, and every four months send me a quarterly statement of my finances, which were healthy. I had told him not to forward any but the most urgent-looking of mail, and I do not blame him for sending the envelope return-addressed *Portmann Institute, Paris, France,* and marked, in French—the words underscored in red—*Please Forward!*

It was from Dr. Bousquet, asking me, imploring me, whether I had reconsidered and would I please call him as soon as possible to arrange for tympanoplasty? I shredded the envelope, tossed it in a wastebasket, and burned the letter. I cabled my business manager and told him *under no circumstances* was he to forward any more letters from the Portmann Institute. Perhaps I should have worded the message a bit less vehemently, because it could have been interpreted as indicative of an imbalance of some kind, as indeed it was. I discovered the details only later, but apparently Dr. Bousquet, after his first letter went unanswered and his second was returned to him unopened, called my manager and explained the situation. My manager, who doubtless already thought I didn't have both oars in the water judging by my refusal to return home to Sonoma, allowed himself to be persuaded by Dr. Bousquet that I was still suffering from depression, that I was irrationally rejecting the only opportunity I would ever have to restore my hearing, and my career.

My manager relented and gave him my address on Mykonos.

Dr. Bousquet sent a cable to me at that address.

I wasn't in when it arrived; but Sia was.

The telegram wasn't overly specific, but its allusions were enough to send Sia to the nearest phone—we had none in the villa—where she called Dr. Bousquet. By the time I returned from my trip into town to get groceries, Sia knew the whole story. And she was furious.

—Why didn't you *tell* me? she demanded.

I was taken off-guard, but managed to keep something of my wits about me before replying. —It was my decision to make, I told her.

—I have no say in the matter?

—It's my life.

—*Our* life. A decision like this affects *both* our lives.

—If I made any decision *other* than this, I insisted, —"*our*" life wouldn't even exist! All I'd have to do is hear your voice, and the love that we have would be rendered as false, as meaningless, as any of the empty relationships you've talked about in the past.

She barely acknowledged this, quickly shifting the subject. —Dr. Bousquet says that you might regain enough of your hearing to compose again . . . possibly even *perform* again. I've seen you, John, these past weeks, trying to compose without hearing, trying to create without seeing what it is you're creating! It's tearing you apart.

—*Was* tearing me apart, I maintained. —I realized it couldn't be done, so I've stopped trying.

She paled at that, her face a tense mask as she spoke. —It couldn't have been as casual a decision as that, she said stubbornly. —Can you stand there and tell me, honestly, that not being able to compose . . . to perform . . . doesn't matter to you?

I considered only a moment before answering.

—No, I said truthfully. —It does matter. It's just that . . . you matter more.

I tried to explain what I was feeling . . . the sense that my own frustration seemed insignificant compared to her sacrifices . . . but far from placating her, she became angry and defensive.

—I don't want you staying with me out of pity, damn it! she snapped.

—It's not pity, I said quickly. —It's . . .

I hesitated. How could I articulate what I was feeling? *Was* it just pity? No; it was more than that. But—

She snapped up her purse, slung it over her shoulder, and started for the door. —I have to go, she said, chilling me until she completed the sentence: —I have my first set at six. I have to go set up.

—I'll come with you.

She turned, stopped, and the anger in her face had turned to confusion. —No, she said. —Please. I need to think. I can think when I'm singing.

Seeing the fear in my eyes, she added, —I'll be back. I promise. All right?

I nodded wordlessly. She turned and left. Damn, I thought. You can't win. Even when you make the right decision, you get screwed. I stayed in the villa for the next five hours, trying futilely to get through one-third of one-fourth of the *Alexandria Quartet*, terrified that the clock would pass eleven, twelve, one o'clock, with no trace of Sia; but a little past eleven-thirty the door opened and she entered, a small smile on her lips as she saw me look up from my book. I got up, embraced her, kissed her long and tenderly. Without preamble we went into the bedroom, slowly took off each other's clothes, kissed each other's hands, arms, legs, caressed each other's backs, then slowly and tenderly made love. No words were spoken; it was as though we were gauging the extent of each other's love through touch and kiss alone, dispensing with the words and sounds that had created this barrier, this encumbrance between us. We made love again and again, until finally, sometime in the middle of the night, as the meltémi drew a long sigh through the hot, soundless room, she turned on her side and faced me, touching my cheek with the back of her hand.

—It's difficult for me, she said, with no trace of anger or

defensiveness now. —I'm the daughter of a muse, and when I look at you, I see a man deaf to his muses, a man in pain. And I don't want to be responsible for that.

I cupped my hand to the back of her neck, stroked her long black hair slowly. —And I don't want to be responsible, I said, —for taking away the first real happiness you've known. I can't hurt you that way.

—You'd rather hurt yourself? she asked.

—Yes.

—As would I, she replied.

I had to smile. —Have you ever read O. Henry? I asked.

—No, she said. —Why?

—Nothing. Doesn't matter.

I held her close to me, as though trying to bind our bodies together. —I love you, Sia.

She pulled back so that I could read the words, and the sad smile, on her lips. —And I love you.

We fell asleep holding each other; I drifted off aware of the warmth of her body, the beating of her heart. But when I woke the next morning, there was no one in bed beside me, and what few belongings she had were gone from the closets. She left a note, thanking me, telling me she loved me, and wishing me long life. Health, and long life. Not without a certain rueful irony.

I searched for her for the next six months; searched all the Mediterranean, the coast of Africa, any city in Europe on the banks of a river or a lake or an inlet sea. Her manager in Athens, Karlovassi, was the first person I contacted, but she'd broken off their relationship and he didn't have a clue to her whereabouts. I wrote to every personal manager my contacts in the music business could muster; I didn't expect her to use her real name again, but I described her in detail and hoped that one of them might provide a lead. Most had heard of me and wrote back respectful, friendly letters, but none had recently signed a Greek-born singer like the one I'd described. With the skill of someone who'd done all this before, too many times to consider, she had covered her tracks expertly.

I searched from Cyprus to Sicily, from Morocco to Abidjan; but there was nothing that said she couldn't as easily have flown to South America, or Australia, or even the U.S. After six months I realized it was futile—a deaf man who couldn't even use the phone, relying on letters and cables and personal visits to a hundred different clubs in dozens of seacoast cities. After six months, I surrendered to the inevitable and returned to Paris, where Dr. Bousquet was happy and relieved to see me.

The tympanoplasty was successful, and today I have perhaps fifty percent of my hearing restored in my right ear—enough to hear people's voices, enough to compose, even enough for the occasional small club date. When I first returned to the Portmann Institute, it was as a man defeated; I felt ashamed for my failure, my surrender. It was only as my hearing slowly began to return that I realized something important; something most people are never even aware of, something even I, while deaf, had not truly been conscious of.

I started listening to people talk, at the same time watching them as I had trained myself to watch them while deaf—and I realized that what they were saying did not, in most cases, even matter; their intentions, their feelings, their souls, if you will, were all there in their eyes, and hands, and faces. In the way they smiled, or frowned, or swatted at an insect; in the way they shook your hand, or touched your shoulder, or raised a hand in greeting. The words helped for more abstract concepts, but the essence of them was there to be seen, not heard. The voices truly didn't matter. And that was when I started looking for her again.

Back in Sonoma, I can call any agency, any manager in the

world; I can fax a drawing I had made of her to any club I want; I can access, through my Macintosh, newspaper reviews of singers at small cabarets the world over. I'm getting closer; it's only a question of time. When I think I have a good lead, I arrange a club date in that city, or that area, and I look. I look for long black hair and sad eyes and a café thronged with devoted fans. And I don't worry about what I'll hear if I find her. Because I can't believe any gods could be so capricious as to condemn a woman to eternal loneliness, just for the sin of vanity, long repented.

According to legend, Odysseus, while passing the isle of the sirens, had his crew stuff their ears with wax, then bind him to the mast, so that he might hear the exquisitely beautiful music, yet not fall prey to it. But the legend, like many legends, is wrong. I alone have heard the true siren's song, and it was silent.

Queen of the
Magic Kingom

On Thursdays (she decided) she would spend half an hour each morning watching the Country Bear Jamboree. She liked the fat gray and brown bears, Big Al and Teddi Bara and the rest, the easy way they sang or strummed their banjos; it was a good way to start the day. She thought it terribly rude when the audience never applauded at the show's end, though they certainly laughed well enough during the performance. Unthinkingly she clapped her hands fiercely as the curtain drew closed, her applause abruptly hushed as the other members of the audience stared at her, some smiling, some suppressing smiles, others shaking their heads. You didn't applaud machines.

Well, damn it, *she* did. And she refused to be embarrassed about it, either. With an exaggerated elegance she left the Jamboree building, up the cool, sloping corridor and into the early morning heat. Her blouse was already clinging to her skin after only a few minutes of walking; she paused and pressed smooth her magenta skirt, trying to iron out the few wrinkles made during sleep. There should have been more of them than there were, actually, considering the cramped closeness of the crawlspace above the Jamboree, the forgotten attic area no more than—what?—three feet deep, four feet wide? But she had tossed and turned hardly at all, had had a completely peaceful night—the first in years, it seemed.

The only two restaurants in Bear Country served just lunch and dinner, so she walked the short distance into Frontierland and lingered outside the River Belle Terrace, where the seductive odors of waffles, bacon, sausage, and ham brought back (just for a moment) the morning smells of her daughter's home.

She checked her purse and wallet: four D tickets, three Es, a few wrinkled dollar bills, and some change. She counted the loose coins and decided that although she could afford a large order of eggs and sausage, her little remaining money would not last very long that way. Instead, she went up to the counter, ordered a cup of coffee and two thin pancakes—all she really needed anyway—and found an empty table.

She ate slowly. A few employees sat at the next table (they called the place "Dismal-land") also eating leisurely breakfasts, and for the length of her meal she felt the most delicious sense of belonging, more delicious than the food itself. Already she felt more at home here, hundreds of miles from Tulsa, than she ever had at Maureen's house.

Leaving the Terrace, she roamed wistfully around Frontierland, passing the shooting galleries, the Arcade with its antique gun collection, and the Golden Horseshoe (showtime 11:45). She wandered down to Fowler's Harbor and watched the still green waters ripple and eddy at the approach of the *Mark Twain*. The steamboat glided silently to the dock, picked up a light load of passengers, then glided off down the river again.

The island rafts followed it, and in their wake drifted one or two canoes.

She waved at one of the canoes, in which three or four teenagers were merrily attempting to drown one another; they took a moment to wave their paddles in response, then disappeared from view as the canoe rounded a bend, toward the waterfall.

Luckily she didn't need a ticket to sit under the cool green verandah next to the pier or to listen to the white-and-gold-trim player piano beneath it. The stately *Columbia* sailed by as the piano played a lazy western tune, and she thought to herself, *well, why not,* and got on the ship. That was a D ticket. The tinny sounds of the piano faded as she sailed on down the river, around and around Tom Sawyer Island, never tiring of the view.

Afterward, she left Frontierland, passing through the main plaza on her way to Tomorrowland. She liked Tomorrowland best; she enjoyed the bright functional architecture, the soft pastels. Although she had been there just yesterday, she entered the Circlevision exhibit—reasoning that it was, after all, *free,* and her tickets would have to be as carefully rationed as her money.

Inside there were some two hundred people in the large lobby, waiting for the next show to begin as a digital clock ticked off the remaining minutes. Girls in blue uniforms were speaking through microphones to the crowd, asking the tourists the names of their home states, telling them to shout it out in a proud cacophony of territorialism.

Yesterday *she* had joined in that shout, her yell of "Oklahoma!" lost amid the general tumult. But today that claim was no longer true. The girls asked the crowd to shout out their home states.

She called, "California!"

She felt good about that.

The doors to the theater opened and she entered, careful to get a spot in the middle of the circular room. She gripped the handrail in anticipation as the 360-degree screen lit up, and the honey-voiced announcer so familiar to her from Sunday evenings made her feel calm and secure.

The aerial tour of the country never failed to awe her. (Mental accent on *never*: she'd only seen this once before, she'd only been in California one day, but already the past was beginning to blur and the hours she'd spent wandering the golden streets had turned to years. Slowly she was building a new past for herself. And so: it *never* failed to awe her.)

But then the camera glided over the Western plains to focus briefly on Oklahoma, on Tulsa with its doll's-house homes and trimmed green lawns, and her new past was eclipsed by the shadow of the old, forcing her to remember. Maureen, grown bluff and harsh since childhood; David, forced to live not only with the dead pulp of his dreams but also with a mother-in-law he barely knew and rarely cared to; and the children, who *had* to be awake during those long nights of argument, counting the many ways three people could tear themselves apart. The most recent battle had pointed up the ultimate uselessness of a mother, a mother-in-law, or grandmother, and she was all three; the next morning she was gone, savings account tapped for bus fare. Her baggage was still in the hotel, but she hadn't used the other half of her monorail ticket and never would. She was here to stay. She was here to live.

The film ended, the lights came up. She blinked once and left the building, pausing briefly to examine the picturephones in the lobby.

Once outside she left Tomorrowland for Main Street, USA, finding an empty spot of curb where she could watch the morning parade. Her knees were stiff as she sat down; bending, she knocked over a young woman's purse.

She picked it up and handed it to the girl. "I'm sorry. My bursitis."

"That's all right." The girl smiled; apparently she was there with three other young people, two boys and a girl.

Her bursitis, the night's sleep, it didn't matter what caused the stiffness in her knees as she sat down next to the four youngsters. She felt a need to talk, to hear other voices besides the running commentary inside her own head. "Do you—do you come here often?" she asked them.

The first girl shook her head. "Once or twice a year. It's hard to get away."

"Do you like it? I do, very much. I've never seen anything like it. I'd like to stay—" She caught herself. "—all day. Two days."

The young people, college students perhaps, approached her enthusiasm with a certain bemusement. One of the boys said, "I don't guess it's the park itself that's so much fun. They've got some good attractions, but some real losers, too. Stay away from the Tiki Hut. It's like anyplace else—the important thing is being with people you like; otherwise it's all just, you know, so much noise."

She nodded, but any reply she might have made would have been lost in the swell of sudden music that filled the street. The parade was beginning. Mickey, Snow White, the dwarfs (or were they elves?), dancing down the street to a familiar rhythm. She knew it to be a childish thrill she felt as she watched the costumed characters, but it had something to do with what that boy had said: Friends were very important here, and these— these were her friends, of a sort, in a way.

(She remembered the desperate loneliness she'd felt grow large within her during the long bus ride from Tulsa, a sense that her world was receding from her, falling away, and soon she would be lost and drifting. Then she stood in the Greyhound terminal in Los Angeles and *knew* she was lost, and the loneliness became an awful panic, a soundless inner groping for someone/ something/somewhere she could grasp and hold, but her fingers always locked on empty air. She was ashamed at her own half-heard whimper as she walked unfamiliar streets: "Maureen, David, Maureen," whispered like a rosary. Until she had fled to Anaheim, and the panic ebbed, receded, died.)

She watched the characters dance happily down the street; she felt a closeness, and no guilt for that closeness. Her searching hands had found something to hold . . . the first thing she'd held since Len had died. Odd; usually when she thought of her husband, even briefly, it depressed her, but now, here, she didn't have the time to be depressed. She was so busy.

Too soon, the parade was over. She stood, feeling her leg muscles twinge uncomfortably, and waved goodbye to the college students.

She spent the morning in the shops along Main Street, and, later, in those in New Orleans Square. She stood in the Cristal d'Orleans and watched a young glass cutter carefully engraving a crystal ashtray, his quiet eyes set on the milky water and the spinning grindstone. She watched the portrait artist in the square do sketches of nervous tourists. She waited on line outside the Golden Horseshoe for forty-five minutes just to catch the (free) Western Revue; then once inside she defeated her own caution by ordering a small Pepsi at the inflated prices. But it was a good show.

She became so engrossed in her wanderings, and in those free exhibits that she found, that she forgot lunch. By the time she realized she was hungry it was almost five o'clock. She approached the Plaza Pavilion, scanning the menu posted at the gate, then balked; one meal here and her savings would be gone.

(In any event they would be gone soon, too soon. What then?)

Don't think about that, she told herself, heading for Tomorrowland. She knew this world well enough by now to locate its other face; she slipped between two buildings and found herself "backstage," back with the parking lots and employee banks and administration buildings. She made her way past the half-costumed performers and found a group of vending machines tucked away in a corner, a makeshift cafeteria for night workers. With some of her remaining change she bought a sandwich and a container of orange drink. Later she would splurge and have a "mint julep" in New Orleans Square, or perhaps a fritter, and listen to the jazz bands that played there toward midnight.

Next to the vending machines she found a rack of costumes—frilled, expensive things, laden with rhinestones and sparkle. She fingered the heavy fabric of a gown and wondered if it would be worn by some lucky girl tonight in the Electrical Parade. She held the sleeves in her right hand and stroked the dark velvet trim with her left; the dusk-born panic of two days ago now seemed a far thing, light-years remote—there was a permanence to the sleeve, to this gown, and she held it as tightly as she held the memories of her marriage.

But this was so much more *real* than those memories, somehow. If she had to let go of one of them, she might . . . but no. No, it was only a dress: cloth and glitter. That was all.

(But if she *had* to let go—)

She took the dress from its hanger, holding the thick vanilla-colored material to her chest, glancing about her with guilt but not embarrassment. Quickly she located a ladies' room used only by employees (most were gone by now) and hid the costume beneath a sink. Even more quickly she left, and then, giddy with her adventurousness, she went over to the Mint Julep Bar and had a julep *and* a fritter, waiting and listening to the sleepy jazz, watching the summer dark descend.

At eight-thirty she returned to the ladies' room. The gown was still there; locking the door first, she put on the costume, feeling at once foolish and regal. Standing there pulling on the white satin gloves, the sequined blouse, the velvet skirt and translucent shoes—standing there she felt like a twelve-year-old, a girl gone to the attic to slip into the costumed guise of Mother. And like a twelve-year-old, she enjoyed the feeling.

She slipped out of the restroom, glanced at her watch, and headed toward Fantasyland by way of the parking lots. En route she passed a man in a staid business suit heading toward her—no, heading toward his car, but noticing her nonetheless. He smiled as they neared one another.

"Hi," he said. His gaze unnerved her, she knew she was magnifying its intensity in her mind but she couldn't help it.

She managed a nervous smile. "Hello." Her heart was pounding beneath the quilted fabric.

He nodded toward the spires of Fantasyland as he began to unlock his car. "You in the parade tonight?"

They can't know everyone. She took a breath, and her heart stopped beating quite so fiercely. "Yes," she said, nodding timidly. Then, with assurance: "Yes, I am."

"Thought so. Jesus, isn't that thing hot?"

She laughed. "No," she said, though it had been a moment before. "Not at all, really."

She arrived a few minutes before the parade was due to begin. The line of electric floats extended far to the rear of the "Small World" exhibit. She blinked in awe at the brilliance of the display—the men in blazing tunics carrying neon banners; the fluorescent trains, the phosphorous animals; all the colors tended to mix and blur back here, shining, sparkling, very much like being at the center of an exploding fireworks display.

No one noticed a woman in a non-electrical costume dawdling toward the very end of the line; perhaps they thought her a new addition, perhaps they didn't care. In either case she kept her distance, out of earshot of the last marcher but still within the recognizable scope of the parade. She shivered pleasantly as the music began, the bouncing repetitive beat to which the paraders began to move. And from the loudspeakers, that familiar Sunday-evening voice, speaking now of her:

"*Ladies and gentlemen . . . we proudly present . . . the Main Street Electrical Parade!*"

The music grew louder, crowding out all thought, all deliberation, leaving only a reflex of dance to carry the marchers through the night. Flecks of light detached themselves from the common brilliance, becoming scrupulously constructed thousand-kilowatt floats. The parade began.

She followed. Past "Small World," down the streets lined with grinning visitors—children, like her grandchildren, smiling as they never had, not to her; women with faces soft as Maureen's could have been but never was; hundreds or maybe thousands of people squatting on the warm summer pavement, watching the floats, watching the lights, watching *her* . . .

She followed. Past the Matterhorn, the glare of the bulbs (red, white, yellow, blue) partially obscuring the crowds. The music blared merrily, filling a void within and without. Flashbulbs popped in her face, giving her permanence in someone's scrapbook, giving her immortality denied her when Maureen was found barren and had to *adopt* . . .

She followed: up, down, along Main Street, belonging to this night and place more than she had ever belonged to Tulsa or Maureen—or—or Len, yes, damn it, more than that! She marched. She danced. She sang to herself and was filled with the music of a joyous communion.

And at the end of the parade, after they had doubled back to Fantasyland and most had begun shucking off their costumes, she stood with her hands over her ears, watching the fireworks birth and die like suns gone to glorious nova, the explosions striking secret resonances within her.

The euphoria waned slowly. The last of the fiery pin-wheels sputtered and turned to ash. The crowd thinned and dissipated, scattering to all corners of the remaining night—leaving the lady in the unlit gown alone under a starless sky, alone and smiling.

She took the dress back to the racks from which it came, changing in the ladies' room once more. She wandered again for a while, dimly searching for that music which had filled her earlier, but neither the soft rock on the Tomorrowland Terrace nor the slow rhythms of the Blue Bayou Pianist was what she was looking for. But she kept searching.

Time seemed to drift loose of its moorings. She went onto the dock where the *Mark Twain* waited, shut down for the night, and sat down beside the player piano again. No sooner was she within earshot of its tinny refrains then, quite unexpectedly, the music returned to fill her.

It was a silly kind of music, honky-tonk blues that sounded like a jangle of crystal drops in a tin can, but she suddenly and completely was in love with it. She couldn't explain why. When she and Len were first married, in the good days, Len had played that same kind of jangling music on their battered pianette, and she had never liked it. Noise, she had called it. She wondered why it should mean so much more to her now.

She listened for what seemed minutes but must have been longer, the darkness around her growing deeper, the green bulk of Tom Sawyer Island turning gray, then brown, then black.

Finally, from behind her, a cool, friendly voice. "Ma'am?"

She turned to see a young man in the blue cavalry uniform of a security guard—the white kerchief, the floppy cowboy hat, the fake gunbelt.

"Yes?" she said.

"We close in half an hour, ma'am."

"Oh. Of course." She smiled. "I'll be along in a few minutes. I'm just listening to the music. I want to hear the end of it, that's all."

He nodded. "Fine," he said and quickly left.

She turned back to the piano and listened, at first hearing her daughter's shrill tones in the higher notes, gradually forcing that voice from mind and memory till only the music remained, the music and the calming waters below. The *Mark Twain* fell dark. Rafts were tied to piers, then abandoned. The canoes bobbed in the water, as if dancing to the honky-tonk, the jangling, the . . .

"Ma'am?" The guard again. His tone puzzled, hesitant. "Can I—can I do anything for you?"

"No, no," she said, not turning now, just shaking her head politely. The piano glimmered in the moonlight, white as a bridal gown—no, not so, white as the gown she'd worn this night. "I'll be along, don't worry. I'm just listening to the music."

"Yes, ma'am." And gone again, more reluctantly this time. He didn't matter. She sat and stared and listened and loved. She could admit that now, it wouldn't *hurt* to admit that now. She'd needed something to love for so very damned long; that was very basic, that was very natural; and this place, this world of strangers in familiar smiles, *this* was the one thing she'd found that she could love that wouldn't draw *back, stay back* at her touch . . .

"Ma'am, I'm afraid we're closed. You'll have to go."

She turned. The guard stared at her, his eyes kind but firm. He repeated the words: "You'll have to go, ma'am."

No. No. It was because she admitted it, it always happened, it always hurt. If she'd kept it from herself, if, if, if . . .

She found herself grasping tightly the bench she sat on. "No," she whispered, and recognized her tone as the same in which she had called for—called for whom? Called for when? She couldn't remember. It didn't matter.

"But, ma'am . . ."

"No, you don't see," desperately, now, "I can't, I, I want to stay here, I want to *live* here—"

The guard blinked, his mouth opening a little in amazement. She shut her eyes; she shouldn't have said that and now it was too late. She opened her eyes and looked at him. "Please. I wouldn't be any trouble, really I wouldn't. I could live above the bears, I did last night, it wasn't bad. I could do things, work, little things—"

A second guard had come off the *Mark Twain* and now stood behind her; he did something to the piano, choking off the music. She gasped as if her own throat had been gagged. "Oh please," she said, the two men gently taking her arms, causing her to slowly rise, "I just want to stay, that's all, I just want to—"

"Well sure," the first one said, trying perhaps to be kind. "Sure you can."

She felt a helpless anger at his lie. The two of them held her by the elbows and began shepherding her away from the dock; with quick pride she wrestled herself from their grip. "That isn't necessary," she said flatly, and the guards drew back respectfully—flanking her now, leading her through the empty kingdom like nervous courtiers.

Healer

There was another disturbance in the Citadel today; Ta'li'n saw it from his hidden room in the temple atop the Pyramid of the Sun—a short, bloody skirmish between followers of the Old Order and proponents of the New. The latter were armed not merely with clubs and daggers, as in the past, but with atlatls, as well—spears tipped with gray or green obsidian points—and Ta'li'n noted with sadness that the followers of the Old had taken up weapons of their own: daggers, slings, a few knives edged in black obsidian. The confrontation was more evenly matched than previous ones, and briefer; both sides dispersed upon arrival of the Priests' Guards with atlatls of their own, the two factions leaving a bloody trail both north and south along the broad, two-mile-long avenue that bisected the City—a road that would one day, Ta'li'n thought ruefully, be aptly known as the Avenue of the Dead.

Past, present, and future all seemed to be fighting for dominion over the priest's soul. The past was a glorious lure, a dangerous seduction on which he could not afford—yet could not avoid—dwelling. From up here, the City was still beautiful, still vibrant, the undisputed capital of a continent; not even the Maya had built a home as large, as populous, as this City which the Aztecs would rechristen Teotihuacán—whose true name would be as obscured by time and history even as its temples, its pyramids, its courts, and its palaces would be covered over by mounds of dirt and tangles of guayule scrub. But now, at this moment, it was still alive, some twenty square miles of it, and he could see, from this tallest pyramid at the center of the City, the ceremonial platforms lining the broad, expansive Avenue; the Pyramid of the Moon to the north; the—what would they call it, centuries from now?—the temple of Quetzalcoatl, to the south. The frescoes and facades blazed with vivid colors— bright reds, whites, golds—and the marketplace thronged with merchants and traders from as far away as the Gulf Coast, bartering for the City's famed obsidian, or its Thin Orange pottery. Ta'li'n's people had lived here, in peace and prosperity, for nearly seven hundred years; and staring out now at the City, the rioters no longer in sight, business as usual being conducted in the Great Compound, it was easy to believe that it would continue so forever. But the present, that eternal Now, was as dangerous a lure as the past; only the future mattered, as terrible and unfathomable as it was, or would be.

Returning to his meditation, and to the peyote which induced it, he placed another of the mescal caps on his tongue; it burned, sharply, for several moments, then all sensation was lost as the vision took form behind his closed eyelids. For an instant he hoped that this time, perhaps, the future would show him a different face, a kinder countenance—

But it was the same vision: always the same. The City, center of light and peace for six and a half centuries, in flames.

The Temple of X'l'o—the god renamed Quetzalcoatl by those who would follow—would be stripped of its color, the plumed serpents adorning its face reduced to dun reflections of their present glory, and the City itself, the thousands of private dwelling places . . . all that, set to the torch. A fire that would burn for days, turning nights into a kind of constant dawn, a flickering orange glow that could be seen as far away as Oaxaca. Pillars of black smoke would rise from one end of the Avenue to the other, eclipsing even the massive presence of the sacred mountain, Tenan, for centuries the home of the water goddess, X'la'n—or Tlaloc, as she would be known.

Tlaloc. A strange name, he thought, invented by they-who-would-follow; yet somehow the idea that they would never know her true name, nor even that of the City itself, gave him odd comfort as he watched that city's destruction—better, perhaps, to be an object of anonymous mystery, than of indifferent notoriety. He did not care if such thoughts seemed stoic, or overly philosophic; he had seen the vision too many times, these past months, to spare any more tears for it—especially now that the event itself, the reality of it, was so frighteningly close.

If he was to save any of his golden city—to preserve any of its achievements, these past six and a half centuries—he would have to act, soon.

A drifter lay sleeping at the mouth of the alley, a two-day-old *Times* wrapped around him like a blanket, a rain-soaked carton for his pillow; if he heard or felt the rat scuttling at the tattered cuffs of his pants, he gave no indication of it—no more notice than he gave the short, somewhat feral young man at the far blind end of the alley. Dark-haired, bony, with a build more likely to be called wiry than strong, Jackie Thompson nervously tugged on the straps of the rope harness as he slipped it over his stooped shoulders; he hated this thing, hated the way the straps cut into his skin no matter how many layers of clothing he wore—he still had rope burns under his arms from the last time he'd used it. Nervously glancing toward the mouth of the alley and the lighted street beyond, he reeled in the twenty feet of rope and fingered the rusty grappling hook at its end; he knew it was too dark for anyone to clearly see him from the street but he couldn't help it, couldn't help the pounding of his heart or the sweat on his palms or the small twitch at the corner of his eye. Even after fifteen years of second-story work he had to take deep breaths, had to ignore that small mocking voice inside that told him he was no good at this, that he was a loser and a screw-up and a putz. Rubello's voice, sometimes; sometimes, his own.

It was probably only his stubborn defiance of that voice that had kept him in this business, all this time; that even now made him raise the grappling hook and, winding up like a swarthy Mickey Mantle, let it fly—up onto the roof of the two-story museum. It landed with an unwelcome clang, but Jackie was too busy trying to stifle a cry of pain to pay it any mind—he'd wrenched his shoulder, still tender from the fall he'd taken last month, that botched jewelry job on Fairfax. Doing his best to ignore the pain, he yanked on the rope, just enough so that the hook snagged on an outcropping of ledge; then, gingerly testing its hold, he took the rope in two hands and began slowly ascending the brick wall, half-expecting his luck to unravel along with the rope—relieved and a little amazed when he actually made it to the second-story window.

He took a glass cutter from his jacket pocket, placed a small suction cup on the bottom half of the window, and began cutting a hand-sized half-oval in the glass. Earlier he'd broken into the museum's alarm box and rigged a parallel circuit at the junction controlling this wing of the building; now, as he gripped the suction cup, pulled out the half-oval of glass, and reached inside to raise open the window, that parallel circuit was telling the alarm system that everything was just copacetic, that the perimeter alarm on the window was intact and the sensors under the plush museum carpeting were likewise undisturbed as Jackie clambered inside. He slipped off the rope harness and left it dangling—uncomfortably resembling a noose—from the roof; taking out his flashlight, he began to make his way through the deserted museum, the red wink of motion sensors in far corners noting his presence, but unable to get their warning past the bypass circuit Jackie had installed. At the same time he'd been careful not to place the circuit board *too* far downline: shunting the downstairs alarms out of the system could potentially have attracted some attention.

Still, for all this, he felt no less nervous. He'd breached the museum, as intended, in the Mesoamerican wing, the section his sources had told him was least patrolled, most remote from the guard station on the ground floor. Padding silently through, he swept his flashlight beam from side to side, illuminating statuary too large to transport: a reclining porcelain figure of Chac Mool, the Aztec rain god; a fresco, bright even after the bleaching of centuries of sun and dust, of the water goddess, Tlaloc; a bronze metalwork of Quetzalcoatl, the Feathered Serpent—

A phone rang.

Jackie stopped dead. The ring was muffled, distant, from downstairs; after another short ring, someone picked it up, and he could hear the indistinct drone of someone's voice—a guard, obviously—talking.

Suddenly impatient, he began casting about for something small, something he could snatch and grab and get the hell out of here. He stopped at a glass display case, and in the wash of his flashlight he saw a bronze plaque: TEOTIHUACÁNOS RELIGIOUS ARTI-FACTS, CA. 650 A.D.—COURTESY MUSEO NACIONAL DE ANTROPOLOGIA MEXICO CITY. Inside were half a dozen objects, none larger than ten inches across: a mask made of some dark green stone, with slits for eyes and a broad flat nose; some sort of gray vessel in the shape of a jaguar's foot, one of its six claws broken at the joint; another jaguar, this one a black obsidian figurine; a stone model of a Teotihuacános temple, with its distinctive, four-tiered *talud-tablero* style.

Dimly he was aware that the voice downstairs had ceased; he stood, frustrated, at the display case before him and swore silently to himself.

All the research he'd done on the museum's collection was doing him damned little good just now. He had assumed, naively, that the more valuable artifacts would be identifiable by their material—gold or jade, say, easy to recognize, easy to carry. But none of these looked particularly—

A door shut, downstairs, followed hard upon by the sound of footsteps—ascending stairs.

Jackie's first instinct was to run, but that mocking voice within him would surely torment him later should he leave without something to show for his efforts. He swung his flashlight along the display case again—

And this time, his attention was caught by a polished oval stone perhaps two inches high, flashing a lustrous green in the lamplight; it looked marbled, with black highlights. Jackie's heart raced faster. Jade? Yes, of course; it had to be. Hurriedly he jimmied the lock on the display case, lifted the glass cover—

And an alarm sounded throughout the museum.

As the klaxon began its shrieking alert, Jackie's bladder chose to empty itself at the same moment. Oh, Christ, he thought. He thought he'd gotten the full scope on the system, but in his caution not to disable *all* the alarms he must've placed the circuit not downline *enough*; he'd accidentally left the systems functioning in this room. *Damn* it! He'd fucked up royally this time—he had to get *out* of here. He snapped up the smallest object in the case—the oval stone, burnished like metal and yet, somehow, not metal—and bolted out the room, frantically retracing his path. Behind him he heard the sound of footsteps pounding up the hardwood stairs, then softening as they took to the thick museum carpeting. He felt a wave of relief— prematurely—as he reached the window through which he'd first entered, he opened it again, started to reel in the rope harness—

"Hold it!"

Jackie whipped around to see a security guard silhouetted in combat stance in the doorway, a .38 gripped firmly with both hands, pointed directly at the fleeing thief. Jackie froze for an instant, then, panicked, forgot about the harness, spun round and started to clamber out the window.

The guard fired.

Straddling the window, Jackie took the bullet in the abdomen and cried out in pain; that and the velocity of the bullet's impact sent him pitching sideways out the window. The world turned upside-down, there was a fire in his stomach and he was falling, two stories, the ground somehow *above* him, a thin cord of blood streaming out of him like a vapor trail—

He plummeted twenty feet to the ground, a messy fall broken inadequately by a couple of garbage cans and a mound of rancid trash. Stunned and in shock, he caught a glimpse of the guard poking his head out of the window above, then vanishing. *Move,* Jackie told himself. *You've got to move.* The lancing pain in his stomach intensified as he staggered to his feet; it became unbearable as he took a step forward, nearly buckling on what was probably a broken ankle. But something propelled him forward, something sent him stumbling down the alley, around a bend, and into another alley; in one hand he still unconsciously clutched the jade stone he had stolen, while with the other he sought to hold his lacerated skin together, blood streaming out between his fingers as he stumbled on. Oh God, he thought, oh,

Jesus, please, please help, I'm sorry, I'm sorry, please *help* me . . .

There were sirens now, and above the roofs of nearby buildings, the red flashing corona of police cars drawing closer. Finally, in an alley behind a dry-cleaning store on Figueroa Street, the pain became too much; he could go no farther. He slumped behind a low wall separating this store's parking lot from the next, he held his hand uselessly over the bleeding wound . . . and, soundlessly, he began to weep, and to pray: Jesus, oh Jesus, I'm *sorry*, I'm an idiot, I'm a thief, but please, let me *live*—I'll get it right next time, I swear, just let me live, oh sweet Christ, just let me *live*—

Slowly, he became aware of something other than the pain in his stomach, or the throbbing in his ankle. He became aware of a growing warmth in his right hand . . . a soothing warmth that he soon felt, as well, in his wounded abdomen, a warmth that blotted out the pain. He looked up at his balled-up hand . . . and saw *light*, a pulsing white glow leaking out from between the fingers of his fist. Oh God, he thought. Was he dying? Don't you see white light when you die? He uncurled his fingers long enough to see the stone—no longer jade-green, no longer marbled, but white-hot, like the heart of a star—yet he felt no pain, no scorching heat, just . . . warmth. There, and in his stomach. Dazed, he closed his fist around the stone once more, not understanding but waiting until the warmth totally obliterated the pain; then he got to his feet and began running, still holding his side, still clutching the stone, afraid to let go of either. He ran strongly, as strongly as you can on a broken ankle, and within minutes he had made his way through the maze of alleys and side streets of downtown Los Angeles, losing himself amid the homeless who peopled its quiet corners.

When he was far enough away from the sirens and the police cars, he leaned up against a brick wall and, for the first time, looked down at himself. Slowly he took his hand away from the blood-soaked sweatshirt he was wearing; the warmth had dissipated, but the pain had not returned. He rolled up his shirt, steeling himself for what he was certain he would see—

And instead saw . . . nothing. No gaping bullet wound, no powder burns, no blood . . . just smooth, unbroken skin. As though he'd never been shot at all.

Stumbling half from disbelief and half from his swollen ankle, he made his way to a pay phone and fished in his pockets for a quarter to call Harry. Harry would come, and pick him up, and then he'd be safe. Harry was always there. Harry would always be there. He found the quarter, dropped it into the slot, and stabbed, a little dazedly, at the touchpad; and as the dial tone was cut off by the click of connection, Jackie exhaled a long breath—allowing himself to believe, at last, that he might live, after all . . .

Even the shadow of sacred Tenan offered little relief from the blistering sun; Ta'li'n felt drained, light-headed, after his long ascent up the steep slopes of the valley. Or perhaps it was the sight of row upon row of failing crops, maize and beans and squash dying on the vine, that made him sway and teeter; he stopped, turned, and looked back down into the valley, seeing terrace upon terrace of irrigation canals lying parched and dry. For centuries Tenan, and the rain goddess, X'la'n, who dwelled within, had provided water to this thirsty land, these otherwise infertile slopes whose crops fed the hungry City below. X'la'n had shaped the volcanic mountain in such a way as to capture the rainfall, to channel it into a stream that fed the canals. The dwelling structure at the valley floor—home to the hundreds of farmers who tilled this land, and the priests who administered them—was adorned with a brightly painted facade, nearly all the bas-relief statues carved in the squat likeness of the water goddess. The correct rituals were still performed each day, the just and proper offerings made in Her honor; but the canals were still dry, and the sound of the river that ran inside the mountain—once a constant, mighty rumble—was now just a thin whisper on the wind.

One of the administrator-priests from the dwelling below drew abreast of Ta'li'n; he had followed at a respectful distance, and now stood beside his superior and offered him a small jade figurine in the shape of the goddess. The high priest closed his eyes, wrapped his hands around the small carved devotion, and prayed.

He stood, motionless, silent, for a full minute—until a brief cooling around him caused him to open his eyes. He looked up; a gray storm cloud pressed low over the valley, blocking the sun, so near it seemed to touch Tenan itself. For a brief moment the priest allowed himself to hope, and, hoping, closed his eyes once more, hands tighter around the talisman as he continued his prayer. It seemed like hours before the first raindrops, carried on the southerly breeze, brushed his face; he opened his eyes again—but far from feeling joy at the light mist which had fanned across the valley, he felt only misery. He had conjured similar mist before, with this talisman, once even a steady rain that had lasted nearly twenty minutes—but what he had been praying for was a cloudburst, a downpour that would split the skies with thunder and fill Tenan, and the canals, with water. He had prayed that the crops might be restored, the exodus from the starving city halted, the unrest within it quelled. And instead he received a light mist which was passing even now . . . the storm cloud dissipating in the hot, dry wind, exposing the brutal sun.

He had prayed, yet known his prayers would be fruitless: he had seen the future, and it contained neither rain nor food—merely ash and flame. The other priest had observed such failures before; he looked respectfully away, to the west, where the sun was falling into the abyss from which it climbed, triumphant, every morning.

"I shall take this," Ta'li'n announced suddenly, weighing the jade figurine in his hand, "back to the temple, where I might consult the Tonalpohialli." It was a lie—the Tonalpohialli, which the high priests used to predict the coming cycle, had yielded the same bleak answers as the peyote—but a convincing one. "As you wish," the administrator said hopefully—then turned and headed down the terraced slopes, to carry a glimmer of false hope back to his fellows.

Ta'li'n hefted the small devotion. The talisman still worked, up to a point; the power vested in it by the gods still lingered. But it, and the two or three others like it used so successfully over the centuries, possessed not nearly enough power to replenish the barren canals. Only the gods, working through the talismans, could do that.

He turned and looked down at the City; the Great Compound was crowded not just with merchants and traders, but pilgrims drawn to the City's great shrines—hundreds of them making the journey each year, to worship and to honor. They called the City "the home of the gods"—would continue to call it that, the priest knew, even in its nameless future—and yet—

And yet there were other cities—Oaxaca, Xochicalco, El Tajin—and other cultures—the Zapotecs to the west, the Mayans along the Gulf, even the warlike Toltecs to the north—rising in ascendancy across the continent. Was it possible—could it be that—

The priest shivered despite the oppressive heat.

Could the gods have found another home?

Harry Faulk was an owlish man in his late fifties, with thinning brown hair, watery eyes set deep beneath arched eyebrows, and a cast to his face that made it seem as though he were always frowning: as though gravity and age had permanently turned down the corners of his mouth, making the creases and wrinkles of his face look forever disapproving, or cynical. Certainly he was frowning when he picked up Jackie at the corner of Figueroa and Temple; he helped the younger man, who could barely take a step without pain, into the car, then looked at him—at the ankle swollen to the size of a grapefruit—and sighed heavily. "We'll stop at a 7-Eleven," he said, shifting the gears of his dilapidated Oldsmobile, "and pick up some ice for that ankle." He turned his gaze to the road as he swung left onto Temple, toward the Harbor Freeway. "But first let's put a little distance between you and wherever you were." The car swung onto the freeway on-ramp, and Jackie felt himself relax, at last, as the Olds merged into the anonymous stream of cars heading north on the 110, carrying him safely and forever away from police cars, from flashing lights, from gunshots in the dark.

Jackie told him where he'd been and what had happened— omitting the gunshot and the wound, the bloody traces of which couldn't be seen in the dimness of the car; omitting too the aftermath, the stone, the healing—and Harry's face grew even more disapproving than usual. "Christ," he said in disgust. "How many times have I told you, museums aren't worth the trouble. Half the stuff's too big to carry and the other half's too hard to move once you've boosted it." Just ahead, the Harbor split in two, on the left becoming the Pasadena Freeway, on the right, the Hollywood. Harry veered to the right.

"No more museums," Jackie promised distantly. His hand, hidden from Harry's view, still clutched the stone, no longer white, no longer warm—a deceptively cool, green stone. He wondered how he would tell Harry about it, and what had happened back in the alley. Harry would never believe it—he could hardly blame him for that—but there had never been any secrets between the two of them, and Jackie was not going to start now, not when he'd been given this second chance . . . a chance he wanted desperately to share with his friend.

Harry Faulk was the closest thing to a father Jackie had ever known; his own father was a dream, a memory of beard stubble and big callused hands holding his son aloft—a lingering scent of aftershave or cologne, and that was all. He had left when Jackie was four, and to this day, Jackie could not recall his face. Jackie and Faulk had first met, briefly, ten years ago, back when Jackie was a runner for Joseph Rubello; three years later, Jackie found himself sharing a cell with Harry at Vacaville, the younger man serving ten months for burglary, the older a year and a half for mail order fraud. When Harry got out, Jackie found him a cheap one-bedroom in the two-story, yellow stucco courtyard apartments on Fountain, off Highland Boulevard in Hollywood, where Jackie had already taken up residence. Since then they'd executed a succession of seldom risky but only marginally profitable swindles, scams, and the occasional burglary—usually enough to pay for food and rent, but not much more. And on their sporadic solo efforts—like Jackie's, tonight—there was an unvoiced, unwritten understanding between them: if either made that big score first, he would cut the other in.

Harry took the Highland exit off the freeway and headed toward a convenience store a few blocks north of Hollywood and Highland. He dug in his pocket for change. "I got a buck in here for some ice," he began. "I'll stop and—"

"Forget the ice," Jackie said suddenly. It had just occurred to him how he would convince Harry of all that had happened this night. "I won't need it."

"What the hell's wrong with you?" Harry said. "You got an ankle the size of an emerging nation, you might've broken it—"

"I did break it," Jackie said. "I felt the bone snap."

"Then we get you some ice, take you to an emergency room, and get that taped or splinted or whatever the hell they do, and—"

"I *won't need it*, Harry," he insisted doggedly. Somehow Jackie convinced him that he wasn't in shock, wasn't delirious or drunk or stoned, and got him to take him not to the nearest hospital, but home—finally by lying, by telling him that the security guard at the museum saw him hobble away and that showing up at an ER with a broken ankle might not be such a good idea just now. "Okay," Harry allowed. "We'll wait till tomorrow, find a private doctor. But we still stop for some ice."

Back in Jackie Thompson's bleak little single apartment, with its scuffed linoleum floors and its foam-rubber couch that doubled for a bed, Harry Faulk watched as the young man showed him the green marbled stone he had stolen; watched as Jackie closed his fingers around it; then cupped his other hand around his broken, swollen ankle; watched as light spilled out from between the fingers of Jackie's fist, and as the swelling began to perceptibly shrink before his eyes. He stood, transfixed, as Jackie, eyes shut, seemed to concentrate . . . seemed to *will* the swelling smaller and smaller . . . until, finally, the white light faded, Jackie took his hand away from his foot . . . and Harry stood staring in awe and disbelief at the perfectly normal, unbruised, unswollen ankle. Jackie stood up and grinned; not only could he stand without support, he even danced a few giddy tap steps, to Harry's utter astonishment.

"Jackie . . . how in the *hell*—"

Jackie told him, then; all of it. And now, no longer in the concealing darkness of the car, Harry could see Jackie's blood-soaked sweatshirt, which rolled up to reveal absolutely nothing —nothing, certainly, to account for the dark, mottled stain on

Jackie's shirt. And Harry began to believe. Not in the way Jackie believed, but the power of the stone, that he began to accept. He asked if he could hold it a moment, and as he turned the stone over in his hand, staring at it in wonder and dawning realization, he said softly, "My God, Jackie. You realize how much something like this is *worth?* We could have every goddamn hospital and research center in the country down on their *knees* for this—we could set our own *price*—"

"No," Jackie said, with a steel and a suddenness that surprised him as much as it did Harry, who looked up, startled. Jackie lowered his voice. "I struck a . . . a deal, back in that alley. To . . . change . . . if I got out of there alive."

"A *deal?*" Harry said derisively. "With who? God?"

"Maybe," Jackie said. "Why not?"

Faulk sighed, sensing his friend's determination, and backed off.

"Okay. Fine," he said. "No more burglaries. No more scams. Man, we won't *need* any of that penny-ante shit if we sell this. Look: it's simple. We find some doctor with a Beverly Hills address to front for us, he brokers the rock and gets a commission; by the time the buyers find out it's stolen property, they won't care. They'll hush it up, and we'll be set for life."

"If they hush it up, they won't go public on it, and it won't reach the people it needs to reach," Jackie said adamantly. "They'll keep it to themselves, Harry. They'll test it, and X-ray it, try to figure out ways to duplicate it—and if that doesn't work, they'll keep it to themselves and use it to cure billionaires with lung cancer. That oughta be worth a new wing to the hospital, eh? Or how about Alzheimer's? Two wings and a parking structure. Maybe even—"

"So what the hell," Harry snapped, exasperated, "do *you* want to do with the damn thing?"

Jackie hesitated only a moment.

"I want to use it to heal people," he said quietly.

Harry stared at him in disbelief.

"Jesus H. Christ," he said softly.

Ta'li'n did not tell the other priest-rulers of his plan; they were too busy squabbling among themselves, arguing how best to appease the gods, how to put down the uprisings and nullify the proponents of the New Order. The dissension that was tearing apart the general populace had spread to its ruling elite, and Ta'li'n knew there was no way he could stitch the Council together any more than he could avert the coming catastrophe. So he set about on his own course, quietly procuring as many of the sacred talismans as he could, hoping to preserve, at least, some small part of his culture.

He secured the amulet of Pe'x'r, goddess of fertility, a necklace of polished obsidian chips strung on a fine gold strand; barren women wore the necklace for seven days and seven nights, and their husbands made love to them on the seventh and last night, planting the seed that invariably took root where none could grow before. He acquired, discreetly, the cloak of Ya'n'l, god of springtime, of renewal, a god known also in Oaxaca as Xipe Totec; at the spring rites, Ta'li'n often wore this cloak himself, helping to celebrate and honor the renewal of the land. And he obtained the small golden figurine of Qo't'l, the fat god, bringer of luck and prosperity, entrusted for times to families beset by death or ill omen: the small figure squatted on the hearth of the accursed family, speaking, it was said, in its own tongue to the spirits of misfortune which plagued the home, convincing the demons to move elsewhere.

Each of the relics and talismans still possessed the power invested in them at the time of their creation, when they were kissed by the breath of the gods on the hot, dry ceremonial platforms lining the central Avenue. Ta'li'n tested each one before he locked them away in a chest in his private chambers.

Pe'x'r, Ya'n'l, Qo't'l, X'l'o—all the major deities were represented, save for X'la'n, the plumed serpent, whose talismans were beyond even Ta'li'n's political authority; some of the more recent, and more sanguinary, additions to the pantheon like Za'd'e, god of the curved knife; and H'ue'na, god of medicine and health, healing, and well-being. For this last talisman, the priest would have to seek out the healer, Ch'at'l—and for that reason he suspected that procuring this one would be almost as difficult as obtaining the serpent's. If not more so.

The Shrine Auditorium was packed to capacity tonight, as it was each night, three times a week; Jackie peered out from the wings, holding back the curtain to make the narrowest of slits through which to see the crowd. It never failed to amaze him, the size and the reverence of the audience, the low whispers in which they spoke, as though afraid to speak too loudly their hopes and hurts; and it never failed to frighten him, either, as he scanned the line of supplicants, noting their disabilities or deformities, wondering at those whose afflictions were not readily apparent, and realizing that they had come here to see *him*—that for most of them, he was their last best hope, their final recourse along a torturous path of pain and disappointment.

Tonight he saw three people in wheelchairs, one ravaged by the blight of Lou Gehrig's Disease, the other two paralyzed from the neck down; behind them stood a small girl, thin, emaciated, with no hair, obviously the result of a chemotherapy or radiation treatment that had not worked; and half a dozen men and women with the gaunt, wasted look of AIDS victims. Jackie knew that for every one of these sufferers who would leave tonight weeping with joy at their miraculous recovery, there would be at least two who would leave disappointed, or buoyed with false hope; the stone was not, he had learned, infallible, and it was difficult to predict which ailment or which sufferer would be healed by it. To date, Jackie had failed to cure anyone of AIDS, and had only arrested, not eliminated, the growth of several cancers—turning malignant tumors to benign, and at least one case of leukemia into remission. Viral and neoplasmic diseases like these were most resistant to the stone's power; it had better luck dealing with simpler, though no less crippling, ailments, as though those were the ones it was originally designed to treat: bacterial infections, metabolic and nutritional diseases, "mechanical" trauma caused by physical injury—paralysis, muscular and skeletal damage. The stone could cure arthritis, but not MS; gangrene, but not, say, chemical poisoning . . .

Like that first day, six months ago; that first morning, in Lafayette Park, when a scared, nervous Jackie had shuffled into the park, stood on an outcropping of rock, and, the stone hidden in one hand, began calling out to the homeless people scattered —sleeping, eating, talking to one another or talking to themselves—around the park. "My name is John," he told them, using a name he had not heard since his mother died, years before, "and if you're hurting, I can help you." They thought he was a nutcase, of course, at first, and ignored him—until one old woman, perhaps a quart low herself, stumbled up and asked if he could do anything for the bursitis in her left hip. Jackie gently put a hand to her hip—so tiny and frail he was almost afraid to apply too much pressure—palmed the stone, keeping his hand behind him so no one might see the glow as he closed his eyes, trying to will this woman well again . . .

And succeeded. And then, all at once, it seemed, they

were upon him: battered, hurting people with arthritis, or cataracts, or emphysema, and so busy was he in healing them that he didn't notice until an hour into his labors that there were now news cameras trained on him, videotape whirring away and a news van from Channel 11 parked on Wilshire Boulevard . . . brought there, Jackie later discovered, by an anonymous tip from Harry. He'd called all the local stations, and though the three network affiliates ignored him, independent KTTV had sent a team; as soon as the cameras started grinding, Harry was there, shepherding the supplicants as he would do on a much larger scale later on: "Brother John will see you all," he'd said, Jackie hearing the designation for the first time; "Wait your turn, sisters, brothers, wait your turn . . ."

Jackie wasn't comfortable with the title, nor with the religious trappings of all this—the Church of the Brotherhood, as they came to call it—but Harry had convinced him that it was the only way the public could accept what he was doing. It was probably the shrewdest move of Faulk's career: after the recent, bitter disappointments and breaches of trust by so many evangelists and faith healers, at the appearance of one who could actually *deliver*—one whose results were, in fact, verified by baffled physicians—people flocked to Brother John, happy to finally find one Man of God worthy of their faith. And Jackie had to admit he liked it; for a man who had never in his life been treated with even the most minimal respect, this newfound adoration was . . . intoxicating.

"Jac—John?" Harry's voice, behind him. He turned, amused as always to see Harry looking so respectable in his smartly tailored gray three-piece suit. "Better get ready," Harry suggested. "We go to floor in five minutes."

Jackie nodded and went to his dressing room, where a petite young woman applied his makeup for him; before leaving, he checked himself in the mirror, impressed at the man he saw reflected back at him: his hair neatly trimmed, his tendency toward five o'clock shadow even at noon artfully concealed by the makeup, his cream-colored suit impeccable and tasteful. For the first time in his life, he could look at himself without the slightest hint of self-disgust, without hearing that inner mocking voice harping at him, belittling him. For the first time in his life, he actually felt proud—of himself, and of what he was doing.

"Brothers . . . sisters . . ." He could hear Harry, always and ever the advance man, warming up the crowd. ". . . if you think no one cares . . . if you think no one can help you . . . you're wrong."

Jackie left the dressing room, waiting in the wings as Harry finished his introduction, feeling a rush of excitement and anticipation as he listened. "We don't pretend to be infallible," Harry was saying reverently. "That's reserved for a Higher power than ours. But we can try. We can try to take away the pain, and we hope you'll let us." A susurrus of voices from the crowd murmured eager agreement. Harry went on for a while longer, delivering the pious homilies and righteous platitudes the audience seemed to demand, finally concluding with, "My friends, I give you . . . Brother John."

A burst of heartfelt applause greeted Jackie upon his entrance; it never failed to move him, to expunge his doubts and get the adrenaline surging. As usual, Harry had handpicked the line of supplicants that stretched from the lip of the stage, up the aisle, to the back of the auditorium—there were only so many people they could treat in a two-hour telecast—with the simpler cases, the rheumatics, the deaf, the vision-impaired, up front. That way they led the hour with immediate and tangible successes, and by the second hour they could afford the occasional failure or non-visible healing (cancer cures, being internal, didn't make for especially good television). Jackie disliked the artifice of it, but knowing the limitations of the stone, it was necessary . . . though Harry liked it because the more dramatic the cure, the bigger the "love offerings" the next day, and Jackie was constantly fighting to keep the quieter, less showy sufferers on the bill at all.

The first person in line was a classic Faulk choice; yet the moment he saw her, Jackie could hardly fault Harry for it. She was a ten-year-old girl, with pretty green eyes and limp blonde hair, sitting in a wheelchair; behind her her mother hovered nervously, her eyes pathetically searching Jackie's face as he turned to them—a silent, desperate plea that Jackie had come to know only too well. He purposely averted his gaze from the mother, squatting down to look in the little girl's eyes; she looked self-conscious, embarrassed, but had none of her mother's reek of desperation.

"Hi," he said softly. His body mike picked up even the faintest of whispers and made them echo in the vast auditorium.

"Hello," the girl replied tentatively.

"I'm John. What's your name?"

"Amanda," the girl said with a shy smile.

"How long have you been in that chair, Amanda?" Jackie asked gently.

The mother answered for her: "Almost three years, Brother John. She was . . . hit by a car. They never did find the driver . . ."

Yes, of course. Multiple sclerosis, muscular dystrophy, they were more problematic; Jackie's success rate with them was low. Harry would never put one of them on first. Simple spinal break, that was better, more potentially dramatic. Jackie sighed inwardly. Right now, he didn't care; right now he just wanted to make this little girl well.

"The driver," he told the girl's mother, "will answer to God's judgment. All that concerns us here is Amanda." He reached up, one hand palming the green marbled stone, and laid his hands lightly on her legs. "Don't be afraid," he said, smiling. He slid one hand—the one clenching the stone—behind Amanda's back, touching her spinal column. The stone didn't have to be in contact with the afflicted area to function, but this served to hide its glow from the audience and the camera. They had decided, when they'd made the transition to television, that the glow would seem too phony, give skeptics a chance to claim they were just using fancy video effects—so Jackie either hid the stone, as he was doing now, or covered it with a black felt cloth inside his cupped hand, which damped the glow without diminishing the warmth, the power.

Jackie closed his eyes and began to concentrate. "Dear God," he said softly, "help this child. Help her walk again . . ." Harry was always trying to get him to make his speeches more flowery, more pious, but the words sounded unnatural to Jackie; *help me* or *help her* seemed sufficient for the occasion. He felt the stone growing hot in his hand, felt that warmth spreading through his clenched fingers, then beyond—

"Mommy," he heard the girl say, "it feels *hot*—"

"It does?" The mother's voice was full of hope. "Honey, are you sure?"

"God's love is warming her," came Harry's voice, booming and sententious. "Praise be!" The audience chanted in unison: *"Praise be!"* Jackie tried to ignore it, tried to concentrate on nothing but the task before him—for the briefest of instants he felt something shift, felt something seem to fall into place in Amanda's back, and then the stone began to cool. When the heat was totally dissipated, Jackie opened his eyes. He drew his hand from behind her back, pretending to wipe perspiration on his jacket but in reality pocketing the stone; then he took the girl's hands in his, smiled, and began to stand. "Stand with me, honey," he said gently. "You can do it."

The girl came to her feet, tentatively . . . Jackie let go of her hands . . . and she stood. Unaided. The audience cheered. Amanda took a step forward, away from her wheelchair, a look of wonder and delight on her face. The audience roared. "Praise God!" Harry shouted. *"Praise God!"* the crowd bellowed back, filling the auditorium with their cheers. The mother embraced her daughter, and then the daughter, spontaneously, ran to Jackie and hugged him around his waist. Jackie, genuinely moved and pleased, stroked the girl's hair—

Only to find Harry, a moment later, hustling the little girl and her mother offstage as quickly as possible, to make way for the next supplicant . . .

At the end of the evening, an exhausted Jackie left the stage to wild applause and exuberant cries: "We love you, Brother!" they shouted, and Jackie felt drained but happy, depleted but exultant. "Praise the Lord!" Then, finally, Harry took the podium to deliver his fund-raising pitch: "On behalf of Brother John, thank you for coming tonight. And those of you watching at home—won't you take a moment to count the blessings in your life, and perhaps share some of them with others? Anything you can give, to do the work He has charged us with, would be deeply appreciated. God bless you all, and good night."

That night and the next morning, the phones in the Church's small offices off Cahuenga Boulevard rang incessantly with credit-card pledges, even as an overworked staff opened letters containing checks, money orders, dollar bills, and sometimes even pennies from a child's piggybank.

Jackie had his misgivings about all this, but the fact was, it did cost money to rent the Shrine, lease video equipment, hire technicians, and, most expensive of all, purchase airtime on the two hundred and fifty TV stations across the country that carried the program. By now Harry and Jackie had moved from their dive on Fountain to a pair of pleasant townhouses just above Sunset; to Jackie the modest condos were palaces, but Faulk, it developed, took a broader view.

The day after the broadcast, Harry drove his new white baby Mercedes down Sunset to an office building a few blocks east of Vine. It was a twenty-story, steel-and-glass tower, and Jackie thought they were going there to a restaurant for lunch; but the elevator instead delivered them onto a deserted floor filled with empty offices, plush carpeting, and stacks of boxes containing what seemed to be personal computers, phone systems, and office equipment. "Welcome," Harry announced, "to the new headquarters of the Church of the Brotherhood."

Jackie's jaw dropped. He'd put all the financial dealings in Harry's hands, but this—"The whole *floor?*" he said, with quiet astonishment.

"Five floors," Harry corrected him, "and the penthouse. C'mon. Let's take a look at our new home."

Numbly, Jackie followed him to the three-thousand-square-foot penthouse that perched atop the tower. This was in better array than the offices downstairs; Jackie followed, dazed, as Harry led him through a home the like of which he had never imagined he'd see in this lifetime. There was a huge living room with a three-cornered, sixty-foot wall of windows overlooking the city: to the east the mirrored facade of the Bonaventure Hotel, five glassy cylinders dwarfed by even higher structures, gleamed in the afternoon haze; to the west, Beverly Hills sprawled lazily from Sunset to Pico, stands of palm trees marching down wide, immaculate streets; west of that, the sleek towers of Century City shimmered in the heat and the smog, seeming, in tandem with the skyscrapers of downtown, to bracket the Basin.

Off the living room was a formal dining room already furnished with sleek Scandinavian tables, chairs, and hutch; beyond that, a state-of-the-art, fully equipped kitchen with three microwaves and a cooking island the size of Catalina; down a T-shaped corridor, a cluster of four bedroom suites. Harry's and Jackie's were at opposite ends of the corridor, each one enormous, with breathtaking city views, full baths, and small kitchenettes off the bathrooms.

Jackie sank, stunned, onto the soft king-size bed in his room, but Harry grinned and pulled him to his feet. "Tour's not over yet," he said, leading Jackie to a private elevator that took them to the roof—and an Olympic-sized swimming pool surrounded on all sides by majestic views of the city.

"Jesus, Harry," Jackie said softly. "We're not actually going to *live* here?"

"Why not? 'Appearances'? It's legitimate, we use five floors for office space, and the rest—hell, who's going to begrudge a few luxuries to a man who's helped so many people?"

Jackie felt uncomfortable; he didn't know whether he wanted to be convinced or not. "Why do we need so much money?" he asked. "Ninety percent of the people who contribute won't even be able to get on the show, just by sheer weight of numbers. Not that the stone could handle so many, anyway, but—"

"I'll give you one very good reason we need so much money, my friend," Harry said soberly. "You and I, we don't have the cleanest of slates in the world. You have any idea how many of our old pals from Vacaville have turned up lately? In need of funds?"

Jackie started. "You've been paying blackmail?"

"Pin money. Most of them are so stupid they ask for a hundred thousand, I bargain them down to fifty, they go away happy. It's the reporters who're more savvy; they ask for more, and I have to deliver."

"Oh, shit, Harry, maybe we should forget this whole—"

"Don't be an idiot. This *was* your idea, wasn't it? *You* wanted to heal people, right?"

"Yeah, but—all this—it doesn't seem—"

"Fair?" Harry said. "For a man who's made cripples walk . . . made the blind see . . . the deaf hear? Why the hell shouldn't you have a few creature comforts? After all the shitholes you've lived in, after all the good you've done in the last year—you're telling me you don't deserve a decent *home*, for the first time in your miserable life?"

Jackie wavered. In that moment of hesitation, Harry put a hand to his back, started walking him along the pool, the two of them taking in the city below. "Besides," he said, "I think we can eliminate the danger of extortion, with a little grease applied to the right wheels. Our records, our convictions, our down time—the only place it really exists is in the state computers, right?"

Jackie began to see where this was going. "You want to bribe somebody to go in and wipe out our records? How the hell much will *that* cost?"

"Not as much as you'd think." Harry smiled. "I've done a little checking. Seems the deputy commissioner of prisons for the state of California has a wife, with cancer. Terminal. I think a deal could be struck . . ."

Jackie said nothing. He looked out across the dazzling blue swimming pool, toward downtown; from up here, that night in the alley—all the nights in all the alleys—seemed utterly remote. He felt safe. When was the last time he'd felt safe? He couldn't remember. He didn't care. Harry was talking about profit margins and satellite time and promotional items. He listened to Harry, he nodded, and he did not protest.

The healer lived in a dwelling identical to those of the majority of the City's inhabitants: single-story, white-walled buildings of adobe brick, each compound containing some thirty apartments clustered around a central atrium; there were no windows in any of the apartments, but no walls facing the center court either, only hanging curtains that most of the day remained open, admitting sunlight into the comfortable rooms. At the entrance to the compound a doorkeeper greeted Ta'li'n with a solemn nod, respectfully stepping aside to let him pass. The laughter of children carried out on a gust of wind, and the priest felt a twinge of pain, knowing how soon that laughter was to end.

Most courtyards had at their center a small brick temple, a miniature of the ones atop the great pyramids, each one adorned with the likeness or symbols of a particular god; this one, understandably enough, was an altar to H'ue'na, god of medicine. Around the fringes of the atrium, small children chased one another, laughed and giggled; at the priest's approach they hushed momentarily, but as he made his way to Ch'at'l's apartment, they quickly resumed their games.

Outside the healer's room—its curtain drawn, for the moment—some half a dozen people lingered in a casual line, each injured in some way, or visibly ill. Ta'li'n hesitated, weighing the extent of their afflictions; but told himself he could not let that sway him. He pushed aside the curtain and entered the healer's apartment.

Ch'at'l was seated on a pillow in the middle of the sparsely furnished room, eyes closed in concentration, his left hand on the stomach of a woman who looked to be about five months pregnant. The room was lit only by candlelight, but even in the dimness the priest could see a distinctive glow—a pure, white, pulsing light that spilled out from between the fingers of the healer's right hand. He seemed not to notice Ta'li'n's entrance or, if he did, paid it no mind. The priest kept a respectful silence, watching the old man for some moments, then letting his gaze drift to the bright frescoes painted on the plaster walls: pictures of running children, laughing women, crying infants, strong and vibrant men. Ta'li'n had almost forgotten how uniquely beautiful the healer's quarters were; each apartment was adorned with similar murals, but Ch'at'l's burst with life and health and light, even in this semidarkness.

After several minutes the glow in Ch'at'l's hand subsided, and the healer opened his eyes and nodded with satisfaction. "The child will be fine," he told the woman, who exhaled a long breath of relief. "The birth canal was twisted, askew. It is repaired. The birth will occur, now, unimpeded."

The woman hugged him gratefully, and as they stood Ta'li'n saw how small the old man was—perhaps five feet tall, with browned, leathery skin taut over a brittle skeleton. If height were a measure of authority, Ta'li'n would have had no problem fulfilling his task. But not even the authority vested in him by his robes was sufficient to intimidate this frail old man.

The woman left the room, and only then did Ch'at'l look up to greet his visitor. "Most Holy. Good day," he said with deceptive humility. "Is there an ailment that plagues you? How may I help?"

Ta'li'n found himself straightening, mustering as much authority as he was able. "No ailment," he said. "I—have need of the stone."

The old man blinked his large black eyes, eyes set deep in a lined and furrowed face; his bald head seemed somehow too large for his frail body. "I do not understand," he said, but something in his tone made the priest feel that he did understand, that he was somehow expecting this. "If there is no ailment, why then do you have need of the stone?"

"The Council," Ta'li'n lied, "requires it for a ceremony. It will be returned to you when we are done."

"I am not to join in this . . . ceremony?"

"No."

The healer looked at him with those black, penetrating eyes. "I have been entrusted with this stone," he said quietly, opening his hand to reveal the green marbled stone in his palm, "for over sixty years, and not once has it left my sight." He met the priest's gaze evenly. "I do not take my trust lightly."

"No. No, of course not," Ta'li'n said quickly. "But it is but for a short while, and will be returned to you as soon as—" He groped for a convincing falsehood. "—as soon as we are able," he concluded lamely.

"But what of those in need of it?" the healer asked, nodding toward outside, toward the waiting line of ill and injured. "How long must they suffer?"

Ta'li'n was growing more frustrated and impatient. Damn the old man for his stubbornness. "It is not our intent that *anyone* suffer," he said, taking a step forward, raising his voice, "but we *must* have the stone. You are directed to give it to me, in the name of—"

The old man took a step forward, raising his hand in a placating gesture before the priest could invoke any deities. "High One—please," he said quietly. "I know why you need it. You need not dissemble."

Ta'li'n bristled at the old man's impiety, accurate though it was. "How dare you suggest that I—"

"You are not the only one," Ch'at'l said simply, "to whom the peyote sings its sad chorale."

Ta'li'n started. The healer moved slowly to a table crowded with urns and bottles, all filled with various herbs and roots; he took the lid off one jade bottle, drawing out a small white mescal cap. Ta'li'n stared at it, in disbelief. The old man hobbled toward him, the tiny white cap held aloft on the tip of one small, bony finger. He smiled.

"Teotihuacán," he said, and the priest flinched, as though at an insect's bite. "That is what they will call us, in the time to come, is it not?"

The priest nodded, dully, taken completely off-guard. The healer smiled again, but there was no trace of mockery in it, just a gentle reassurance. "I know what is to come," he said, "and I know what you are trying to do. And when the time is right, I shall give you the stone. But in the meantime, there are many ailments to be seen to, and many sufferings to be eased."

Ta'li'n frowned ruefully. "Only to die," he said in a low voice, "along with the City."

"Not all of them," Ch'at'l said. "The City will die, but many will escape. Who can say that a fractured bone I repair today will not carry a man out of the City? With perhaps a woman, or a child, in his arms?"

Ta'li'n hesitated, but the healer put a hand reassuringly on his arm. "When the time comes," he said again, "it will be yours. I promise." A hint of mischief gleamed in Ch'at'l's eyes. "Or don't you trust me?"

The priest smiled, for perhaps the first time in days. "After sixty years," he sighed bemusedly, "who am I to begin to doubt?"

The old man laughed, then hobbled over to draw back the curtain and admit his next patient.

The wife of the deputy commissioner of prisons had a malignant tumor in her left lung, and, according to the latest magnetic resonance scan, the cancer had begun to metastasize to her right lung and upper colon. Despite his worries over the stone's spotty success in dealing with cancers, Jackie did his best, half out of concern for the woman—she was only forty-one but looked nearly sixty; drawn, haggard, wearing an obvious wig to hide the effects of chemo and radiation treatments—and half out of concern for himself, and Harry. If this worked, they would be beyond blackmail; if it failed, who was to say that the commissioner himself might not expose them, out of bitterness and disappointment? Jackie did his usual number, the stone covered in black cloth to hide the glow, did the laying-on of hands, and, for the next three days, waited anxiously for the results of new tests from Cedars-Sinai.

On the morning of that Friday's taping, the word came in from Cedars: the growth of the tumor in the left lung had been arrested, and the cancer in the right lung and colon had similarly been halted. She wasn't cured, but she was in remission—and that was enough for her grateful husband. Within twenty-four hours, all traces of Faulk's and Thompson's criminal records—arrests, convictions, detentions—had been expunged, neatly, from the state computer system.

Jackie was surprised at the extent of relief he felt upon hearing the news; amazed at the sense of freedom it brought him. Even before Harry had told him about the extortion, a part of him had worried, every time he stepped onto that stage, that someone, anyone, everyone would see through the neatly tailored suit and the salon-trimmed hair, to the frightened second-story man beneath. Now he went on stage and felt only confidence, and pride, when the crowd cheered at his entrance, or when he made a lame girl walk, or a deaf man hear. He was growing to like that sound, that applause and adulation, more and more—

And, conversely, coming to hate the awkward silence and unspoken disappointment when it *didn't* work—when the young man with MS *didn't* get up from his wheelchair and dance a little jig, when the AIDS victim's sores did not heal on the spot, and the emphysema sufferer failed to stop coughing and gasping for air. Jackie came to hate those moments, wanted less and less to hear that disillusioned silence and more and more the cheers and approbation.

So when Harry decided to allow no more AIDS victims on the broadcast, Jackie readily agreed. When Harry continued to front-load the program with simpler afflictions that made for more dramatic cures, Jackie no longer objected. And when Faulk began screening the supplicants more carefully, weeding out the cancer and leukemia sufferers—not because there was no chance at saving them, but because even if they were cured, it was impossible to see on the spot, because it didn't make for good *television*—Jackie kept his silence. They still took on the occasional private patient with cancer, of course, and when the results were positive, trumpeted them to the press; the failures were smoothed over with large monetary donations to the deceased's family. Tax deductible.

The streamlined program was cut to ninety minutes but broadcast, via satellite now, four times a week instead of three; the net effect was approximately the same number of people healed, but an increase in profit margin. The Church of the Brotherhood quickly expanded to fill all five floors that Faulk had rented; donations increased by 55 percent over the next six months, bringing in an average of 115 million dollars a year; competing evangelists chafed over the inroads the Church had made into their congregations, and at their inability to find any kind of sex or embezzlement scandals to discredit and dethrone the new king of televangelism.

Harry was very careful not to give them any ammunition, either. Brother John's penthouse home was expensively, but not opulently, furnished; most of the luxuries in which Jackie indulged himself could reasonably be called deductible: state-of-the-art video and audio equipment, spa and gym facilities (how could Brother John be expected to heal others if he didn't take care of his own body?), and an abundance of foods Jackie had never had the money to even taste before (with Faulk always careful to donate a fraction of what they spent on food for themselves to some charity for the homeless and hungry). Compared to many evangelists' self-styled Disneylands, it all seemed positively modest.

As for women, Harry screened the supplicants very carefully for potential entertainment purposes: disfigured or crippled women were especially grateful when John's healing touch wiped away the scars that had made them feel like pariahs, or reawakened feeling in parts of their bodies long numb with paralysis. Such women were uncommonly thankful and loyal, and unlikely to sell their stories to the *Enquirer.*—especially after being feted and gifted with jewelry, clothes, and cars.

Jackie no longer asked why they needed to make so much money. Jackie no longer asked any questions, to speak of. He was content to revel in the love and applause of the audience, and in the comforts which that love provided. He was still doing good, after all—wasn't he? And wasn't that what mattered, in the end?

They were going over last-minute scheduling details for that evening's telecast when the intercom in Jackie's inner office buzzed. "Brother John?" came his secretary's voice, rich and mellow. "There's someone here to see you. He doesn't have an appointment, but he says his name is—Joseph Rubello?"

Jackie exchanged a quick, startled look with Harry.

"Son of a bitch," said Faulk, a nasty smile coming to him, slowly. "You going to see him?"

Jackie considered a moment, then smiled back.

"Why not?" he allowed generously. But when his finger toggled the intercom, there were the beginnings of a satisfied, and not altogether pleasant, smile on his lips. "Send him in, Bobbi," he said, settling in behind his wide teakwood desk. Harry perched on the arm of a sofa across the room, looking like an owl about to watch a kill from the safety of a tree limb.

Bobbi ushered Rubello into the inner office, then discreetly shut the door behind her; Jackie rose from his seat and extended a hand to the visitor. Twenty years ago, in his prime, Joseph Rubello was a physically powerful man, broad, square-shouldered, barrel-chested; even now, in his late fifties, with more fat than muscle, his was still a commanding presence, though one tempered by age, infirmity, and . . . something else. Something that Jackie had never seen in him before; something like fear.

"Jackie," he said with a near-genuine heartiness; his grip was weaker than Jackie remembered it—not that Rubello had ever had much call to shake Jackie's hand before. "Good to see you. *Really* good . . ."

"Been a while, hasn't it, Joe," Jackie agreed. He had never called him "Joe" before; if the old man was affronted, he didn't show it.

"Yeah, must be, what, five, six years . . . ?"

"Eleven," Jackie said evenly. "Last I heard from you, your thugs put me in the hospital for botching a delivery for you. You sent flowers and a card. Thoughtful as hell."

Rubello paled, then laughed nervously.

"Hey . . . Jackie. That's history. I mean, c'mon, eleven years; you're not gonna hold that against me, are you?"

"John," said the younger man suddenly.

"What?"

"It's John. My name is John, now. Not Jackie."

"Oh. Sure. John." Rubello glanced appreciatively around Jackie's office. "Sweet little place you've got here."

He wasn't here for blackmail, that much Jackie was certain of; his demeanor would be entirely different. And surely, with his contacts, Rubello knew that digging up evidence for extortion would be nearly impossible now. That left only one possible reason for this visit.

"Something I can . . . do . . . for you, Joe?" Jackie asked quietly.

Rubello looked him square in the eye, and Jackie saw not just that glimmer of fear again, but the sweet complement of desperation, and need. "You . . . you really can do what they say?" he said. "It's not some kind of scam?"

Jackie smiled. He nodded.

"I can do it," he said. Then, with a trace of amusement in his voice: "What is it, Joe? Cancer? All those Honduran cigars catching up with you?"

Rubello hesitated—Jackie could almost see the struggle inside him, his dignity warring with his desperation—then took a short breath and shook his head. "Atherosclerosis," he said. "I had quadruple bypass surgery last year, cleared out two of the arteries, but I—" He winced slightly. "I had another heart attack, six months ago. Nearly died. Just a matter of time 'til the next one."

"All that high living and rich food, eh, Joe?" Faulk said, speaking for the first time. Rubello glanced at him, a flicker of disgust crossing his face, then quickly gone as he nodded tightly. "Yeah," he said, swallowing his pride. "I guess so."

Jackie breathed a silent sigh of relief. Just an excess of fat cells, clogging his arteries and blood vessels; a nutritional disease, not a viral one, nothing the stone couldn't tackle handily. Rubello turned from Faulk, looked pleadingly at Jackie.

"Ja—John," he said quietly. "Please. Anything you want, just name it. A blank check. Hundred, two hundred thousand dollars . . . whatever it takes, it's yours."

But Jackie stood his ground, voice flat, gaze cold as he stared at the older man.

"You treated me like shit, Joe. Like you treated all your runners. Like you treat everybody. And now you want me to cure you . . . give you another ten, twenty years to go *on* treating people like shit?" Jackie shook his head, started out from behind his desk with a quick nod to Faulk. "C'mon, Harry. We tape in another couple of—"

Rubello blocked his path, as Jackie knew he would. His lower lip trembled with rage and fear, his voice was disdainful and imploring at the same time. "What do you want me to do, Jackie? 'Scuse me—*John*. You want me to beg?"

Jackie gave him a chill smile. "That'd be nice."

There was a long pause, then Rubello nodded once and said, "Okay. Revenge. I can understand that. Maybe I'd do the same thing. Maybe I deserve it. Okay, Jackie—I'm *begging* you. Help me. You want me to get down on my knees? I'll do it. I don't care. I want to *live.*"

Jackie considered a long moment, then nodded with satisfaction.

"Okay, Joe," he said offhandedly. "That's fine. That, and, say, one million, ought to do it."

Rubello paled. "One *million?* Are you out of your—"

"Price just went up. One million five."

"Jackie, for God's sake—"

"Two million. I've got overhead, Joe, serious overhead."

At that, finally, Rubello caved in; the resistance seemed to leave him in a rush, like air from a slashed tire. "All right," he said hoarsely. "Two million. Just *do* it, goddammit. *Do it!*"

Jackie smiled with satisfaction. "Sit down," he said, nodding toward the chair opposite Jackie's desk; while Rubello's face was turned, Jackie palmed the stone, wrapped in its black velvet cocoon, then went to Rubello, put his other hand over the old man's heart, and closed his eyes.

The stone became warm in Jackie's hand—but not very. Something was wrong; it was far cooler than it should have been, cooler than Jackie had yet felt it. The last several weeks, he'd noticed, the stone's heat had been gradually lessening, but he'd attributed that to overuse—had deliberately skipped the taping before tonight's, in fact, to give it a rest. But now he realized that it had not helped. It felt about as warm as a cup of tea, rapidly cooling to room temperature.

He didn't tell Rubello this, of course; and, a day later, when Rubello called, joyously, to tell him that the latest blood tests showed a significant *decrease* in the number of fat cells in his system, he graciously accepted the mobster's thanks, as well as the two-million-dollar "love offering" that was messengered over that afternoon.

But all through the taping the night before, Jackie had felt the stone growing less and less warm . . . until, halfway through the program, he surreptitiously ditched the velvet cloak, thinking that perhaps that was inhibiting the stone's powers, and risked using it in his bare hand, risked exposing the glow. But there *was* no glow, to speak of; only a faint glimmer of light that people on stage could easily have mistaken for stage lights, and which was too dim to be picked up by the TV cameras.

Two weeks later, Jackie opened his morning paper to find a grainy photo of Joseph Rubello staring up at him beneath a twenty-point headline reading *Reputed Mafia Chieftain Dead of Heart Attack.*

One day later, a pale and shaken Harry Faulk entered

Jackie's inner office and announced, shakily, that the wife of the deputy commissioner of prisons had died the night before, of lung cancer.

The end, when it came, came quicker than Ta'li'n could have imagined; for all his prescience, it caught him unawares and threatened to unravel his carefully woven plans.

He had known the final conflagration would occur sometime that spring, but had not guessed that it would arrive on the very first day, in the very middle of the Rites of Renewal. He himself stood on the main ceremonial platform in the middle of the Avenue of the Dead; he himself wore the cloak of Ya'n'l and spoke the sacred words of celebration and rebirth, all the while gazing out at the parched and blistered valley of Tenan, his own voice ringing hollow in his ears. He did not notice until he looked down that a fight had erupted in the crowded street; he watched with horror as combatant pushed combatant, as attackers jostled onlookers, drawing them into the melee—as the violence rippled across the face of the crowd until the congregation had become a mob, and the ceremony a riot. Ta'li'n tried to continue, tried to shout the ritual words over the din of battle, but from deep inside the fray came a chant that drowned him out: *The old gods are dead. The old gods are dead!* The Priests' Guards were pushing into the crowd, shields and atlatls raised, trying to separate the combatants, but succeeding only in being forced into the fight themselves as daggers, spears, and knives were thrust at them.

"*Stop it,*" Ta'li'n shouted, trying to make himself heard above the din, "*stop*—"

Suddenly one of the fighters—a boy of no more than nineteen—launched himself at the ceremonial platform, scrambling up its wooden foundation, screaming obscenities at the priest. Another young man joined him; they hoisted themselves up onto the platform, blood in their eyes, the priest the object of their imminent violence—

But a contingent of Guards had already surrounded Ta'li'n and was hurrying him down the steps to safety, even as other Guards battled the rebels who had desecrated the platform. The phalanx of soldiers surrounding Ta'li'n pushed their way through the crowd, rectangular shields warding off the thrust of daggers and knives, forging safe passage; dazed, stunned, and despairing, the priest saw that nearly everyone in the crowd was now armed—daggers, obsidian blades, atlatls—and in the distance he could see the first awful flicker of torches being lit . . .

The guards were steering him toward what they believed to be the sanctuary of the temple atop the Pyramid of the Sun, but the priest commanded them otherwise: "Not the temple. Take me to Ch'at'l. Take me *now!*"

They protested, but he insisted; and soon he found himself back at Ch'at'l's apartment compound, only this time no door-keeper greeted him, and inside, in the central court, the laughter of children had been replaced with the moans of the injured, or dying: dozens of wounded lay bleeding on the tile floor, or sat hunched in corners, holding themselves and whispering soft prayers. Ta'li'n had not fully comprehended the extent of the riot, the depth of its violence, until this moment; the injured looked up at his entrance, reaching out to him as though the gods' power would pass from him into them, healing their wounds—but aside from the priest's murmured prayers and words of comfort for them, the only significant mark of his passage through the atrium were the bloody streaks staining his stark white robes. He was helpless to aid them; and now, he knew, he was about to take away the one thing that *might* . . .

He entered the healer's quarters and drew a short breath of surprise: it, too, was crowded with injured people. Ch'at'l was at the far end of the room, kneeling beside a semi-conscious young woman; he was force-feeding her a liquid Ta'li'n recognized as an herbal remedy for concussion. Cries of pain were a constant background noise, but even the quiet rustling of the curtains caught Ch'at'l's attention; he looked over, saw the priest standing awkwardly in the middle of the room, and without hesitation nodded toward a young man with a bleeding wound in the chest. "Tend to him," he said, pressing the priest into service. "I must keep this woman conscious, but his wounds are just as severe."

"How—?" Ta'li'n began—and was startled when the healer pressed the green marbled stone into his palm, then half-pushed the priest toward the injured man.

"You have used it before," Ch'at'l said, returning to the young woman.

"Yes," Ta'li'n said, albeit uncertainly. When first initiated into the holy order, Ta'li'n had learned how to use all the charms and talismans of the gods—but as he'd risen into the ranks of the priest-rulers, such practice grew less and less frequent. He prayed to X'l'o that he still remembered how. He knelt beside the young man, grasping the stone in one hand, placing his other on the gaping chest wound—

And recognized the injured man—*boy*—as one of the rebels who had incited today's riot . . . one of the proponents of the New, the one who had tried, dagger in hand, to climb the ceremonial platform and attack Ta'li'n. The priest paled, trying to ignore the tangle of conflicting emotions he felt, and shut his eyes. He concentrated on healing the wound, on stanching the flow of blood; he tried to visualize arteries mending, blood vessels closing, slashed flesh knitting together—

But the stone was not getting warmer, as he knew it should have been. He redoubled his efforts, but the stone remained cold in his fist. *Fist.* Yes. That was the problem, wasn't it? He opened his eyes and saw that the young man's wound was still bleeding profusely; he had had no effect on it whatsoever. And then he felt someone brushing him aside, prying the stone from his stiff fingers.

Ch'at'l took the stone from the priest, placed his hand on the young man's chest, and shook his head. "The eye cannot heal," the old man said, without apparent rancor, "what the heart cannot see."

Ta'li'n watched as the stone began to glow white-hot in the healer's hands. He lowered his gaze. "Were I truly the holy man I profess to be," the priest said, ashamed, "I would be able to care for my enemies as I do for my fellows."

But Ch'at'l merely shook his head. "You are a man," he said with no recrimination. "All men have their limits." He took his hand away from the rebel's chest, and Ta'li'n saw that the blood had stopped and the wound had begun to heal. But the healer did not seem particularly happy; he looked around the crowded room, at the suffering and the injured, with great sad eyes. "Even as I," he said softly, "have *my* limits . . ."

"No one can heal an entire city," Ta'li'n said gently, "dying like a frightened beast in the night."

The old man looked up at him, his eyes now veiled. "The time has come?"

Ta'li'n nodded silently.

The healer hesitated only a moment, then, with a quick nod, put the stone back into the priest's hand—standing up as he did. "Go," he said, returning to the young woman and her herbal medicine. "Save what you can . . . while I save what *I* can."

Ta'li'n turned and left, his guards enclosing him as they left the compound. In the street people chased and stoned one another, fought one another with sling and dagger and atlatl; they bellowed with rage, cried out in mortal pain, giggled with manic laughter. In the east, Ta'li'n saw the first hot lick of flame appear from behind the Butterfly Palace. He told his guards to hurry, praying that there was still time—praying to gods who seemed no longer to be listening.

Jackie could feel the stone growing colder and colder with each successive use. Harry was now weeding out all but the simplest, most easily cured ailments from the program: they were reduced to mending broken arms and compressed disks, torn tendons and sprained ankles. And as the more serious and more dramatic cases were shunted off the air, revenues began to dip—not much, at first, but by the end of the week contributions had dropped by 15 percent.

At the same time, people who Jackie had "healed" within the last few months began to appear, their injuries and illnesses abruptly returned, at the Church of the Brotherhood's Hollywood headquarters. Some were desperate, some were pleading, most became angry, and indignant, when staffers turned them away and told them there was nothing Brother John could do for them. Hurt, betrayed, they took their complaints to the press. Among these were several women whom either Jackie or Faulk had slept with after being "cured"—and who, their ailments or injuries returned, were eagerly selling their exclusive stories to the *Star* or the *Enquirer*.

Donations plunged by another 35 percent.

The first hard news story about Brother John's and Brother Faulk's prison record broke in the L. A. *Times* a few days later. The reporter, Marnie Eilers, detailed in depth Jackie's history as a second-story man, his conviction for burglary, and Harry's multiple convictions for mail fraud and passing counterfeit money. Apparently the deputy commissioner of prisons had had the presence of mind to retain a copy of the data when he had wiped the state's mainframe clean—though he'd covered his tracks well enough not to have been caught doing it. One minute the information wasn't there; the next, it was. As quickly as it had been initially expunged.

"Love offerings" bottomed out to nothing.

Harry laid off most of the Church staff and was scrambling to liquidate whatever assets he could—Rubello's "family" was demanding restitution of their two million dollars, alternately payable in blood—when the bunco squad sought and obtained a court injunction freezing the Church's bank account pending investigation of "improprieties." The time had come, Faulk decided, to pack up, cut their losses, and get the hell out of the country before either the IRS or their moral counterpart, the mob, got to them.

Jackie, leaving the building on Sunset for the last time, had to push his way through a crowd of ill and injured, people whose faces he vaguely recalled but for whom he felt nothing; all he felt was fear and disbelief, stunned astonishment that it had all fallen apart so quickly, so completely. Harry was a few steps ahead, trying to clear a path. "Please—let us through, just let us—"

"Brother John—please—"

"Brother—help me—"

"—you son of a bitch, you *promised*, you—"

"Oh, God, Brother, help my boy, you helped him once—"

Jackie looked up and saw a mother, arms wrapped protectively around an eight-year-old boy. He recognized the boy, dimly, as a mute he'd given voice to, only—what? Two months ago? The last of those whom Jackie had truly, even in part, cared about . . . or the first of those for whom he had not. He felt a stab of guilt, of shame—

The mother stepped in front of him, blocking his path. "Brother John—please—"

"I *can't help* you!" he cried out, in anger and frustration.

"Leave me *alone!*" He pushed her aside, her and the child both, away from him and into the crowd—

And with the next step he took, he felt a sudden, jolting stab of pain in his abdomen—so intense that he doubled over, crying out in inexplicable agony, hands going to his stomach—

His hands came away smeared with blood.

His blood.

He screamed. With an effort he straightened, looked down at himself: blood was soaking through his shirt, his once-immaculate white suit, a bright red stain growing larger and larger, product of what Jackie knew, instantly, was an open wound.

Those in the crowd closest to him saw the blood and jumped to an understandable—and, in a way, accurate—conclusion: "Oh Jesus," someone shouted, "he's been *shot!* Somebody's shot him!"

The crowd disintegrated into chaos as the former supplicants scattered, rushing to avoid becoming the unseen gunman's next victim; Jackie staggered forward, arm outstretched, imploringly: "No," he managed to choke out, "please—somebody, you've got to help me—"

But no one listened to his pleas; within moments the only person within twenty feet was Harry, who caught Jackie as he began to fall, lowering him onto the sidewalk as the blood continued to gush—staining his pants, now, a long red finger running down the inseam to the cuff. "Jackie! What in *hell*—"

Jackie groped in his pocket for the stone, not finding it at first, fighting back a wave of terror until he felt it in his other pocket. He clenched the stone in his right hand, as he had in a deserted alley many months ago; now as then, he placed his left hand over the wound and closed his eyes. *Oh God*, he thought, *oh Jesus, I'm sorry, please* help *me* . . . He concentrated on healing, concentrated with all the failing strength and faltering will he could muster—

But when he opened his eyes, he saw the blood flowing from between the fingers of his left hand, and he knew instinctively that this time—this time it wasn't going to work . . .

He forced the stone into Harry's hand. "You've got to do it," he said, voice a hoarse whisper. "Please, Harry, you've got to do it!" He grabbed Faulk's other hand, put it on the bleeding wound—

Harry recoiled, drawing back his hand in horror and disgust. "Jackie—I can't—"

"Harry, you *have* to!"

"I—" Harry clenched the stone in one hand, working up the nerve to put his hand near the wound again; he was perspiring, clearly terrified. "I don't know *how*, Jackie, I don't—" He suddenly tore his hand away, bolted to his feet, and dropped the stone on the sidewalk beside the injured man. "I *can't*, Jackie!" he cried out, backing away into the building. "I just can't!"

Jackie stared at him, disbelievingly, as though seeing him for the first time. "*Harry . . . ?*"

"I'll call an ambulance," Harry promised, and then he was gone, swallowed up in the revolving glass doors to the lobby. Jackie called after, weakly, but to no avail: Harry was gone.

Jackie closed his eyes. An ambulance, he knew, would arrive far too late. He fought back his terror, trying to come to terms with what was happening to him; trying to come to terms with death. Because he *was* going to die this time. He'd been given a second chance and he'd blown it, pissed it all away— allowed himself to be corrupted, by Harry, by the money, by the applause and the approbation. All right. He blew it. Time to pay the piper; time to accept his due. But God, he was frightened. Suddenly he felt like he was falling into a deep black well, enclosed by a solid darkness with a definite shape, like a tunnel; but far from the white light he'd heard people saw at the moment of death, he saw only the blackness above him, and below him a fevered babble of voices—the damned, perhaps, crying out in pain, giggling with crazed glee, calling out to greet him, to welcome him to their ranks—yes, he could even feel himself growing warmer, felt a fire growing inside him. He was going to Hell, no two ways about that, and he was—he was—

He was no longer falling. He'd stopped, somehow, though the fire inside him continued to grow hotter. And then— abruptly, inexplicably—he felt almost as though he were *rising* again, carried aloft on a hot gust of wind, ascending as quickly as he'd been dropping moments before—

He opened his eyes.

An eight-year-old boy—the mute boy he'd pushed aside, along with his mother, lifetimes ago—was squatting beside him, eyes closed, left hand on Jackie's stomach, right hand pulsing with a hot white luminescence. His mother stood behind him, looking first anxious, then relieved as Jackie regained consciousness and began to stir.

He saw, Jackie thought dazedly. He saw what Harry tried to do—what Harry couldn't do—and he—

The boy kept his eyes closed until the light ceased to issue from his hand—until the stone cooled—then opened them. Jackie reached down, unbuttoned his shirt . . .

. . . to reveal smooth, unbroken skin, and no blood save for that which stained his clothes.

The boy smiled triumphantly, exchanging a silent grin of victory with his mother. And in that moment, Jackie understood. Why the stone had stopped working; where it had all gone wrong. Where *he* had gone wrong. Without even thinking about it, Jackie gently took the stone from the boy . . . held it tight in one hand . . . then cupped his other hand around the boy's throat, covering his larynx. Jackie closed his eyes, concentrated, and felt the stone growing warm in his hand . . . a warmth he hadn't felt this intensely in months. He'd forgotten how good that warmth could feel. After thirty seconds, it began to cool again; Jackie opened his eyes, took his hand away from the boy's throat.

Jackie remembered, now, the look on the boy's face when he had cured him the first time; remembered the smile that came to him, the raspy, inchoate sounds he had made with his newfound voice. Now that same smile lit up his face, but though his voice was at first raspy from disuse, he had apparently learned something of how to use it in the few short months he had been able to speak.

He looked up at Jackie and said, very slowly and carefully, "Thank you, Brother John," his grin growing broader with the completion of the sentence.

The man in the bloodstained suit tousled the boy's hair and smiled back. "No . . . thank *you*," he said softly. "And please . . . call me Jackie."

He looked up and saw one or two members of the former crowd lingering at the end of the block: an old man, Jackie recalled, with severe rheumatitis, and a young black man with an ulcerated colon. Jackie motioned them to come closer. "Don't be afraid," he said gently. "Come on." He stood, started toward them even as they began to move hesitantly toward him; even as, to Jackie's right, Harry Faulk stepped out of the building, looking absolutely stunned.

"Jackie! Jackie, are you—"

Jackie paid him no mind, walking past him as though he no longer existed—all his attention on the two injured men who needed his help. He took the old man's gnarled, rheumatic hands in his, and he thought: No; not attention—concern. That was the secret—wasn't it?

From atop the Pyramid of the Sun, Ta'li'n could see the last of the five young priests to whom he had entrusted the sacred talismans making his way up the terraced slopes of the valley of Tenan—far from the flames which were consuming the City, a wall of fire marching down what was now, truly, the Avenue of the Dead. Seared, charred bodies lay strewn in its wake; just ahead of it, one-time rioters fled, sparks blown before them on the hot, dry wind, igniting their clothes, turning the fleeing figures into living torches who ran and stumbled a few feet, a few yards, before falling before the oncoming flames. The Pyramid of the Moon and the Butterfly Palace—the first to feel the torches of the rebels—were no longer temples, but furnaces. Up and down the length of the City, pillars of black smoke rose to touch an uncaring sky; directly below, the heat from the oncoming sheet of flame was peeling the bright red and gold from the plaster facade of the Pyramid. Soon, it, too, would be engulfed; only Ta'li'n remained in the temple, all others either murdered, immolated, or escaped.

The priest turned away from the open gateway, already feeling the intense heat rising up from below; he retreated to his meditation room, sat, took a last mescal cap from its jar, and ate it, waiting for the peyote to carry him away, even as his five young priests had been carried away—they to safety, and Ta'li'n to a different sort of refuge.

Ta'li'n had chosen them well: young enough not to have become involved in the internecine political warfare among the priest-rulers, yet old enough to be expert at the use of the talismans, and able to pass that expertise on to succeeding generations. Why that was important to him, the priest only dimly understood; he knew, from his visions of time to come, that no memory of him or his people would remain—their names, their language, their grand accomplishments, their greatest failures, all would be but blank parchment to they-who-would-follow. Why, then, even bother to preserve the talismans? Why bother to save these relics of a religion that would itself be nothing but a mystery years from now?

Perhaps simply to remind the future . . . that the past was once the present. That for a time—a brief, golden march of centuries—the gods had made their home here; had blessed the City with their love and power, their only remembrance in the form of two jade and gold figurines, a long leathery cloak, an amulet of small obsidian chips on a golden strand, and a green marbled stone polished by the sweat of countless hands and countless healers. Even if no one remembered the rites, the divinations, the sacred words, these small enchantments would serve to remind that once, for a time, the gods had lingered here . . . in this place, in this City . . . before moving on.

The smell of smoke now filled the temple, intruding even into Ta'li'n's meditation room; once it filled with the noxious black fumes, he would die very quickly. Now he cast out with his mind one last time, his soul riding the crest of the peyote, searching—longing—for some glimpse of the talismans in the days to come, some affirmation that his actions had had meaning. Eyes closed, images raced through his mind: the City, bleached of color and life; a woman—Mayan, perhaps—the necklace of Pe'x'r around her neck, life stirring in her womb; a park—

A park surrounded by tall structures—taller than even the tallest pyramid, roadways of some smooth black material ringing the island of grass and trees—

And a man. Dark hair, dark eyes, dressed in what looked like holy white—but a white streaked, oddly, with red; with blood. Like Ta'li'n's own robes. The thin, wiry young man knelt beside an older, injured man—an indigent of some sort—one hand on the man's chest, the other glowing with a pulsing white light that made Ta'li'n nod in recognition. The image, the glimpse, was gone within seconds—but as the air grew hotter around him, and the first gray fingers of smoke slipped beneath the door to the room, the priest smiled, content in the affirmation that his legacy had/would/did survive, secure in the knowledge that this small part of it, at least, was, somehow, in good hands.

Jamie's Smile

Birthdays are for dying once a year; more often and it's no longer a merry thing. So while my own would pass in a flurry of half-glimpsed Hallmarks, my nephew Jamie's became the focus of my family's masochistic attentions. Some innate sense of proportion allowed them but one sacrificial lamb, and Jamie, God help him, was it.

Once a year, then, I would bundle myself up, hop a bus or hitch a ride, and make my annual pilgrimage to L.A. And once a year I would find myself at my brother Walter's apartment, shrugging off my coat in a dim foyer, and with it any pretense of being a stranger here.

On the eleventh pilgrimage my mother looked very much as she had on the previous ten: thin, bony, very probably more active at sixty-eight than I at thirty-two, her pinched features dry as old parchment. I pecked her on the cheek and hung my jacket on a rather ugly coat rack. "Who died and left you this?" I said.

"That? It was in the old house. Walter went over a few months ago for a last look, to see if there was anything in the attic rooms that might be salvageable."

"If that's what he salvaged I'd hate to see what he deep-sixed." Our family has an unnatural love for the art of reclamation.

"How are you, Judson?"

"Emphysemic," I said. "Between the buses and the smog I may never breathe again."

"You'll find it a hard habit to break, Walter," she called into the living room, "Walter, Judson is here."

We walked into the living room and I noted with a silent resignation that it had not changed since last year: the overstuffed furniture, the piss-yellow wallpaper, and of course Walt himself, the oldest and grayest of its features, today looking more uncomfortable than usual in a vest two sizes too small.

"Jud!" We shook hands; his palm was cold and damp, like a dead fish. "How the hell are you. Drink?"

"No, no thanks, Walt."

"Oh hell, that's right," he said, going to the bar. "You still don't touch the stuff? Sorry," he added with a small laugh, "can't offer you pot or anything . . ."

"Don't be silly, Walter," my mother said. "You know Judson doesn't go in for that sort of thing."

Walt shrugged. "Well, it's been a year and all. I don't know."

I felt the old knee-jerk urge come back to me, the urge to snap at my mother for tying me to a preset mode of behavior. Walt was right, I wanted to say, a year can bring a lot of changes; but this year hadn't, damn it; Mother was right and any argument would have been absurd. I felt confined again, boxed into another's idea of what I was. My own birthday suit, as it were.

"So how *are* you doing down there in Laguna, anyway?"

Walt asked, sipping his gin, one thumb hooked into his frayed belt. God, how he'd gained weight.

"Two steps removed from starvation. The usual."

"You don't look it," Mother said. "Or did you mean that symbolically?"

Walt laughed. "Artists have to starve, it's in their blood."

"So are low sugar levels," I said, surrendering to the banality. "When do we eat, by the way?"

"After interrogation and debriefing," Becky said from behind me. "I should think you'd have learned the procedure by now." She entered the room smiling warmly, her thin sandy hair now shoulder length, longer than it had been when I last saw her. I liked it better this way.

She came and took my hands·in hers, examining me with her glinting brown eyes. "Toulouse, you've grown."

"Platform knees, mademoiselle."

"I thought as much." She kissed me coolly on the cheek, then drew away. "Good to see you, Judson."

"You too. Where's Jamie?"

"In the bathroom," she said, "washing his hands. He insisted on not using the IV today."

I started at that. "Insisted?"

Mother said, "He's eating with us?"

Becky nodded. "Yes, he thinks he can."

"Insisted?" I repeated.

Becky shrugged lightly. "The hand signals were rather— fierce. He stood firm." An embarrassed silence. "I mean he was adamant. Oh hell, you know what I mean."

"Of course."

Walt wedged himself into the conversation: "Darling," he said to Becky, "why don't you show Jud what we got Jamie for his birthday?"

"Before he opens it?" I asked.

"Oh, I think he knows what it is already," Walt said. "He's very—"

"Perceptive," Mother prompted.

"Something like that, yes."

"I'd rather wait," I said. "I got him some new books. They're in my jacket. We can give them all at once."

I can't say I usually cared very much what they had bought for Jamie. I supposed it was some art supplies, in which case it would be incumbent upon me to tutor Jamie in their use, as I had tutored him in charcoals and inks. If so, I wanted to do it, but for Jamie and not because it was expected of me.

"Then I guess we'll open them after dinner," Walt said, "if that's okay with—"

I stopped listening to Walt. The grinding whir of Jamie's wheelchair began quite suddenly, souring my stomach all at once; it continued in short staccato bursts as Jamie entered the room, the chair grinding its way across the faded tan carpet.

Jamie reminded me of half-finished sculpture, the smooth plaster mold rather than the solid bronze statue. The hand of his creator, whoever or whatever it was, had been snatched away the moment Jamie had been squeezed from between Becky's thighs. His hands were thin, delicate in a way that suggested weakness rather than artistry; there was webbing between the third and fourth fingers, and no little fingers at all, merely stumps. His feet were always covered by socks or slippers, concealing ankles of thin bone, too weak to support his weight. The flesh that covered hands and feet was stretched taut, almost translucent; beneath it could be seen the pulse and flow of capillaries, veins.

His face was much the same, but the skin was paler still, and even his lips lacked color as they lacked form. Those lips—two lines carelessly sketched on the plaster, waiting for further delineation—never parted more than half a centimeter.

At least not since the moment the doctor had pulled him from Becky, slapped him on the ass, and listened as the baby tried to scream—but couldn't. His vocal cords had never developed and, over time, his facial muscles atrophied.

"Well, Jamie," Mother said, "Uncle Jud finally made it."

Uncle Jud *always* made it. Uncle Jud was feeling the same way he felt every year at this time: sick with memory and guilty for that sickness. I smiled and approached Jamie, trying to ignore the patch of sterile gauze on his neck that covered the results of a long-ago tracheotomy.

I took his hand in mine and shook it. I could feel his fingers grasping mine in what had to be an effort for him, and all at once the sickness vanished and I was with my nephew.

"Hello, Jamie," I said, releasing his hand. He nodded a greeting and a silent communion passed between us. The ritual of strangeness was over. No emotion showed on his face, but I sensed in him an almost desperate gladness to see me. To see anyone beyond the immediate family, I supposed.

"I'll get dinner ready," Mother said. "You've done enough, Becky."

"I'll go in and change, then," Becky said. "Jud, why don't you talk to Jamie awhile? Walt, clear away the junk on the dining-room table."

"Anything you say, love." Walt had a habit of adding an endearment whenever he was being subservient. It was one of the things that grated on my nerves—that, and the way he had seemed to die in the mind years ago, the slow dissolution of morale that had let his body go to fat while his ambition went to hell.

I watched him slosh over to the dining-room table and pull off the newspaper and other crap strewn over the scratched Formica top. How could a man that large look like a burst balloon? I didn't know. I think I hated him. He was everything I was trying desperately not to be, but I didn't know whether or not I was succeeding and so I hated him all the more.

And he was only four years older than I was.

I turned and looked down at Jamie, and found a knowing and an agreement in his half-shut, watery eyes.

I knelt by his side and put my hand over one of his. "How are you, Jamie?"

Walt had been doing some minor engineering work at Edison's nuclear power plant at San Onofre. Landing a job on the initial staff was one of the few good moves he made in his life—that, and marrying Becky—and for half a year he was as happy as I'd ever seen him. For half a year he was also soaking up trace amounts of spillage, radiation falling unnoticed on flesh and seed. Edison discovered the leak before the exposure became lethal, but not before Jamie had been conceived.

Walt lost his hair, grew it back, developed cataracts and had them removed at the company's expense. Edison agreed to pay some piddling compensation and Walter, being Walter, accepted the offer. They didn't suggest aborting the child until it became apparent that it might actually live. But Walt was quite effectively sterile from that time on, and the doctors were saying that Becky should not attempt to have any more children after what was sure to be a difficult birth—or a difficult abortion. Confused, shaken, they decided to chance it.

Horror stories circulated in the family that fall, forgotten deformities from all branches of the family tree brought to new light in the atomic glare. For my part I had stray visions of fetus and embryo, saw Walt in a plane flying silent above Nagasaki, kneeling beside a bomb dropping through irising bay doors. And then the bombs would fall, becoming small and blurred and soft, and Walt would continue to kneel there, slamming them home to target, driving, driving . . .

If it had been Jamie and Jamie alone, an afternoon or a weekend of teaching him how to use those pale hands for something beside writing brief, functional notes in lieu of speech—if it had been that, I would not have minded. Instead, it was Walt and Becky and my mother, celebrating a birth they would rather damn—that was what I hated. That was what I feared, in my selfish way, all year.

I escaped into the bathroom a minute, and as I came out I passed Jamie's bedroom. I noticed that his bed was closer to the window now, almost flush with the wall. The room was still painted a sickly green with cream trim: my mother's doing, I recalled. My mother, once a registered nurse, now Jamie's nurse, who couldn't help turning this room into a hospital ward. My gaze fell on the IV stand tucked away in a corner, its long tube falling in a languid loop to the floor.

There were quite a few new books; one entire wall was obscured by shelves of glossy paperbacks and worn hardcovers, frayed-edged magazines and torn, yellowed newspaper clippings. Jamie loved to read: novels, news stories, philosophy, pornography . . . anything that spoke of a world beyond his own narrow universe. I knew the feeling.

I went into the kitchen where Mother was juggling dishes and pans. The odor of steamed fish permeated the room; on one burner a soft whitish concoction that looked like baby food bubbled obscenely.

I nodded toward it. "That for Jamie?"

Mother grabbed a saucepan with a quilted pot holder. "Yes, it's a vegetable concentrate. He eats it sometimes, for the sake of eating something. Through a straw; he can manage that.

My God, it must be awful to have to take all your food through that damned tube."

"It must be difficult for him to do otherwise. You're sure he really wants to make the effort and join us?"

"Don't be silly, dear, of course he does. These parties are as special to him as they are to us. Did you see the way he smiled when he saw you?"

I suppressed a weary sigh. "Mother, Jamie can't smile."

"Well of course he can. He can smile with his eyes. You can see it in the way he looks at you . . . the way he watches what's happening."

"Have you seen that—smile—very often?"

She poured some steaming water into the sink, her back to me. "Every . . . once in a while, yes," she said. Her voice was odd and I felt she was deliberately keeping her face from me.

"Well, I'm glad to hear that," I said. Not believing her for a minute. Perhaps Jamie *had* smiled on seeing me—but why would he ever have occasion to smile at any other time, here, with them, caged?

Mother turned abruptly and faced me, her eyes hard, almost fanatical. "Things have worked out very well for Jamie. You were wrong to think they wouldn't. He may be a cripple, but he can do things and be happy. The art, he loves the art. And his books." She turned back to the sink and dropped the pan into the basin with a sharp clang. "And to think that bitch wanted him dead. Thank God Walter didn't listen."

She went over to the stove to turn off the oven, the fierceness gone from her eyes. "Better go inside, Judson, dinner will be ready in a few minutes."

I hesitated a moment, then backed out of the kitchen. I had never become used to my mother's flares of cold temper, those icy novas that burned briefly in her eyes, then faded. They always took me by surprise.

In the dining room Becky was setting the table. Off somewhere I heard the grind and hum of Jamie's wheelchair, and the rattle of ice cubes in Walt's glass.

Becky smiled at my entrance but did not look up. "Well, Toulouse? Finished inspecting the Bastille?"

"Oh, God damn it, Becky, knock it off. If it's that much of a prison, get out. Stop banging your wine glass against the bars." I was surprised by my own vehemence. So was Becky; she looked up and stared at me.

She smiled grimly. "Sorry. But who else is going to listen, Jud?"

I sighed and wrapped my arms loosely about her waist in what I hoped was friendly in-law fashion. "Beck, Beck . . . damn it, I always listen. You're the one who turns a deaf ear." Her arms encircled my own waist, her fingers gently finding the small of my back; despite myself I began to run my hands along her thighs, along the tight seam of her skirt, the touch and rhythm of it all-too-suddenly familiar. I fought to keep myself from getting hard, I fought to remind myself why this could never work. "Becky, I—"

I didn't notice Walt's approach until he had entered the room. He paused in the doorway, blinked once, and for a moment I thought I saw a pale fire in his eyes.

Becky and I disengaged ourselves, but Walt was already leaving. "Sorry," he said tonelessly. "I'm sure you two have things to talk about." He disappeared into the foyer leading to the bathroom.

I watched him pass. "Jesus!" I said, suddenly angry. "That's what you don't want to leave? That *shadow*? My God, he's just like Mother. For a moment they allow themselves anger or rage, then they damp the fires and turn to ash."

"I can't leave Jamie, can I?" Her face was impassive—a trick she'd learned from them, no doubt. "And I can't support him by myself. He needs someone to look after him constantly, Mother does that here, but she'd hardly come with me, would she? A nurse costs money, Jud, and I'm not trained for anything more than steno."

"Then just get the hell out. Leave them, the three of them. Edison still pays some compensation benefits, don't they? Walt could make up the difference for medical costs, and Mother could go on tending Jamie. And you'd be free."

She stared at me a second. "Walt hasn't worked in nine months," she said quietly. "Even before that I had to bring in something to add to those glorious benefits. That something grew larger and larger every month. Now it's everything. I'm the support around here, I'm the foundation, not Walt, not anybody else."

I didn't know what to say. "I—Jesus, Beck, I didn't know—"

She laughed shortly, not a nice laugh. "No, of course you didn't. How much of a damn do you give for us? Once a year is all you have to suffer. You tell me to get the hell out; all right, if I do, will you give up your days and watch Jamie? Or go to work to support his IV, his chair, the whole thing? Can you divorce yourself from your damned artists' colony as easily as you have from your fami—"

She stopped suddenly, as if hearing herself for the first time. She sank into one of the dining-room chairs and lowered her eyes.

"Oh God," she said. "I'm sorry, Jud. You're free and I'm trying to make you feel guilty about it." She looked up, tried to smile. "Forget I said anything, will you?"

I nodded. "It's forgotten." But she was right, damn it. I'd tried to divorce them from my life, all of them, but could anyone ever annul his own past?

"But do you see—" She watched me, seeking absolution.

"You do see how it is? I can't give up on Jamie. We owe him. It's not his fault he's alive, it's mine—mine for not being strong enough to refuse the tracheotomy. Does that sound awful? Maybe it is. But it would have been better for all of us if Jamie had never found a way to breathe. For once in my life I was weak, and for once in his life Walt was strong, and we were both so goddamn wrong."

She stood up, trying to regain that lost impassivity that Walt and Mother so loved. She took my hands again. "Weird relatives you have, eh, Toulouse?"

"No," I said. "Weird family I have."

She smiled at the word. I smiled at having said it.

And from the kitchen Mother called out that dinner was ready. "Give me a hand, Becky. Walt? Jamie? Jud?"

Jamie sat between Walt (at the head of the table) and Becky (to Jamie's left), holding between his middle fingers a spindly straw. I sat opposite him, Mother opposite Becky. No one said grace; as I've said, my family has an innate sense of proportion, and the saying of grace would have tipped the delicate balance of irony.

Jamie nursed that straw of his like a child at the breast, sucking that dreadful cream-of-crapola slowly but forcefully from the shallow dish. I kept my gaze down, making a careful study of the bone china plates I ate from. Eating became something of a ritual as I tried to avoid watching Jamie, and I was almost grateful for the tepid questioning that went on throughout the meal.

Mother: "What have you been working on recently, Judson?"

Me: "Nothing, I'm afraid. Haven't felt right about anything. For a while there I thought I might do some sculpture, but—"

Walt: "How do you survive if you don't produce regularly? Not that I'm criticizing; hell—"

Me: "I manage. I still have some of the cash I got from that portrait commission a while back."

Mother: "A while back! Seven months. And how much, only two, three hundred dollars?"

I was about to say that I didn't need much, about to become argumentative, when I became aware of Jamie's hand; he had moved it toward a pitcher of milk and it was abruptly in my field of vision. I felt a momentary shock and a subsequent guilt over it; the hand—I almost thought of it as separate from Jamie—the hand was vainly trying to reach the distant pitcher.

Walt reached for it. "Here, Jamie, I'm closer." Jamie withdrew his hand, knocking over the sugar bowl and spilling its contents over the tablecloth. Becky sighed heavily.

"Don't sweat it," Walt said, and clumsily extended his reach to try to right the bowl; but his slow, uncoordinated arms succeeded only in knocking over Jamie's dinner dish, spilling the vegetable contents into Becky's lap.

I stared. Jamie blinked. "Oh, shit, Becky, I'm sorry," Walt stammered. "Here, let me—"

Becky stood up, allowing the creamed vegetables to drip on the carpet. Walt grabbed a napkin and went to her side, trying to wipe the stuff from her skirt, but Becky recoiled at his touch. Her eyes burned with brief resentment.

"Keep your fucking hands to yourself, will you," she snapped, wiping the cream from her leg herself. "You've done enough as it is." She turned and headed toward the bathroom, leaving Walt standing there, uncertain, embarrassed. I felt a horrible pity for him at that moment, the pity one feels for a lost animal and not at all the pity one should feel for a human being.

He put the napkin down on the table, looked at Jamie as if

remembering something, and then moved the pitcher of milk nearer to his son's arm.

"Here you are, Jamie," he said absently. "Excuse me, Jud? Mother?"

He too left the room, heading in the general direction of the bar. Mother was already up and brushing the sugar off the table and into her cupped hand. Jamie started his wheelchair, bound for his bedroom; I got up and followed Walt into the living room, something familiar tugging at my thoughts.

He was mixing a drink, of course, the hands preparing it trembling like fallen branches. I felt uncomfortable; I felt the gap between us, wide and deep; and for the first time in how long, I wasn't sure I wanted that gap there.

I joined him at the bar. "I, uh—I'll have that drink now, if you would," I said, the words taking me by surprise as much as they did Walt. I saw something stir in his eyes; a kind of foggy pleasure—that someone would share something with him? I don't know.

"Sure," he said, managing a crippled smile. "What'll you—I mean, gin, or Scotch, or—"

"Scotch. Whatever," I said. He nodded and poured me the drink. I sipped at it, trying to enjoy it, but soon Walt began to slip back into his fog of inaccessibility and I began to feel uncomfortable again.

Finally he looked in the direction of the bathroom. "Christ," he said softly. He shook his head, once, then stared down at the top of the bar.

"Wasn't your fault," I said in an undertone. "I'm sure she didn't—"

"I'm sure she did. She always does." He took a large swallow of his gin.

I fumbled for something to say. "Well, look—maybe she felt embarrassed after you came into the, uh, dining room. With the two of us like that. Maybe she still felt embarrassed, and that made her tense up, and snap at you like that."

"Yeah." I don't think I convinced him. "Shit, Jud, I hope you don't think I'm mad about that. I mean, I know how much of a thing you two had going before she married me. I guess that kind of thing doesn't die as easily as—others."

Marriages? I wondered. "It's not that, Walt."

He didn't hear me. "You were more her age in the first damn place," he said. "You should have married her, Jud. You spoke the same language."

"But different dialects. Would've never worked, Walt."

"And this has? So maybe you'd be starving in a garret somewhere, using diapers for canvas, how should I know? At least you wouldn't have been caught dead near any—goddamned nuke plant . . ."

"Hey," I said, "c'mon, knock it off. You love that kind of work. Don't put it down just because—"

"Love doesn't mean shit these days," he said. "I'm a good nuts-and-bolts man, Jud, *you* know that, always have been. Remember all those wacky contraptions I used to build in the garage when we were kids? The firecracker factory, and you'd agent the stuff around the neighborhood?"

"Hell, yes. You almost blew up the whole damn block with that thing."

He chuckled. "Yeah. And the time the tornado almost did it for us, the blackout—"

"—and you made candles out of a couple of bottles of shaving lotion, and some wicks—"

He laughed, but at length the laughter faded, his gaze becoming remote, his voice soft. "But that's not where the money is, today. Nuts-and-bolts are a dime a gross. Theoretical men are the ones in demand, and I—I've never been too good on theory."

The pleasant mood of nostalgia drew away like a soundless tide. I stared down at my drink, saw I hadn't had much, and quickly took a burning swallow.

He glanced again at the bathroom. "Christ," he repeated, turning back to me. "God damn it, Jud, I *do* wish you'd married Beck. You'd have given her a good life. I mean that. What have I given her? A full-time job and a millstone in the shape of a son. Christ—I wish . . ." He let the sentence trail off.

I stared at him, trying to understand the feeling I had for him now after so many years, a feeling different from the animal pity I'd felt at the dinner table.

On impulse I asked, "Are you hurting, Walt?"

His voice was tired. God, was it tired.

"I hurt all the time, man," he said.

We didn't talk for a long time after that, not until Becky returned from the bathroom, but by then it was too late: I'd seen my brother in his eyes.

"Getting late, Becky," Mother said. "We should really give Jamie his presents now, before Judson has to go."

Becky sat splayed in a large overstuffed chair; her body seemed to tighten like a watch wound to midnight, and there was an odd tone to her voice. "I'm sure Jud doesn't have to leave—quite so early, do you, Jud?"

"Well, I—"

"Open them now," Walt said, entering the living room with a large flat package tucked under his arm. "It'll give Jamie and Jud some time alone with the presents."

"Walter, you'll give away the surprise," Mother admonished him.

"Not if we open them now," he insisted, and plopped the package down on the coffee table in front of Jamie. He moved to Becky's side. "Jud, why don't you open it for Jamie?"

I went over and picked up the package. Out of the corner of my eye I saw Becky stand up, apparently trying to escape one more ritual, but Walt took her by the waist and held her close to him, proudly. Becky's face went pale, her facial muscles tightening Jamie-hard. Walt was beaming happily, perhaps attempting to forget the brief honesty he had shared with me.

"From both of us, Jamie," he said as I unwrapped the present: the large white sketch pad, the canvases, the tray of expensive watercolors, the thin brushes with stems as thick as Jamie's fingers.

"Hey, nice," I said, putting them on Jamie's lap. "Damned good canvas, Walt."

"Thanks. I looked for days to find the right kind. I was a little worried it wouldn't be."

I didn't doubt it; Walt's kindnesses were clumsy but sincere. Becky seemed unaffected, however—Walt's sweaty grip held her in a vise tangible only for her, visible only to me.

She broke away from him and walked quickly past Mother. "Why don't we get dessert ready, Mother, and let Jud show Jamie a little about the supplies?" Already heading toward the kitchen.

"I'll give you a hand," Walt said, following her. Becky slammed open the swinging kitchen doors with the flat of her hands; I felt a sudden upsurge of sympathy for her, a returning anger at Walt: *Leave her alone! Stop pawing her, making her one with you, this family!*

But that was ridiculous. She was already one with the family, or the cage that the family had become. Mother paused a moment as Walt disappeared into the kitchen, and then she followed him in.

I turned to Jamie. He was trying to open the oversized sketch pad with his undersized fingers. I crouched down to help him. "Here, Jamie, let me—"

His hands clenched suddenly into tight, angry fists. The

effect was of two pale, fragile spiders abruptly turned compact and venomous. Startled—no, let me admit it: frightened—I drew back.

His fists unclenched, but the rigidity did not leave them; slowly, methodically, Jamie opened the sketch pad and allowed the large floppy cover to fall over his knees. He ran his left hand over the smooth bond surface while his right hand reached for a number two pencil. In one unbroken motion he began to sketch—to doodle—on the paper.

"Well," I said inanely, "maybe we should go over some of the basic techniques. We don't have much time, I know, but—would you like that, Jamie?"

The pencil continued to scribble and between absent-minded doodles Jamie wrote *Yes* in the middle of the sheet.

"Okay." The hands continued their random pattern across the paper. I watched them, fascinated, and tried to collect my thoughts; I spoke, hardly listening to what I was saying.

"The thing you have to remember," I said, "is that art is life and life is movement; we move, the world moves about us. The interface between the inner movement—us—and the outer movement—the world—is touch. Touch is very important in art . . ."

(But how could anyone who would never move more than an inch at a time know of inner movement or outer movement or any interface between the two? Without movement, could there be touch, could there be sight?

(I made my art from that interface of environment and ego. But Jamie had only *one* environment—unchanging, save for tantalizing glimpses through books of a world outside; static, stale, dying. Had it stunted his ego? What kinds of dreams could he possibly paint?

(Only wet dreams that would never be more than that, only an aching need to move and be moved that would never be filled. Only the family. Until they died and Jamie was put in a home, until then it would be only the four of them, trapped in a world without sky, turning year by year into figures from that faded yellow wallpaper . . .

(As they had almost done to *me*?)

"Jamie," I said. He continued scribbling. "Jamie"—my voice low, my heart pounding—"I don't know if you can understand this, I don't know if I do, but—

"You can't let them define you, Jamie. Do you see? You can't let them make you into what they think you are. What they think you can be. They almost did it to me—Mother and Walt first, but Becky too, she wanted a dull steady man and she almost made me into another Walt. They almost did it, Jamie, that's the important thing—they *almost did it*."

Jamie's pencil ran across the page, guided by seemingly absent fingers: *You escaped.*

I stared at the words and they seemed to lose their reality for me. "I hope I did, Jamie. But *you* can, too. Just by being—what they don't expect. By being alive, God damn it."

Something stirred in his eyes. His hand-action became savage, rough.

Alive, he scrawled.

The pencil snapped between his fingers.

I turned away just as Becky and Mother and Walt reentered the room with the birthday cake. Eleven candles burned with that same weak, flickering fire I had seen in all the eyes in this room. I felt off-balance as I stood up from my crouch.

"Happy birthday, Jamie," Mother said. "Walter, why don't you blow out the candles?"

"Sure," he said. "But hey, why don't we sing first? Hell, we haven't done that in years. Right, Beck? What the hell. Come on, Beck, let's sing."

I saw Becky's eyes go cold as frosted glass, and though I

could not read the thought behind their sudden opacity, looking at them I felt a lingering chill.

"We still have one present to open," Becky said tonelessly. "Excuse me, I'll get it." She went quickly into the bedroom. I tried to catch her attention with a glance, tried to telepathize my fear; *Don't do it, Beck. Whatever it is, don't do it.*

Walt called out to her, his tone a bit hurt: "I thought we were giving a joint present, Beck. I mean, I thought it was from the two of us."

Becky (from the bedroom): "This isn't for Jamie."

Walt (puzzled): "It isn't?"

"No," and she reentered with a small, fat package. "I've been thinking about giving it for a—long time now . . . It's for you, Walter."

"Me?" The confusion in his voice was mixed with a dull, unquestioning pleasure. He couldn't detect the sharp edge of secrecy in Becky's voice, as I could; maybe that was one of the things she wanted from a husband. He took the box from her hands, his fingers fumbling with the wrapping. I looked only briefly into Becky's eyes before I had to glance away. I felt sick. I wanted to run. I wanted to escape.

"Hell, Becky, you shouldn't have . . ." He was touched, I could feel it as he threw off the last of the wrapping. He ripped off the lid of the box, and his eager smile turned empty. His face turned that peculiar white that faces pale to before nausea. He looked up and stared at Becky as if she had shot him.

He dropped the box. A gun fell out, a .45 I think it was, its muzzle covered by a thin, taut piece of—*rubber* . . .

"Actually quite functional," Becky was saying, and I wondered if she even heard herself; "used by French army officers during World War I—protection from mud, and rain, and—"

Walt clenched his hand into a fist. "Bitch," he whispered, over and over, "bitch, bitch, sweet *bitch* . . ."

Their choreography was perfect. She turned; he grabbed at her, missed; she ran into the bedroom, slamming the door shut, locking it, and then Walt was banging away at it, slamming the hard wood with raw knuckles, his raging pathetic voice carrying back to us in the living room . . .

Mother's eyes were closed. I stared at her. "They'll kill each other," I said, a world away. "Mother, they'll kill each other."

She opened her eyes and shook her head. "No. They never do."

And then I turned to Jamie and knew that my words to him had been unnecessary, my fears of him groundless in themselves but seeds for new fears that I might nurture to full ripeness. Jamie was himself, no one else. Jamie was sitting quietly, listening to his parents' screams. Jamie was smiling.

Steel

The glen was quiet this time of night, the last stars dimming over the horizon, the sun's light cresting the near hills. Ken abandoned his star-gazing and poked his way through the underbrush, moving back toward the cabin. The thorns scratched his fingers, but did not, of course, draw blood; his bare feet trod uncut over the sharp pebbles and bits of broken glass. Coke bottles. Ken picked up the pieces, disgusted, balled his hand into a fist and crushed the glass to powder. Then, stuck with the deadly powder, he had to dig a hole in the hard clay and bury it—harmlessly, he hoped—half a foot under.

He returned to the cabin—more a cottage, really, nestled in the rapidly despoiling woods—and, to avoid waking either Laney or the kids, didn't enter by the creaking front door but instead leaped up to the second-story window. Gently he pried it open, climbed in, and padded down the hallway to their bedroom.

Laney was already awake, brushing her graying black hair absently, an old nervous habit. She looked quite as beautiful as when Ken had first seen her, so long ago, when they had both worked on the same paper; she turned and smiled at his entrance.

"Out in the glen again?" she said. He nodded. Her quick eyes misted over a moment, sadly. "Why now? You've let it go by for thirty years. Why worry about it now?"

He went to the window, seeing his own reflection—the strong face, tousled black hair graying prominently—against the lightening sky. "I don't know," he said distantly. "I never used to think it was important. I mean, I just assumed . . . that this was my place, and that it didn't matter where I was born, or why I'm—the way I am."

"And now?"

He turned, half-smiling. "Now I want to know."

"Middle-aged identity crisis?"

He laughed. "Like none the world has ever seen."

She touched his arm. "Let's go to breakfast."

They ate a light meal, bacon, eggs, toast, while the radio droned on about the crisis in the Mideast in the background. Ken sat staring out the verandah window into the distance for some minutes, finally smiling and looking back at Laney. "Raccoons about fifty yards into the brush. Have to tell the landlord about it."

She nodded. She was used to nodding mutely at his sudden pronouncements of things she couldn't see. It might only have been a raccoon in a bush, or a car on a distant road, but it might as well have been half a world away for all that she could see what he saw.

"When should we start back to the city?" she asked. Ken shrugged. "Day after tomorrow," he said. "Unless you want to get back early."

"Me? God, no. I don't relish putting together the August

issue." In point of fact, she did not relish putting together *any* issue; editing a women's magazine for an audience she didn't understand and only marginally believed in was a long way from where she had once hoped to be.

He touched her hand, his eyes no longer focused distantly but firm and penetrating. "I know how you feel." And the hell of it was, he did.

The kids whooped in just then, Lucy promptly spilling her grapefruit juice all over her jeans, Tom laughing uproariously at his sister's clumsiness. Looking at them, Ken felt a recurring gladness, a sense of accomplishment. Years ago he would have laughed at the idea of simple paternity counting for anything in this world, but that was years ago. Things had changed a good deal since then.

And thank God they hadn't inherited his—strength. His curse, his glory. He didn't know why, exactly; genetically he should have passed on some of his—abilities—to them; but no, they were normal, and thankfully so.

And, in the end, they might turn out to be his only vindication.

They returned to the city two days later, the kids to school, Laney to the offices of *Fem*, Ken to his editorial desk at *Life*. There was a sheaf of photos waiting for him—several sheaves, in fact: some blurred shots of the fighting in the Middle East, a couple of hot exclusives showing the ultimate dissolution of the League of Nations peacekeeping force, some spectacular color shots of Mars taken by one of the Mariner probes . . .

Ken stared at the Mariner photos a long moment, at the rugged terrain, the wasteland grayness in between the darknesses. Not there, he thought. Not anywhere in the whole damned solar system. *Where? How? Why?* He put aside the space scenes and thumbed the intercom.

"Rose, have Jim come in, will you? I want to dummy up the war pages right away . . ."

By lunchtime, Ken had had quite enough of spectacle and famine; he left Jim in charge of the office and hurried out of the building, pleading a headache. The magazine ran well without him; he had no qualms about leaving.

That afternoon, for the first time in months, he flew.

He stripped in an alley, jogged to its mouth, and leaped up. Within moments he was airborne, arcing halfway across the city before he realized that he had no place to go. No matter. He rarely had anywhere to go these days. The important thing was that he was flying, skirting the tips of skyscrapers, chasing the clouds, high above the smogline. Up here, the city was a gray tundra, soot and mist cloaking the skyline like London fog.

Disgusted, he veered west, toward open country.

(But below, he could see the small blurred figures of men and women, pointing, waving, shouting his name, and he was pleased that they remembered, even now.)

He flew into the night, seeking the darkness and the stars. He sought and named to himself the constellations; he squinted, trying to discern the planets as they popped into view. He picked up speed as he progressed, a blue streak against blackness, until he noticed ocean below him; then, reluctantly, he turned and headed home.

That night, in bed beside him, Laney stroked his face and kissed him lightly on the lips. He drew her closer to him, always careful to be gentle, afraid of the power in his arms, and they made love slowly, and didn't speak of it at all.

Word of the attack came Friday, just after the issue had gone to press. There was no deadline rush, no frantic writing, as in the old days; everyone knew all too well that there might not even *be* a next issue.

The Israelis had tactical nukes; everyone had known that. The Arabs had nuclear reactors; everyone had known that, too. Why in God's name had no one expected what had to come? Ken had, though, even as he anticipated this moment in his career—the moment in which he would, ultimately, have to pit himself against everyone, take no one's side, act from his own morality.

Laney rushed into the office minutes before he left. "Ken, for God's sake," she pleaded, taking him aside, "let them kill themselves. You can't stop it."

He licked his lips and touched her face. "I've been trying for thirty years, love. If I stop now, I . . ." He paused, forcing a thin smile. "I never could break old habits, Laney."

Within minutes he was over the Atlantic, the wind tearing at him savagely. There were limits to his strength, and he was straining those limits, now; he could only go so fast and so far before the force of his own speed battered him into unconsciousness. But he kept at it, and within two hours he was over the Mediterranean.

The fleets were converging, Americans to the south, Russians to the north. The fools who had started it all were nursing their radiation burns and had no time for the end of the world; they would leave that to the major powers. Miles above, the Chinese satellite eyed the tableau with patient silence.

Ken swooped down, the dazzling blue waters of the ocean nearly blinding him; half-sightedly, he dropped toward the U.S. flagship, snapping the aft cannons in two as he fell.

Machine guns turned on him. Volleys of ammunition pounded at him, sending him toppling backward but doing no further damage. At least he was drawing their fire away from the other ships, he thought, and then suddenly a starboard gun began firing from the Russian fleet. Damn it! He leaped up, hands outstretched, and shot toward the second cannon. It exploded, the concussion catching the flying figure off-balance. With a grunt of pain, Ken fell back into the water.

The Russian ships began their counterattack . . . but their missiles were quickly intercepted as a fount of water shot up between the two fleets. The geyser knocked the missiles off-course and they fell harmlessly into the sea.

At the tip of the waterspout, Ken halted his upward flight and the water cascaded down into the ocean again.

He made for the Russian flagship, dodging the cannon fire, snapping their guns in half with a curse. It was getting too damned hard, all this exertion after two hours' flight; he felt drained, he wanted time to rest. Perhaps they would stop now, pause at least to rethink their positions.

When the two American and Russian missiles hit him simultaneously, he knew that they were not going to stop. Not now, not ever.

He fell into the sea, letting the cold biting waters refresh him. The damned fools. They needed him, once, or said they did. As long as he was capturing bank robbers or mending broken dams, they needed him; as long as he flew above the city, lending his power and courage to their lives, they wanted him, or the symbol of what he was.

Not now, though. Not now.

With a sudden, bitter anger, Ken dived to the very bottom of the sea, touching the ocean floor. He stood there, holding his breath, clenching his fists . . . then, with one surge of strength, he vaulted up, up, through the waters, above the waves, surface tension slamming into him like a brick wall, and into the sky.

He peaked at a distance fifty yards above the two fleets . . . and then came down.

He plunged through the Russian carrier, feet first, screaming as the tough steel tore at his limbs—but he plummeted all the way through, four, five, six decks, out the bottom of the hull and into the sea once more.

He zoomed out and into the air again, heading for the American ship, repeating his actions: down through the bowels of the carrier, steel splintering around him, and back into the ocean.

When he flew shakily out of the water, exhausted, the two ships were sinking rapidly and lifeboats were being dispatched from the other carriers. Picking up the sound of radio signals, Ken heard the first halting overtures toward a cease-fire. Perhaps his intervention had slowed the battle long enough for Washington and Moscow to reconsider their options; Ken found that he no longer cared. He hovered a moment in the still air, then shut his eyes and veered to the east, homeward.

He landed in the glen, unseen, he hoped, near dawn. His costume was tattered and he was bleeding slightly, but he would live. Easily. Still as strong as ever, he thought bitterly. But they've gotten stronger. He lay down and breathed heavily.

Behind him, he heard the crackle of dry grass, and he turned around. Laney stood in the clearing, holding her bathrobe tightly around her. She ran to him and they held each other.

After a while, Ken kissed her, and then he lay back once more in the soft grass, his eyes shut to the stars.

"I know where, Laney," he said quietly, unmoving. "I know, now."

She looked at him, so large, so impervious, so deathly afraid of his own strength. All those years, she had had to have enough courage for both of them; had to give him strength enough to touch her. He was a man who never wanted to hurt, but they had forced him to hurt, in their name and their justice;

and it had taken her years to convince him he would not, could not, harm her. And he hadn't. Not once in thirty years.

"Where?" she said softly.

He opened his eyes and looked up at the sky. "They made me," he said quietly. "They needed me for a time, or thought they did. The time was right. I was there." He shut his eyes again.

She took him gently by the arm and got him to stand. "Come on," she said. "Let's go to bed."

He looked at her and smiled. "If it weren't for you . . . and the kids . . . what the hell would I have to show for it all?"

"Let's go to bed."

He nodded. Together they poked their way through the thick underbrush, and Laney thought she had never seen him quite so happy.

The Third
Sex

I couldn't have been more than three years old, that night I wandered into my parents' bedroom; I'd had the dream again, the one where I was being crushed between floor and ceiling, unable to breathe or break free. Shaken, I raced down the hall, pushed open my parents' door—then stopped as I saw what they were doing.

Locked in a sweaty tangle of sheets, they were jerking back and forth, making short, breathless sounds; for a minute I thought maybe they were having the same bad dream I'd just had. Their arms were wrapped around one another, the two of them lying face to face, so close I couldn't tell where one began and the other left off. When they saw me, my mother called out my name, my father swore, they pulled apart with a wet, sucking sound . . . and as the sheets fell away I saw a thick, curved finger between my father's legs, and between my mother's, another pair of lips. I rushed up, fascinated, asking a million questions at once; my father just looked at my mother, sighed, and tried to answer my questions—what is that called? what is that *for?*—as completely and honestly as you can, to a three-year-old; and when I went to bed that night, I reached down under my pajamas and touched the smooth, unbroken skin between my thighs, and dreamed of the day—Daddy never mentioned it, but I knew it had to come—when my own penis or vagina would start to grow. But somehow, it never did.

I'd been a perfectly normal newborn infant in all other respects, though not the first of my kind to appear. At first no one had a clue what to put on the birth certificate, much less what to name me, so they equivocated and the name on the county records is Pat; Pat Jacquith. Later, of course, they realized I had to have some identity, and since they were hoping for a daughter, that's what I became . . . at least until that night in their bedroom. "You're Daddy's little girl," my father had always told me, but if I *was* a girl, why didn't I have what Mommy had, that second pair of lips, that bristly hair? All I had was a pee-hole; it hardly seemed fair. And in years to come, when Mommy would take me out, shopping for skirts, or dolls, or frilly bedclothes, I knew I wasn't *really* like Mommy, would never *be* like Mommy . . . and I felt ashamed. Ashamed to be seen in clothes I didn't belong in, pretending to be something I wasn't.

So I started picking fights, at school . . . jumping hedges, shinnying up hills, sliding down cliffs . . . anything to get my pretty dresses torn, or dirty. We lived in a woodsy suburb called Redmond, and between the ages of six and thirteen I could usually be found in t-shirt and jeans, hiking, bicycling, or swimming in Lake Washington. I was a bit taller than the average girl, a bit shorter than the average boy; my voice was pitched a little lower than most girls, a little higher than most boys, but with a scratchy quality that somehow made it acceptable for either sex. I had no curves to speak of, and as the girls began to blossom with puberty, I stayed pretty much the same, going on hikes or playing shortstop in sandlot baseball games; but even this new, tomboy role would start to feel wrong, in its own way, soon enough.

I was fourteen; it was summer; a dozen of us, guys and girls, were camping at Lake Sammammish. I was wearing a one-piece bathing suit, my only concession to femininity, and when I dressed in the bushes I was careful, as always, to keep my distance from the others. To my left, Melissa Camry was suiting up behind a stand of bushes; to my right, my friend Davy Foster—a tall, loping blond who'd been my best pal for years—was stripping off his clothes in back of a tall tree. I caught a glimpse of Davy's genitals, and a peek at Melissa's impressively large breasts, and I felt an erotic tingle, but for which one, I didn't know; and then they were dressed and into the water, and swimming between them I continued to feel excited, but confused, as well.

Afterward, Davy and I went hiking, our trail coming to an end at the crest of a low, but steep, cliff. The rockface was intimidating; neither of us could resist the challenge. We descended carefully, finding ample foot- and handholds for the first ten feet; then, midway down the bluff, Davy flailed about, looking for a foothold, not finding any: the cliff was sheer granite for the next ten feet. Davy called up to me, "Hard way down," and, propelling himself away from the cliff, plummeted into the bushes below. In moments I was faced with the same choice, and so, feeling almost like a parachutist, I followed his lead. We found ourselves lying tangled, ass-over-teakettle, in shrubbery. We looked at one another, splayed at weird angles, our legs looped through each other's, and started giggling. And couldn't stop. The harder we tried to untangle ourselves, the harder we giggled; we'd grab at a branch, trying to haul ourselves up, only to have the branch snap off as we fell deeper into the bramble. Davy leaned down to help me, his cheek grazing mine—

And then, somehow, we were kissing. I wasn't feeling the same kind of tingle I had earlier, but it still felt nice; the wonderful pressure of lips against mine, our tongues meeting, licking . . . Before I knew it Davy had his hand under my shirt (withdrawing it when he found that my tits were no larger than his); I slid my panties down around my thighs, part of me knowing I shouldn't, knowing there was nothing down there for him to enter, but not caring. Davy's penis was stiff, the tip of it was flushed red; he guided it awkwardly toward my crotch—

And then he saw.

He stopped and drew back, eyes wide with shock and disbelief. "What—" he started to say, and by then I knew I'd made a mistake, a bad one; but some part of me tried to pretend it would all be all right, and I reached out to him, imploring, "Please . . . Davy, please—" There was fear, now, in his eyes, but I didn't want to see it. "We don't have to. We can just keep on touching, can't we, we can keep on kissing—"

I tried to draw him closer to me, but he jerked back, jumping to his feet, swaying as he sought to keep his balance amid the thick bramble. Wordlessly he pulled up his pants, and despite my pleas, staggered out of the underbrush and ran like hell out of sight.

I cried for half an hour before getting up the courage to head back to camp, certain that I'd return to have them all staring at me, whispering about me behind my back; but Davy not only never told anyone else, he never said another word about it to me, either . . . because when we all graduated to high school the next year, Davy somehow managed to transfer to a different school . . .

I never wanted to see again what I saw in his eyes, that

afternoon; never wanted to feel so *different*, ever again. And so, two months before my fifteenth birthday, I simply decided to deny it. All of it.

Overnight, I was no longer Pat, but Patty. Out went the jeans and sneakers; now, to my parents' shock, I wanted dresses, and nylons, and makeup—I became obsessed with learning everything there was to learn about putting on foundation, blusher, and eyeshadow. Mother was eager and willing to teach me, and my first hour in front of her dressing mirror I was amazed and delighted as my boyish features were transformed, through the miracle of Helena Rubenstein, into a soft, feminine face. My eyes, which had always seemed a bland brown, now looked almost exotic—hooded and sophisticated—with a touch of mascara and Lancôme; and as I carefully applied a coat of coral lip gloss, the image was complete. I stared at the girl in the mirror, so feminine, so pretty . . . and cried with joy and relief as I realized that the girl was *me*. Mother held me, relieved herself that she finally had a daughter again; that perhaps things might work out, after all.

Once I'd had a taste of what I could become, there was no stopping me: I had my ears pierced, and came to love the feeling when I shook my hair out and felt my hoop earrings jiggling to and fro; I even loved the sound my porcelain nails made when I drummed them impatiently on my desk in class. By the end of my freshman summer I convinced my parents to let me color my hair, and so I began the new year as a flirtatious blonde, thrilled that boys would open doors for me, or light my cigarettes for me—each ritual confirming my own femininity.

I dated around. saw lots of boys, but knew I could take the role only so far. The dates would often end up in a boy's car, parked at a romantic lookout, with the two of us necking hot and heavily, his hands roaming my body; my breasts were still nonexistent, but now, taken in the context of my new look, the boys didn't seem to mind. But the petting always stopped short of one point: when the boy's hand reached for my panties. I'd let him masturbate against them, or bring him off myself, but that was all. They couldn't know it was as frustrating for me as for them. They at least could masturbate, but all I knew was the pleasure of touching, of caressing, of kissing. I read about orgasms, listened to my girlfriends talk endlessly about them; the more I listened, the more envious I became. And so I kept searching, hoping that someday the right boy, the right touch, might bring me that release, that . . . fulfillment . . . everyone else seemed capable of. Most of the boys I dated didn't see me more than once or twice before dismissing me as a tease; but that reputation worked to my advantage, too, because there was always a ready supply of boys who saw me as a challenge, a prize to be won, and I was more than willing to let them try.

It was in my last semester of high school that my parents unexpectedly whisked me away for a rare day trip into Seattle. At first they tried to pass it off as a whim, but as the white brick buildings of the university medical center swung into view, they dropped the pretense; they seemed excited and enthused, and I became more than a little afraid at the whisper of zealousness in their tones. I could tell the extent of their preoccupation because when, nervously, I lit up a cigarette, neither of them gave me any grief about my smoking. Whatever this was about, it was important.

They wanted to be with me when I saw the doctor—a surgeon named Salzman, a balding, gentle man in his early fifties—but Dr. Salzman insisted on seeing me alone. My heart pounding for no reason that I knew, I sat in his comfortable office, in front of his expansive desk; I took a pack of Virginia Slims from my purse, then hesitated, but Dr. Salzman just pushed a heavy crystal ashtray toward me and I lit up, feeling a bit more relaxed, but certain that this amiable man was going to tell me I had three days to live.

"You've grown up to be quite a lovely young lady," he said approvingly. "I imagine you don't remember the last time I saw you?"

I smiled, shook my head. "I'm afraid not. Was I very small?"

He nodded. "Seven months." He leaned forward a bit in his chair, saw my nervousness, then laughed, putting me immediately at ease. "Don't look so worried. There's nothing wrong with you, at least nothing you don't already know about." He paused a moment, then, in a slightly more sober tone: "What did your parents tell you? About your—condition?"

It felt so strange, talking about this with someone other than my parents, but there was nothing threatening about this man. "They said it was a . . . a birth defect."

Salzman nodded to himself. "Yes, that about covers it as well as a child could understand. But you're no longer a child, are you?"

Suddenly it was a welcome relief just to have someone to talk to, someone who wouldn't cringe in fear. "It's called— androgyny, isn't it? I looked it up. But that's just something out of mythology, isn't it? How can I be—I mean, why—"

Salzman stood, paced a little behind his desk. "It *used* to be something out of mythology. Your case, eighteen years ago, was the first on the West Coast, but before that there was one in Denver, two in New York, a few in the Midwest . . . the incidences are still rare, less than one hundredth of one percent, but . . ." He circled around and sat on the edge of his desk. "You were lucky; the first few cases attracted the most attention. Lived most of their youth under a microscope, and for all that we still don't know anything about the causes. Your parents wanted you to have as normal a life as possible, so we restricted ourselves to periodic exams. There was nothing we could do until you reached maturity, anyway."

I sat up, snubbing out the cigarette in the crystal ashtray. "'Do'? You mean there's something—"

"Slow down, now," Salzman cautioned. "What you are, you are; you have a . . . different chromosome, not X, not Y, something entirely new . . . and no one can change your genetic makeup. But we *can* give you a closer cosmetic resemblance to a normal female. We can start you on a course of hormone therapy to facilitate breast and hip development, augmented with silicone implants . . ."

I was leaning forward in my seat, my heart racing, barely able to contain my excitement. Dr. Salzman went on, "Now, as to sex organs, we can make a surgical incision in your—please tell me if this is getting too clinical—in your groin; then place a sort of plastic sac just inside the skin, and fashion a vagina and clitoris out of skin taken from elsewhere on your body. This is similar to what we do for male-to-female transsexuals, and it may require a follow-up operation to make sure the vagina remains open, but—"

"Oh, Doctor, *thank* you," I said, tears starting to well up in my eyes; "You don't know how often I've dreamed about—"

He held up a hand. "Don't thank me yet. There *are* limits. Like a transsexual, you won't, of course, be able to conceive children; but unlike a transsexual, whose vaginal lining is made of penile tissue, yours will be relatively insensate . . . no more sensitive to pleasure than any other part of your body. Do you understand?"

My hopes plummeted. "Why not?" I asked, voice low.

He looked at me with sadness and sympathy. "Because, child, you don't have any sex organs, and no tissue of the same sensitivity as a penis, or a clitoris. Perhaps the estrogen will give you some sensitivity in your breasts; perhaps not. This will be a *cosmetic* change only . . . but won't that still go a long ways to relieving your gender discomfort?"

I thought about it a moment, my reservations melting away. I could go to bed with a man . . . get married . . . live something approaching a normal life. What did the rest matter, really? "Yes. Of course," I said. I stood, and couldn't help but hug him in gratitude. "When can I have the surgery?"

"We'll want to do a routine exam on you now, and if everything's satisfactory, we can do it whenever I can schedule an OR. Within the week, if you like."

When I left the office my parents saw at once the happiness in my eyes, and the three of us embraced, and laughed, and cried. All the way back they talked about how long they had been waiting for this day; how happy they were that their daughter was going to have a normal, healthy life. That night, there was laughter from their bedroom for the first time in years. The week until surgery passed quickly. And then, the night before I was to go to the medical center, I told my parents I was going out to meet friends, got into the flame-red Datsun my father had bought me for my seventeenth birthday, and I ran away from home.

I left a note, saying how sorry I was, explaining why I had to leave, and how I knew I couldn't live with their disappointment and betrayal. But I simply couldn't go through with it.

Oh, at first I was thrilled; I lay awake in bed, that first night, dreaming about being a girl, a real girl, for the first time. I had a date the next night, a new boy named Charles: good-looking, studious, and a little nervous. We ended up at the lookout outside town, but as we sat there, necking and petting, I realized nothing was happening—not even the whisper of anticipation I usually felt with a new boy, wondering if this, maybe, was the one who would be *different*—and as his hand reached under my blouse, I pushed him away with a little shove. "Charles, please *don't*. Let's go back to town." To prevent any further moves, I lit a cigarette and used it as a subtle shield between us. Charles turned slowly away, started the car, and headed back.

I caught a glimpse of myself in the rearview mirror and, reflexively, began to primp, more concerned with my own appearance than Charles, beside me. It wasn't until he dropped me off that I saw the hurt and anger in his eyes, and by then it was too late; he was gone before I could apologize. He hadn't even been in danger of discovering my secret; I'd just become bored, and used the same coquettish tone I always did to end the scene, without any thought to him. My God, I thought, what kind of selfish, manipulative little bitch am I turning into?

That night, I undressed in front of the full-length mirror on the inside of my closet door and stood staring at my reflection, taken aback at what I saw. I saw a girl's face, immaculately made up—pink lipstick, blue eyeshadow, a hint of blusher along the cheekbones—framed by strawberry-blonde hair. A girl's face, sitting atop a boyish body . . . not muscular enough to *be* a boy's, but too contourless to be a girl's, either. The juxtaposition seemed suddenly, and painfully, ridiculous. Looking at the head of a *Cosmo* girl sitting atop a neutered body, I *knew* for the first time that I was neither boy nor girl, but—something else.

I slept badly that night, and the next morning could barely bring myself to apply my makeup. As the days wore on, as the date of surgery approached, the operation seemed less like a deliverance than a . . . a mutilation. A plastic sac inside my groin? The thought made me shiver. And if I did go through with it, then what? I'd still have no sex organs, no orgasms; would I make the best of it, get a job, fall in love and marry? Or would I continue to search, irrationally, for that one man who *might* bring me complete satisfaction, in the process hurting how many others who failed to make the grade?

I looked at the fickle blonde in my makeup mirror, and knew which path *she* would take. I left her behind in Redmond that night I drove away; I stopped at a mini-mall on Route 22 and picked up a suitcase full of unisex clothing—jeans, shirts, sweaters. At the nearest salon I had my blonde mane trimmed short, in a style of indeterminate sex; when the blonde grew out, I returned to my natural brown. I drove as far from Redmond as I could manage, with no particular destination, no purpose beyond discovering just who, and what, I really was.

A stranger, looking at me, had little clue to whether I was a man or a woman; depending on the pitch of my voice at any given time, I could be either one. It wasn't unusual for me to sit at the counter of a roadside diner, and for the waitress to ask, "What can I get you, sir?"; only to have the person at the cash register hand me my change with a friendly, "Have a nice day, ma'am." I became a chameleon, my gender determined as much by the observer's biases as by anything physical; and the farther I drove, the freer I felt, a living Rorschach test with no demands put upon me to be one sex or the other.

I worked my way cross-country, waiting on tables, clerking in stores, delivering packages. I gave my name as Pat, which was both true and ambiguous. I'd never overtly state my sex unless it was absolutely necessary—on a job application, or if I was pulled over for a traffic ticket—and then only check "female" out of expediency, since that's what all my IDs read. But such instances were rare. It's amazing how much gender identification is really just in the eye of the beholder; I gave no cues, but each person I met brought his or her own lens to the focus of my identity. If I was driving fast, or aggressively, other drivers treated me like a man; if I was looking in a shop window displaying women's fashions, passersby would assume I was a woman. I could, with impunity, enter either a men's or a ladies' room; context, I discovered, was everything.

For the first time, too, I was free to follow my sexual feelings without playing a role. Working in a record store in Wyoming, I let myself experience, finally, the attraction I felt for women as well as men; I slept with a female coworker, keeping the lights dim, and in lieu of intercourse I spent hours caressing her, holding her, massaging her clitoris with my tongue and fingers. She told me later she'd never really liked sex all that much, but this time was different; this time she was starting to see what it was all about. When a lonely, middle-aged man in a diner made a pass at me, I assumed he thought me a woman; but as we talked, it became apparent he took me for a young gay male. In his hotel room, I performed fellatio on him, and then—careful to roll my underwear down only as far as necessary, explaining it as a minor fetish—let him have anal sex with me; then we just held one another for a long while. And as I lay there, both times, feeling warm and happy, I realized with a start I had given no thought to that all-important "culmination" I had been in search of, so desperately, for so long.

Kansas City, Boston, Fayetteville, New York . . . my odyssey took me across the country and halfway back again. Sometimes I settled in various cities for months at a time, taking college-credit courses in psychology and sociology; but it was impossible to maintain gender ambiguity when you settled in one place for long, and eventually I'd get restless with being either man or woman, anxious to be perceived simply as *me*, and I'd be on the road again, searching.

One thing became clear: with more and more of these cases cropping up, the medical establishment could no longer dismiss them as genetic quirks. And a few times I even got to meet my kindred. In Fayetteville I met a twenty-two-year-old living as a male, his full beard and hairy arms a testament to testosterone; an Army brat, he'd spent a good deal of time under the eye of military doctors, and it seemed to me his macho, swaggering pose was just that—a pose to satisfy his family and government, forcing them to leave him in peace. In New York I was shocked to find another androgyne who'd set up shop as a hooker, catering to any and all sexual persuasions, willing to be either man or woman, stud or harlot; he/she had a collection of wigs, toupees, strap-on dildoes and sponge rubber vaginas, and his/her arms were riddled with track marks. I got out of there, fast, feeling sick and sad. And in Miami I met a young "woman" with long auburn hair, dazzling eyes made up exactly right, full breasts peeping out of a low-cut dress, long red fingernails; the surgeons had done an amazing job on her. We sat in an open-air café as she flirted with every man who passed, preening in her compact mirror, yet if I asked her about her past, what it was like growing up, she found a way to change the subject, a dweller in an eternal, and ephemeral, present.

In Tennessee I finally met someone who'd taken the same path as I: Alex, slender, sandy-haired, living neither as a male nor a female, shunned by family, working as a teller in an S&L. We were astonishingly similar in our outlooks, in the decision we'd both come to, and both of us longed for that same unimaginably distant thing: a sense of belonging, of being loved and needed and necessary. We came together, in desperation more than want, and made love—as best as two neuters, two neither-nors, could make love. There were no sex organs to stimulate, but in our travels we each had learned much about touching, and caressing, and the sensitivities of flesh; we could appreciate, as well as anybody, the gentle brush of lips along the nape of a neck, the sensuous massage of fingers kneading buttocks, the lick of a tongue inside the rim of an ear. It was very tender, and very loving, but when it was over . . .

When it was over, Alex stroked my cheek and said, almost sadly, "We're much alike. Aren't we?"

I nodded, wordlessly.

"I always thought when I found someone like myself, I'd be truly happy," Alex said in a soft Tennessee drawl.

"So did I," I said quietly.

Alex held me, then gave an affectionate peck on my cheek. "I'm sorry, Pat."

We were alike; too alike. Even our sexual responses were nearly identical. It wasn't just the lack of orgasm, it was . . . like making love to yourself; narcissistic, somehow. Patty, the strawberry-blonde, would probably have liked it, but I felt only vaguely depressed by it. Both of us knew, instinctively, that the answer to our problem—if there was an answer—lay not in each other, but somewhere else.

My search, my quest for identity and purpose, was unraveling before my eyes. There *was* no purpose. There *was* no identity. I was neither man nor woman, yin nor yang; I was the line, the invisible, impossible-to-measure demarcation *between* yin and yang, as impossible to define as the smallest possible fraction, as elusive as the value of *pi*. I was neither, I was no one, I was nothing.

Not knowing what else to do . . . I went home.

I'd kept in touch with my parents, over the years; letters, postcards, a phone call on Christmas or Thanksgiving. At the beginning they were furious, even hung up the first time I called; eventually though they forgave me, and lately they'd written of how much they wanted to see me again. They were growing old, and I was afraid that if I didn't go now, I might never get the chance; so I headed west, to Washington, to Redmond, and home.

But the closer home I got, the faster my heart raced, the weaker my grip on the steering wheel; finally, somewhere between Bellevue and Kirkland, I lost my nerve and pulled into a motel off the 405. It was well past eleven, and after checking in I headed down to the all-night coffee shop in the lobby. Exhausted, hungry, and nervous, I sat at a corner table, ordered a sandwich, and began chatting with a man at an adjoining table; he had the smooth, charming sheen of a salesman, and as he flirted with me, I found myself unconsciously changing the way I sat, the way I crossed my legs, even the way I held my glass of iced tea. I leaned forward, my now very feminine body language belying my androgynous appearance. It all came back so quickly, so easily. Before he could make a proposition I realized what was happening and hurried off, feigning a stomachache; I hadn't come this far to lapse back into old patterns.

I slept badly, and wasted most of the next day window-shopping in a Kirkland mall, putting off the inevitable as long as I could. I was eating lunch when I looked up to find a man staring at me from a table across the room; this time I fought off the reflex that had overtaken me last night and simply glanced away, but when I looked up again the man was standing in front of me, a quizzical look on his face . . . a face I suddenly recognized.

"Pat?"

It was Davy. For a moment I was stunned that anyone here would recognize me, looking as I now did, but of course Davy had always known Pat, not Patty. The embarrassment of that day in the woods came rushing back; I must have looked terrified as I jumped to my feet, spilling coffee all over the table, and started to hurry away, but Davy rushed after. "Pat—wait—"

Outside he took me by the arm, but it was the gentle look

on his face, and the softness of his voice, that brought me to a stop. "It's okay," he said quietly. "I'm not going to . . . I mean, that was a long time ago, right?"

He was only in his twenties, and already his blond hair was thinning, but his eyes were still a bright blue, and now they seemed to be looking straight through me. Part of me wanted to run; thank God, I didn't. He let go of my arm, smiling apologetically. "Been a while," he said.

It took me a moment to collect my thoughts.

"I've been—away," I said. "Traveling."

"Back for a visit, or to stay?"

I wished I knew. "A visit. I was going to head over to Redmond later and see my parents."

We stood there, awkwardly, for several moments, before he said, haltingly, "Look. If you've . . . got an hour to spare, I'd . . . like to talk with you. Let me call my office, okay?"

"I really should be getting—"

"Please?" What was that intensity, that desperation, I read in his eyes? "Just an hour?"

We skirted the edge of Lake Washington in his Jeep, a gray mist obscuring the few sailboats out on this drizzly day. We chatted innocuously for the first half hour, pointing out familiar sights, the snowy caps of nearby mountains, but finally, as we stood at a deserted lookout over the lake, Davy worked up the nerve to say what had been on his mind all afternoon.

"I'm sorry, Pat," he said, quietly.

I looked up at him. "Sorry for what?"

"For running," he said, glancing away uneasily. "For cutting you off like that. But I couldn't handle it. You were the first girl—" He stopped, momentarily panicked that he'd used the wrong word, but when I didn't react negatively he went on, hesitantly, "—that I was ever really . . . attracted to. I mean, you have no idea how many times I thought about it, about you, and me . . . when we were out hiking, or swimming, or in school—"

I couldn't help smiling. "Really?" I said. "I thought you just thought I was just, you know, one of the guys."

"Yeah, well, that's the hell of it. Even though I knew— thought—you were a girl, I couldn't shake this weird feeling that you *were* a guy . . . that being attracted to you was wrong, somehow. So there we are, the perfect situation, and I figure, okay, I'll prove to myself she's just like any other girl, that it's okay for me to want her—"

"Oh, God," I said, realizing. "And instead you found—"

"Yeah," he said. "Talk about gender confusion. I freaked. And for a while, I wasn't even sure what *I* was, much less you." He looked away. "Later, I did a lot of reading, found out about . . . people like you . . . and when I was in college, I saw a therapist who helped me out. Then I met Lyn. But all during high school . . ."

I put a hand on his; now it was my turn to feel guilty. "Oh, God, Davy, I'm so sorry. I was so shaken up by it myself, I guess I never gave a thought to what it must've been like for you—your first sexual experience and it's so . . . so *bizarre* . . ."

He put his other hand on top of mine, and the warmth of it was familiar and comforting. "It's okay. I came out of it okay. But I wanted to apologize. For not—" His voice caught. "For not being a friend."

I couldn't think of anything to say, so I hugged him, trying to release some of that guilt that had been dogging him all these years; as we stood there the light drizzle became heavier, and when we separated the sky was darker, the ground turning muddy as a gray slanting rain pebbled the surface of the lake. "I'd better get a move on," I said, glancing at the thunderheads on the horizon.

"Rotten weather to be driving in. Why don't you come home and have dinner with Lyn and me?"

The idea frightened me, I'm not sure why; perhaps it was the warmth of Davy's body, still with me after our embrace. "No, I better not," I said, and in my haste to get back to the car I took the muddy embankment a bit too quickly, my foot sliced sideways, I felt a *pop* in my ankle as I tumbled down the small incline. I yelled, swore, but Davy was right behind me, pulling me up with a strong arm; though the damage, damn it, had already been done. "Take it easy," he said, helping me hobble up the embankment to the road. The pain in my foot was overshadowed, briefly, by the feel of his arm around my waist, but I thought of the last time something like this had happened, the blind alleys it had led us both to for so many years, and I resolved it would not happen again. "I'm all right," I protested, his grip loosening as I moved away—but the moment I took a step without his help all my weight fell on my twisted ankle and a stabbing pain shot up through my knee and into my thigh. I buckled, and Davy was there again to catch me.

"Come on. We'll fix you up back at my place." I was hardly in a position to argue. We climbed into his Jeep, the rain drumming on its canvas roof as we headed down the road, and I cursed myself, wondering if I hadn't done this on purpose . . .

We were dripping wet, our shoes muddied, when we entered Davy's tract home in Kirkland, but Davy led me unhesitatingly to a dining-room chair, carefully propped my ankle up on a second chair, and headed for the kitchen. "I'll get some ice," he said, and as the kitchen door swung shut behind him I saw the flash of headlights outside the dining-room window, then heard the hurried slap of footsteps on the wet sidewalk leading to the house. Oh, great, I thought. I looked around for Davy, thinking that this was going to be an awkward introduction at best, but without him here—

The door opened and, along with a spray of rain, a petite blonde in a damp gray suit entered, at first so intent on closing her umbrella she didn't notice me. Then she looked up, stopped in mid-stride, and stared at me, her face contorting into an almost comical look of apprehension.

"Oh, God," she said in a fast Eastern cadence. "You're not a burglar, are you? I left Chicago after the third burglary. Please tell me you're not a burglar."

I had to smile, but before I could say anything Davy entered with the ice pack, introducing me as an old schoolmate; I couldn't tell from the look on Lyn's face whether Davy had told her anything more about me, but as soon as she saw my ankle she came over, wincing as she touched my foot, lightly. "Ouch. Hold on, I think we've got an ace bandage in the bathroom." Within minutes she was wrapping a long, slightly ragged bandage around my ankle, as Davy took off the icepack. "Mud," she said with a sardonic grin. "There should be mud miners up here, you know, providing the rest of the country with our unending supply. Mud and rain, rain and mud—"

She finished wrapping, secured the bandage with a butterfly clip, then let Davy wrap the ice pack around the ankle again. "There. That should keep the swelling down." She stood, and for the first time I noticed the disparity in height between her and Davy; she stood on tiptoe, kissed him affectionately on the lips. "Guess what, dear heart," she said.

Davy looked apprehensive. "My turn to cook?"

She nodded. Davy sighed, picked up his raincoat from the chair he'd draped it over, looked at me. "You like Chinese?"

"Sure."

"Back in a flash." He was out the door and gone in a shot. Lyn turned, grinned. "Never fails. My turn to cook, I feel this obligation to make veal scaloppini; his turn to cook, he goes out for Szechwan. Would you like some Tylenol for that foot?"

"Thanks."

With the Tylenol came hot coffee and a dry sweater; we shifted my ankle to the coffee table in front of the sectional sofa, and Lyn and I dried out in front of the gas logs as we waited for the mu shu pork and kung pao chicken. I asked her what kind of work she did.

"Loan manager. B of A. You?"

"Retail sales," I hedged. "I've been on the road for quite a while."

"Back to visit your family?"

"Yes. Right."

She took out a pack of Salems, offered me one; and as she lit it for me, over the flame of the lighter I thought I could see her staring at me, oddly, trying to figure me out—not muscular enough for a man, not round enough for a woman. Was I live, or was I Memorex? Or was it just my own paranoia?

"I actually quit," she said, taking a deep drag on the cigarette, "back when I thought I was pregnant." Off my puzzled look she explained, "False alarm. Or 'hysterical pregnancy,' as they put it. If it happened to men, you *know* they'd call it something like 'stress-induced symptomatic replication,' but women, we're *hysterical*, right? Like, 'Oh my God, I burned the roast, and—'" She looked down at her stomach in mock-surprise. "'Whoops! Honey, do I look *pregnant* to you?'" We laughed, and that led to a general discussion of the peculiarities of men in general . . . and as I listened to Lyn's good-natured but very funny catalogue of male excesses, not so different from the catalogue of female excesses I'd listened to from men, something occurred to me, something crystallized after all these years.

All my life I'd felt like a member of a different race, human but not-human, similar but separate. And now I realized that this was, to some degree, how men and women viewed each other, at times—like members of a different species entirely. I saw it even more clearly over dinner, because even though Davy and Lyn had a good, loving relationship, there were the inevitable rough edges. Toward the end of the evening they got into a heated argument, as they were showing me around the soon-to-be-renovated basement, over what color tile would be used; Davy kept insisting it would be red, while Lyn said that wasn't it at all, more like terra-cotta, and they went on like that for almost a minute before I stepped into the breach with:

"Uh . . . Davy? When you say *red*, you mean like a fire engine?"

"No, no, darker than that, more like—like—"

"Brick?"

"Yeah! Yeah, like brick."

"That's terracotta," Lyn said, exasperated.

"Well how the hell am I supposed to know that?"

After a moment, both Davy and Lyn loosened up and Lyn even suggested I should stick around and interpret while they were redecorating the house. We went upstairs, had some wine, watched a little cable—me stealing glances at Davy and Lyn, snuggled up together—and slowly my mood darkened. I liked them, liked them both; Davy's steady presence, Lyn's manic energy. I could fantasize myself falling in love with or marrying either one. Everyone in the world, it seemed, could look forward to that—male, female, gay, lesbian, they could all find a partner. Everyone except me. I was grateful when the movie ended and I could retire, alone, to the sofabed in the living room.

Lying there under a thick, warm quilt, listening to the beat of raindrops on the roof, I drifted asleep . . . and had a nightmare I hadn't had in years, the one that had plagued me so often as a child, the one that drove me to my parents' bedroom, years before.

I looked up to see the ceiling was dropping toward me, as,

beneath me, the floor was rushing up. It happened too fast to do anything but shut my eyes against the coming collision; but when I hit, I didn't hit hard but *soft*, as though both floor and ceiling had turned to feather-down and were now smothering me between them. Out of the corner of my eyes I could see a thin wedge of light on either side, kept there only by the obstruction of my own body between floor and ceiling; then the wedge shrank to a slit, then a line, then a series of small pinpoints. I fought against the pressure but it was useless, the pinpoints of light vanishing one after another; I tried to take a breath but couldn't, my chest in a vise, unable to expand or contract; I was dying, I was defeated, I was—

"*Pat! Pat, wake up!*"

I was in the vise, and I was being held by my shoulders by Davy; my eyes were open, but I was in both places. He shook me, and the vise opened a crack; shook me again, and it fell away. I was in the living room, and I was awake; but I was still terrified. I broke down, as I hadn't in years—not since that day in the woods—but instead of shame and humiliation I felt pain, and loneliness; only the sense of apartness was the same. I held desperately onto Davy, tears running down my cheeks, trying to hold sleep at bay. Davy held me, and stroked my back, and after I'd finished he looked at me, put a hand to my cheek, and said in a soft, sad voice: "I think it's time I made it up to you," and then he was kissing me, tenderly. Part of me wanted to stay like that for the rest of my life, pretending to be what he wanted and needed, suspended forever in illusion; but I drew back, shook my head, tried to pull away. "Davy, *no*—your wife, I can't—"

And then there was a hand on my shoulder; a small hand, not very heavy, and I could feel the tips of her fingers on my skin. I turned. Lyn sat in her nightgown on the edge of the bed, looking not at all angry or disturbed; I started to say something, but she just shook her head, said, "Sshh, sshh," and leaned in, her lips brushing the nape of my neck, her breath moving slowly along the curve of my neck to my face, my mouth . . .

She knew. All along, she *must* have known . . .

Lyn gently pushed me back onto the bed, just as I became aware of a pleasant tickle on my legs; I looked down to see Davy, his hands stroking the knotted muscles of my calves, his lips moving slowly up my legs, covering them with tiny kisses.

Lyn took my face in her hands, put her mouth to mine, and our tongues met and danced round one another in greeting . . .

And then I felt something I had never felt before—a mounting pressure, a thrilling tension, as though every nerve ending in my body were about to burst, but didn't, just kept building and building in intensity—a pleasure I had never known, never imagined I *could* know. And it was then that I realized: the doctors had been wrong; all of them. Very wrong. I wasn't lacking in erogenous tissue. My whole *body* was erogenous tissue.

All it needed was the proper stimulation.

I finally worked up the nerve to see my parents; when Mother opened the door there was a moment's shock at my appearance—so different from the flirty blonde teenager who'd run away years before—but then she reached out and embraced me, holding me as though I might blow away on the wind. Then Daddy stepped up out of the shadows of the living room and did something odd and touching: he reached out and shook my hand, the way he might greet a son coming home from college; and then kissed me on the cheek, as he might a daughter. It was his way, I think, of acknowledging I was both, and neither; his way of telling me that they didn't love a daughter, they didn't love a son . . . they loved a child.

Funny; for years I thought of myself as a freak, a useless

throwback to another time—but despite all the psych courses I'd taken, all the books I'd read, I never really thought about that time, eons before recorded history, when my kind shared the earth with men and women. Why we vanished, or died out, may never be known, but the real question is, why were we there in the first place? It wasn't until Lyn, and Davy, that I began wondering . . . thinking about how, in the millennia since, men and women had had such difficulty understanding one another, seeing the other's side . . . as though something were—missing, somehow. A balance; a harmonizing element; the third side of a triangle. Maybe *that* was the natural order of things, and what's come since is the deviation. All along I'd been thinking of my kind as throwbacks, when perhaps we're just the opposite; perhaps we're more like . . . precursors.

The basement's been converted, not into a recreation room as once planned, but into extra living quarters; I have a bedroom, for when Davy and Lyn want to be alone, and a small library/den where I can study. So far, no one's been scandalized by the arrangement; lots of people room together to save rent or mortgage payments, after all. I've enrolled at the University of Washington, aiming first for my master's, then my Ph.D., in psychology . . . because now, finally, I think I know what that purpose is I was seeking for so many years. If the statistics are right, our numbers will be doubling every ten months; thousands more like me, going through the same identity crises, the same doubt and fear and loneliness . . . and who better to help them than a psychologist who truly understands their problems?

Lyn's quit smoking again, but this time, happily, the pregnancy isn't a—what did she call it?—"stress-induced symptomatic replication." And I can't help but feel that after so many false starts, maybe, somehow, it was me who tipped the scales—gave them that extra little push they needed. After all, who's to say life can't be transmitted just as easily in saliva or sweat as it is in semen or ova? We only have one problem, now: the nagging suspicion that when it comes time to buy baby clothes, neither pink nor blue may be appropriate. Green? Yellow? Violet? Take my word for it: there's big money to be made here for some enterprising manufacturer, one ready to tap an expanding market. Wait and see; wait and see.

Voices in
the Earth

*I*t was a sad, wounded world, its atmosphere a sickly shade of yellow-green—clouds of roiling gas obscuring surface features, tumbling restlessly from pole to pole like a sleeper caught in perpetual nightmare. Knowles watched its yellow disk grow larger, absently noting the shadow of the planet's moon as it crossed the equator. From far off, it seemed, he heard Jacinda's voice as she logged the incoming data from ship's sensors: *Atmosphere at perfect chemical equilibrium . . . predominantly carbon dioxide, with traces of methane, ammonia, water vapor . . .* A small, analytical part of Knowles's mind listened, noted the deadly array of chemicals in the atmosphere, and wondered about the efficacy of the environment suits they would have to wear on the surface. But a larger part of him felt merely sad, and increasingly disturbed by the appearance of the poisoned world ahead. He heard himself saying, softly: "What gives the atmosphere that— yellow hue?"

Jacinda peered into a sensor readout, the display briefly

washing her dark brown skin in an amber light. "Iron oxides," she said matter-of-factly. "From the rusting cities. When life vanished from this planet, the free oxygen bonded to anything that was at hand—iron, mostly, in the abandoned machinery, vehicles, building infrastructures . . ."

Knowles frowned. A tall man with a long face, he looked sober and preoccupied even when he was not; now his bushy eyebrows—grayer, oddly, than the rest of his hair—knitted together. "Sensors show *no* life-forms whatever?"

Jacinda passed a hand over some instrumentation; her body heat spurred a momentary hum of activity as the computers ran; then she shook her head, regretfully.

"Nothing. Not even the presence of simple amino acids in the oceans. The last recon was right: it's a dead world."

Knowles shut his eyes. One of the two technicians on the scoutship, Archer—tall, blond, the gentler of the two, quite the contrast to bluff, impatient Bledsoe—came up behind Knowles and eyed the image on the screen with some degree of interest, real or feigned. "There was a name for this one, in one of the old languages, wasn't there, Professor?"

Knowles opened his eyes, nodded, looked at the dead planet drawing slowly nearer.

"Yes," he said quietly. "Earth. They called it Earth."

The scoutship dropped through the atmosphere like a spider descending on a strand of web, its tripodlike legs opening as it breached the poisonous envelope of gases. Inside, on the small, grayly functional bridge, Knowles could feel the subtle shift in engine vibrations as the ship switched to plasma drive for landing. The thought of all that heat and energy pouring out, in an atmosphere of methane and other potentially flammable chemicals, worried him; but Jacinda had assured him that with no vegetation to replenish the long depleted oxygen supply, no reactions were possible. Knowles sighed to himself. He'd never particularly cared for spaceflight, but just now even the narrow seats in the Proxima-Galthor star liner seemed appealing; disconcerting to travel forty light-years in a small ship like this. He felt as though he'd spent the last two weeks in a barrel dropped over—what was the name of that waterfall on Old Earth? Niagara? That was what traveling in non-Einsteinian space felt like—one long, continuous fall, like a parachutist who never hit the ground. The bigger ships had enormous gravity generators to compensate, but a four-person survey craft was far too small to accommodate one.

"Donald?" Jacinda looked up at him, and Knowles saw two people in the dark oval of her face: the mineralogist, sober, thoughtful, commanding the survey team for ReSource; and the quiet, reflective college student she had been fifteen years ago, sitting in his lecture hall on Galthor, listening with rapt attention to the histories of a dozen worlds. Somehow he had always thought she would go on to become an archaeologist. Though perhaps, in an odd sort of way, she had.

"Island on visual," she said, nodding toward the screen, drawing his attention to the land mass appearing, hazily, through the yellow gases. Knowles leaned forward, suddenly excited, as the long promontory came into clear view. Manhattan Island, they'd called it. In its day it, and the city of which it was a part, was the unofficial capital of this planet—three hundred square miles of living structures, business towers, traffic-ways—a population, at its height in the twenty-first century, of nearly twenty million. Knowles had studied tapes and photographs, knew the history of the city from its colonial beginnings as New Amsterdam to its ultimate fall from glory in the great diaspora. It had been a thriving, dynamic metropolis; primitive, yes, but rivaling the Cluster Worlds for sheer dynamism. And now—

Now it was a graveyard. The buildings were still there,

their concrete skin eroded and pitted over the long wait of centuries; many of the infrastructures had been reinforced with new alloys in the twenty-second century, but after this long, even they were decaying. The rusted stumps of two enormous towers straddled the southwest shore of the island; in the harbor stood the statue of what was once a woman, one arm upraised but broken off at the wrist, large gaping holes amid the folds of her robe exposing the rusted framework beneath. Beyond the harbor lay the ocean, stagnant but for the listless pull of the moon, gray-green in color, with a texture less like water than mercury. No trees, or grass, or vegetation of any kind marked the landscape; and the entire tableau was bathed in the pale, jaundiced light of an aging sun, filtered through the poisonous air of the New Earth.

"We'll land on that plain over there, in the middle of the island," Jacinda said. Archer nodded, adjusted his navigation board; the vibrations changed again as the ship slowed further. It wasn't until they were right on top of it that Knowles realized that the "plain" was, in fact, Central Park—a desolate stretch of bedrock denuded of vegetation. The engines shuddered as the ship touched down, and Donald Knowles—who had spent the better part of a lifetime studying the history, the people, the soul of a planet he had glimpsed only in tapes and books—returned at last to the Earth he had never known.

They worked their way slowly through the bleak, defoliated park, protected by the shimmer of energy membranes generated by their environment suits. The lakes, ponds, and reservoir—once a mecca for lunchtime office workers, or weekend visitors—were long since evaporated. The cages of the zoo stood rusted and decaying; Cleopatra's needle, once a spire standing amid tall trees, was little more than broken pedestal. On the outskirts of the park was the Metropolitan Museum of

Art—empty, of course, stripped long ago of its treasures . . . slowly, over the course of a century, as humanity migrated to the stars.

They crossed Fifth Avenue, probing deeper into the city; though most buildings still stood, many were truncated or fallen in on themselves, massive concrete blocks scattered about in odd-shaped piles, like latter-day Stonehenges. Jacinda and Knowles led the way, Archer and Bledsoe behind them. Jacinda looked around at the remains of Fifth Avenue, moved by the silence and the emptiness, her tone soft. "It's like one of those little ghost towns in the High Desert, back on Elsinore . . ."

Bledsoe was unmoved. "A rock's a rock. They all look the same once they've been mined."

Knowles bristled at that. "It's not a 'rock'! It's the cradle, the birthplace of humanity."

Bledsoe looked around, unimpressed. "Looks like we got out just in time."

Knowles said nothing. Jacinda noted his anger, wondering if Bledsoe's sentiments were genuine or intended largely to irritate Knowles; technicians hated taking civilian observers on duty like this, and the two weeks' travel time to Earth had been tense and uneasy. She decided to ignore Bledsoe's belligerence—for the moment. "Mr. Archer, Mr. Bledsoe: you can start taking your readings anytime. Professor Knowles and I will go on ahead." The two technicians began setting up the sensors that would give them, within a week's time, a spectroscopic analysis of the remaining minerals in the Earth's crust; Jacinda and Knowles walked on, taking in the sad, somber face of the dead city. For a moment, Jacinda felt as though she were back on Galthor, viewing history tapes in Knowles's lecture hall . . . but far from launching into one of his enthusiastic dissertations on terrestrial history, Knowles was oddly silent; awed, perhaps, by the faded beauty around him.

"Donald?" He turned to look at her. "Earth was stripped of significant artifacts long ago. Just what do you expect to find here?"

Knowles shrugged. "A feeling . . . a sense of place . . . what it must have been like to live here when the skies were blue, and the oceans green with plankton. If I can capture some hint of that . . . if I can put it into words . . ." A touch of self-deprecation crept into his voice. "Thirty years ago—*ten* years ago—I wouldn't doubt that I could, but at my age, I suppose, you start putting more credence in your bad reviews than in the good." He looked at her with fondness. "And if I haven't said so lately . . . thank you, Jacinda, for getting me on this survey. I know it couldn't have been an easy task. A kind gesture, to an old academic."

"Not that kind," she said gently, "and not that old." She started to say something more when her communicator buzzed; she tabbed the microphone at the base of her helmet, near her larynx. "Yes?"

"Sensors operational and ready to go." Archer's voice. Jacinda nodded to herself, tabbed the *transmit* circuit: "Be right there. Out." She turned to Knowles, feeling uneasy about what she had to say next. "Donald, I . . . I can draw this out for an extra day or two, but . . . I'm afraid I can't give you much more than that. A week, ten days at the most. After that, I'll have to give word for our mining vessels to move in and extract whatever's salvageable, and—"

"And if I haven't found that sense of place by then . . . there may not be a place *left* to have any sense of?" He nodded. "Yes, I understand."

Jacinda looked in his eyes, saw the pain and helplessness he was trying to conceal . . . and she knew that he did, indeed, understand. Better, perhaps, than any of them.

* * *

He spent the rest of the day walking the ruined face of Manhattan—from Times Square across Forty-second Street to the East River, then north to the broken towers of the George Washington Bridge on the western shore. All the while Knowles tried to imagine himself living here, in one of these concrete blocks, the sounds of traffic waking him in the morning—so unlike Galthor, whose business districts were purposely separated from its residential complexes. He ascended a pitch-black stairwell in one of the steel-and-glass buildings on Fifth Avenue, and with a bit of effort made it all the way up to the third floor; in the skeletal remains of one of the offices, its windows looking blindly out at the street below, he tried to envision himself a twentieth-century worker sitting at one of the dozens of identical desks, his schedule rigorously proscribed even to the time at which he was allowed to eat. He'd studied these customs for years, but sitting here, at a rusting metal desk, the cultural imperatives that dictated such a ritualistic way of life remained as remote, as unfathomable, as ever. He'd hoped actually being here might bring him to a closer understanding of them, but instead of epiphany, or empathy, he felt merely puzzled.

He left the building feeling depressed and aimless; he wandered down Fifth Avenue, passing the delapidated remains of a bench and overhang—a transit stop, obviously, along the path of what had first been noxious internal-combustion vehicles called buses, replaced at the advent of superconductors by more efficient transportation—and he wondered, idly, about the trip to work those office workers took. What must it have been like, heading for the office along with thousands, millions, of other human beings, in such close proximity? Squeezed into rattling metal shells that lumbered up and down these streets, or in subway cars no less dense and—

Subways. Of course. He remembered, all at once, the vast honeycomb of tunnels beneath the island, and his depression lifted, buoyed by the possibilities. Excitedly he searched out the nearest entrance to what was once known as the IRT, and headed down into the darkness of the subway station.

His path illuminated by the infrared beam in his suit, Knowles climbed over the rusted turnstile, studied with fascination the graffiti on the cement walls, walked down the tunnel about half a kilometer to where a subway train stood, lifeless, as it had for centuries. He pried open the door; it buckled easily under his touch, nearly falling off. He stood in the car, feeling suddenly rather pathetic in his desperation to understand, to relate to these vanished people he'd spent a lifetime studying but never fully comprehending; observing—in the tapes and disks taken from Earth during the diaspora—but not feeling, as they felt. He shut his eyes, almost trying to will himself back in time—

And heard voices.

He felt both a thrill of excitement and a stab of fear. He opened his eyes, expecting the voices to fade; dream-sounds dimming with his reverie . . . but if anything, they seemed to become louder. They were the sounds and voices of rush-hour commuters . . . of a hundred people jammed side by side in a subway car, talking, yelling above the roar of the train . . . except there was no roar, just voices, voices straining to be heard above a sound that did not *exist*—

Voices that seemed to be coming from the very next car . . .

Moving slowly, unsure of his own senses, Knowles approached the rear door, opened it, and stepped over the platform linking this car to the next. The voices intensified. They were *there*, in the next car, hidden by the centuries of dirt and grime covering the windows, and he knew, impossibly yet absolutely, that they were real. He grasped the doorknob, his heart pounding, his hands inside his gloves suddenly sweaty. The deadbolt opened, but the latch was so rusty it was almost bonded with the door frame's strike plate; Knowles had to put his full weight against the door to pry it loose. He felt it give on the third try; off-balance, he lurched through the suddenly open door—

The voices ceased, abruptly, as though Knowles had stumbled gauchely into a private party, without an invitation.

He stood there in the sudden silence, feeling like a fool. He'd wanted to hear the past so fervently that he'd deluded himself into thinking that he had. Thank God Jacinda and the others weren't around to see him making such a complete ass of himself. Deciding that he had explored the tunnels enough for one day, he retreated quickly to the surface, back to the sallow light growing even dimmer as dusk began to fall.

He glanced at his watch. Sixteen hundred hours: about half an hour before he had to rendezvous with the others back at the ship. He looked around at the street he found himself on—a commercial district chock-a-block with the gutted remains of department stores, bookshops, and boutiques—his attention snagged by one shop in particular. On the window, dust-encrusted but just barely legible, was the name MUSIC & MEMORIES; and below that, AUDIO—VIDEO—HOLO. His embarrassment overshadowed by the prospect of what he might find in the music store, he hurried inside.

The wall shelves were filled with ancient pieces of electronics equipment dating from approximately the mid-twenty-second century—holographic tape players and projectors, surround music systems—and, in the middle of the store, row upon row of metal bins, most of them empty, but a few still full. Eagerly, he began examining their contents: old laser-encoded discs, ranging in size from two to five inches in diameter. There were no recordings that couldn't be found in any good-sized library in the Cluster Worlds, but that wasn't the important thing; what was important was that they were here, they were made on Earth, centuries ago, and Knowles could listen to them as a native might have listened to them. Theoretically the digitalized music, protected by a noncorrosible plastic, should still be capable of playback—but after so long—?

He took a disc from a bin, went to one of the music players on the wall. He took out a small spherical battery from his utility pack, plugged the player into the battery, inserted the disc—

And heard, clear and crisp as though it had been recorded yesterday, *Rhapsody on a Theme of Paginini* . . . sad, sweet, and beautiful . . . encapsulating, for Knowles, the nobility and the tragedy of this ruined planet. He closed his eyes, briefly, and when he opened them—

The store was filled with . . . *people*. Dozens of them, examining the electronic gear, on line at the sales counter, looking through the bins. The room filled with the sound of their voices as they talked among themselves . . . like the voices on the subway. Knowles jumped back reflexively, choking off a scream. Watching the scene with equal parts fear and fascination.

The people seemed solid enough, but the texture of their skin was subtly wrong, strangely different; their clothes, as well as their flesh, had the same sallow color as the air itself. They looked oddly forlorn, as well, their actions mechanical—as though they walked and talked and moved through habit, rather than inspiration. Fear mounting, Knowles backed away toward the exit; as he reached the door, he turned—

And froze. A young man, sallow and strangely textured as the others, stood blocking the door. There was something both sad and sinister in his face, and in his voice; or perhaps it was the odd way in which sound carried through the nonoxygenated air.

"Don't you remember us . . . Professor?" he said softly.

Knowles screamed and leaped back. The spectral figure seemed to dissolve into dust even before the echoes of his scream had faded. Knowles turned to look for another exit—and saw that the other apparitions were now gone, as well.

Knowles's heart was racing faster than it had in years. He leaned against one of the bins, trying to regulate his breathing, to calm himself; finally, after several minutes, he felt composed enough to call the others on his communicator.

To their credit, Archer and Bledsoe didn't laugh outright when they heard his story, but there was scant sympathy in their faces as they listened to what Knowles realized, even as he related it, was a preposterous tale. Jacinda seemed concerned but it was clear that she, too, could hardly take Knowles's word on face value. Ten minutes later, with Archer and Bledsoe canvassing every inch of the store with their pocket sensors, Archer announced: "Nothing. No energy readings at all, aside from normal background rad levels. If there was anything here, it didn't leave much behind."

"If?" Knowles stepped forward. "Are you suggesting there *was* no—"

"*Every* living thing leaves behind some kind of energy trace," Archer said patiently, "even—".

"Then perhaps it wasn't alive! Perhaps it was some sort of—alien *illusion*."

Jacinda shook her head. "We're the only ship in the system, Donald. If there were another anywhere within half a light-year, we'd know."

"Damn it," Knowles said, patience wearing thin, "I'm telling you, I *saw*—"

Bledsoe, across the room, suddenly spoke up. "I'm getting an energy reading."

He was standing at the far wall, pointing his sensor at the bank of electronics equipment. Knowles breathed a sigh of relief. "There!" he said. "I knew it."

"What kind of energy?" Jacinda asked.

"Simple electrical field." Bledsoe nodded toward one of the machines. "Some residual traces in the solar batteries." He reached out, tapped a few touchpads on the machine . . . and immediately several full-scale holographic images were projected into free space: a man and a woman talking (though the sound was turned off) and walking in the midst of the four space travelers.

Bledsoe's smile was faintly mocking. "Sure these aren't what you saw, Professor?"

Knowles was indignant. "I know the difference between holograms and—and—"

"Ghosts?" Bledsoe was baiting him.

"I didn't say that."

"That will be enough, Mr. Bledsoe." Jacinda's tone was sharp. "You and Mr. Archer can go back to your spectroanalysis. I'll join you in a moment."

The two of them nodded, exited. Jacinda turned to Knowles, her tone softening.

"I'm sorry. We've just had some bad experiences with civilian observers. Try and stay out of their way, all right?"

Knowles sighed. "Do *you* believe I saw what I did?"

"I'd like to. But I can't act without evidence."

Knowles nodded. "Of course."

Jacinda touched him on the shoulder and left. Knowles wandered around the empty store, sighed, and stooped to pick up a fallen music disc. He straightened, then, remembering something he forgot to mention, tabbed the communicator at the base of his throat. Before he could say a word, a voice suddenly issued from his own communicator—a sad voice, with a single question:

"You really *don't* remember us . . . do you, Professor?"

It was the voice of the young man in the doorway.

Knowles lay on his bunk, unable to sleep; each time he closed his eyes he saw the pale, mournful face of the young man, an ineffable sadness in his eyes and in his voice. Odd—so odd: if they were, indeed, ghosts, they seemed more haunted than haunting. He felt, inexplicably, a certain pity for them . . . irrational because he knew nothing of these beings, least of all if they were hostile or not. And yet . . .

Giving up on sleep, he got up, dressed, left his cabin, and headed for the galley to make coffee. Halfway there, he passed the bridge—where, to his surprise, Jacinda sat at a sensor web, making notations, stifling a yawn. He hesitated in the doorway a moment, then stepped into the bridge; hearing him, Jacinda swiveled in her seat, smiled tiredly.

"Donald. You're up late."

Knowles sat down beside her. The readouts washed each of them in soft light. "So are you."

Jacinda sighed, nodded toward the sensors. "Lots of data to log. There's still a treasure trove of minerals in this planet. The inhabitants pretty much bled her dry of fossil fuels, but there's a wealth of basalt, iron, uranium . . ."

For a moment he almost blurted out what had happened to him after Jacinda and the others had left—but fear held him back, fear of what they might think, of how they might keep him aboard ship for the rest of the survey if he exhibited any more aberrant behavior. Instead he merely stared at the readouts, at the taped image of the Earth on the main viewscreen.

"Yes," he said, a bit distantly. "This world was blessed with an . . . abundance of natural resources." He gazed at the planet in the viewscreen, so different from the one he had spent half a lifetime studying. "It was really quite beautiful, Jacinda," he said quietly. "Amazing variety of flora . . . climates ranging from the temperate to the tropical, from arctic to desert . . ."

"And so much of it covered with water. Remarkable."

Knowles's eyes gleamed as he warmed to his subject. "Water. Yes. That was how it began, you know, humanity's—questing spirit? They navigated these tiny ships, propelled only by the wind—the wind!—with strips of cloth strung up on wooden masts. They sailed the oceans, not even knowing, at first, whether or not they'd fall off the edge of the world."

He laughed. "Well, they didn't. They spread themselves to the far corners of the Earth, and they thrived. Ah, and the names, Jacinda, the names! India. Israel. Marseilles. Beijing. Some of them still survive. Your homeworld, Elsinore, is named after a castle in a place called Denmark, home of a mythical prince named Hamlet." He paused a moment; then, softly: "This is where it all began, Jacinda. This is where we began."

Jacinda stared at the image in the viewscreen; her voice was soft. "How could they let the planet end up like . . . this?"

The fond look in Knowles's eyes darkened; the wistful tone sobered. "Greed. Stupidity. The usual catalog of sins. They used refrigerants that slowly ate away the ozone layer. They burned the tropical rain forests to make way for farmland, using the ashes for fertilizer, and the buildup of carbon dioxide eventually turned the entire Earth into an enormous hothouse.

"By the time they'd poisoned the whole biosphere, they had the technology to leave it behind. So they fled into space, and cast the Earth aside like a half-eaten apple."

Knowles shook his head. "You know the irony of it? After all that, the Earth, today, is almost exactly as it was, millennia ago, before life emerged—before that first primordial storm rained nutrients into the oceans." He looked down. "And here we are," he added bitterly, "returned to commit the final indignity on the planet that nurtured us. Here to put the knife to her, one last time . . ."

Jacinda, offended, tried to restrain her annoyance. She stood, her voice and manner suddenly quite cool.

"Our *ancestors* killed this world," she said sharply. "Not us. The law prohibits us from mining *any* living world—only dead ones."

Knowles looked up, realizing his mistake. "I'm sorry—I didn't mean to imply—"

But Jacinda was already up and standing in the doorway, electronic clipboard held up to her chest.

"Like it or not, Donald," she said, a bit softer, "Earth *is* a dead world, now. There's nothing we can do about that . . . except, I suppose, be grateful we finally learned our lesson."

She turned and left the bridge. Knowles swiveled in his seat, leaned his elbow on the sensor board, and put his head in his hands, cursing his own tactlessness. It was some moments before he noticed that each of the tiny monitor screens before him had gone white with static. He looked up . . . and as he did, the static was replaced with the image of—the young man.

"Do you remember us *now*, Professor?" he asked, sadly.

Knowles jumped, stifling a cry. He stared at the screen in astonishment and fear and a curiosity that overwhelmed both.

"Sweet Jesus," he whispered. "What . . . what do you *want* from me?"

The young man looked at him with haunted eyes. "Your help, Professor. That's all." A pause; then: "Can you find your way to Penn Station?"

He made his way downtown, as, in the early-morning darkness, the streets became filled with apparitions: men, women, children, all materializing in mid-stride, walking the streets as though alive . . . but joylessly, definitely not the haunters but the haunted. They wore clothes from every era people lived on this island—from the twenty-second century to the twentieth, from the nineteenth to the seventeenth, all the way back to when this city was known as New Amsterdam. He walked, dazedly, in their midst; once or twice one of them looked at him with yellow eyes, brushed up against him as they passed; they felt solid, material, not at all as insubstantial as they appeared.

He reached Penn Station a little before one, walking through the entry doors into the dilapidated transportation terminal; and as he shut the doors behind him, the first thing he noticed was the air. The roiling gases were not in evidence here; the yellow light which bathed the rest of the Earth's surface was somehow excluded from this place. Knowles looked up and got his second shock: the station was filled, on every level and on every square foot of floorspace, by specters like the ones he had seen on the street. Thousands of them, many gaping in wonder and amazement at him, as though he, not they, were the apparition.

The young man stood at the forefront, smiling. "You won't be needing that helmet anymore, Professor," he said. "The air's breathable in here."

His instruments confirmed it; slowly he removed his helmet. And breathed in real air. "How—how did you—?"

"Difficult to explain," the man said. "We used part of our . . . energies . . . to change the molecular structure of the gases." He extended a hand. "My name is Blaine."

Knowles hesitated a moment, then reached out and took his hand . . . finding it quite solid, but oddly textured, not like human flesh at all, but some sort of simulacrum . . . fashioned, perhaps, out of the same random molecules that made up the air.

So intent was he on the young man that Knowles did not notice until the last moment that the others were drawing closer—not threateningly, but with mounting fascination and . . . hope?

"Are you real?" one of them asked, and Knowles had to restrain an ironic smile. A young boy looked at him with eyes wide. An old man just kept smiling, as though he could not believe his good fortune; an old woman came up, touched him lightly on the arm, and said softly, "We've been waiting so long . . ."

They were all converging on him now, old men, young women, children, teenagers, black, white, Asian, Indian, from every time period, every social class—

"Why did you *leave* us . . . ?"

"Are you back to stay? All of you?"

"Where are the others?"

"Will they follow, in more ships?"

"Yes," said the old woman, "where are they, when are they coming?"

Knowles backed away, overwhelmed by the loneliness and desperation in their pale eyes and plaintive voices. Slowly he began to realize who they were, and why they were here. "My God," he said hoarsely. "All of you . . . you're . . ."

"The ones you left behind," Blaine said sadly. "All the souls who ever were . . . all the ones who stood and watched as your ships vanished, forever, from our sight." His voice became a whisper. "All of us who couldn't follow . . ."

Tears began to well up in Knowles's eyes. "We . . . we never *knew.* We never knew you even *existed* . . ."

"Didn't you?" Blaine asked. "Didn't a part of you *always* know?"

A little boy looked up at Knowles, eyes big, voice small. "You didn't come back to stay?"

Hopelessly, Knowles could only shake his head. Almost as

one, the apparitions exchanged glances, hope dimming in their eyes. Knowles looked to Blaine; the young man sighed. "I tried to tell them. But after so long, they didn't want to lose hope so soon."

Knowles looked again at the crowd, struggling to understand. "But why is it so important to you? To follow us?"

The old man—not much older than himself, Knowles realized suddenly—stepped up. "You're our *children*," he said patiently, as though explaining the obvious. "Our immortality. Since time began, we've walked among you, sharing in your triumphs, your despair—but now—" Bitterly: "Now there's nothing. No children, no future. Just a ruined playground you left behind."

Knowles was barely able to comprehend the concept, much less the immense loneliness and betrayal these creatures must be feeling. He searched, desperately, for some words of comfort, as well as something to ease the guilt forming in his own mind. It was irrational—he, personally, had not betrayed them; he'd been born on a world five hundred light-years, and several centuries, removed from here—but he suddenly found himself spokesman for vanished humanity, the ancestors who had fled this planet so long ago.

"It . . . it doesn't have to be this way," he said, throat dry. "You can follow *us*, our ship—"

Blaine shook his head. "Your ships warp space in ways we can't. Those of us who have tried have come back disfigured, or insane. Can you comprehend that, Professor? Disfigurement, insanity . . . not of mere flesh, but of one's immortal soul?" He seemed to repress a shiver. "No. We can't follow your ship."

"I—I could give you coordinates—"

"And how would we know to get there? We're not gods, Professor. We're human beings. Or we used to be. Could *you* find your way to Tau Ceti, unaided?" His mouth twisted in an unhappy smile. "It's a large universe, Professor. And not nearly as benign as you living like to think it is."

Knowles slumped against a wall, withering under the sad stares of the dead.

"Then what *can* I do?" he asked. "You said you needed my help."

"Put your helmet back on." Even as Blaine said it, the light in the station made a subtle but unmistakable shift toward the yellow end of the spectrum. Knowles did as he was directed. Blaine moved closer.

"I know why you're here," he said. "Not you, but your ship, the crew.

"We're just shadows. Helpless to stop them. But you—you can *do* something. Let them know this planet still contains . . . life. Of a sort." He moved even closer, and as he did, Knowles thought he could see the young man's body become less opaque . . . not translucent, but actually losing its density, the atoms that made up the makeshift body losing their molecular cohesion, breaking up into random bits of carbon and ammonia . . .

"This Earth . . . ruined and gutted as it is . . . is all we have left." His face started to disintegrate, skin flaking off as the soul binding it together merely shrugged it off like a worn coat. The eyes turned to smoke; his hair, his ears, to dust. His voice was fading but urgent in the dimming light: *"Don't let them take it away from us."*

And when he looked up, Knowles saw that he was alone once more in the empty station.

Jacinda stood in the galley, nursing a cup of coffee, trying to collect her thoughts. She had stayed up working till well past one, finally managed a few hours' sleep—then found herself awakened again, by Donald, who now stood before her, telling some incredible story about the ghosts of all who ever died, about abandonment and betrayal and redemption. Good God, she thought, he seems so wild-eyed, so . . . desperate. Could this really be the same man she had studied under, years ago? Suddenly the strings she had pulled, the favors she had called in to get Knowles on this assignment, all seemed like a tragic mistake.

"Donald," she said hesitantly, "do you have any *idea* what Archer and Bledsoe would say if they could hear you?"

Knowles looked at her beseechingly. "All I'm asking is for you to keep an open mind. Give me a chance to prove it to you."

"Prove that the Earth is some sort of—haunted planet? And then what? Suspend mining operations?"

"You've heard stranger tales in your travels, I'm sure."

Jacinda forced a smile. "Not by much." She sighed unhappily. "Donald, we've known each other a long time. Don't put me in this position."

"If I had any choice, I wouldn't. But I don't. Too much depends on it." He added gently: "You were always my best pupil, Jacinda. Let me teach you one last thing?"

Reluctantly, she followed him into the city, two figures enveloped in the shimmer of environment suits, walking through a long-dead city in the middle of a cold, yellowish night. They entered an abandoned transportation terminal; Jacinda set her infrared for widest possible angle, swept the beam through the station. No signs of life. Or anything else, for that matter. Knowles tabbed his communicator. "I'm activating the exterior speaker on my communicator. You might want to do the same. To speak to them."

Jacinda reminded herself that Knowles had been correct: in her work she had seen things equally bizarre as that which he was suggesting; alien life-forms, odd cosmic phenomena. She hoped, desperately, that Knowles was telling the truth . . . as unbelievable as it might appear.

"Hello!" Knowles's voice reverberated oddly in the methane. "Hello, I've come back!"

There was no response.

Knowles cleared his throat. "I—I've brought someone. Someone who can help. Please, let us see you!"

The words echoed off the tiled walls. Jacinda glanced down. Please, she thought. Please, let someone answer . . .

"It's all right!" Knowles shouted into the darkness. "She has to see you, has to know you exist! She can call off the mining, if you just—"

Jacinda said, "Donald," but he seemed not to hear.

Desperation crept into Knowles's voice. Where *were* they? What was going on? "Don't you understand? She can *help*, damn it!"

"Donald, that's enough," Jacinda said softly.

"God damn you, show yourselves!"

"Donald!"

Jacinda's shout made him turn round, quickly. She swallowed, feeling embarrassed and sorry for this old man she loved like a favorite uncle. But now the uncle was unbalanced, and it was up to her to save him from himself, before he humiliated himself any further.

"This is my fault," she said. "I knew what this planet meant to you. I shouldn't have invited you along to watch it be—" She put a hand to his arm. "Why don't I just forget we ever came out here. All right?"

Knowles saw the pity in her gaze and hated it. He looked from her to the empty terminal; there were tears in his eyes.

"Please," he whispered into the dark. "Don't do this to me . . ."

Jacinda took him by the elbow, gently led him out the door and back to the ship. They spoke little on the long walk back; at the door to Knowles's cabin she touched him affectionately on the shoulder, then went to her own quarters. Knowles lay down on his bunk and stared into space, tears forming again in his eyes. Why? Why were they doing this? They said they needed help; they knew he had to convince Jacinda of their existence; *why hadn't they appeared?*

The thought came to him, nasty and unbidden: Perhaps they hadn't appeared . . . because they had never been there in the first place.

He shut his eyes tightly. Ghosts. That was all his life seemed to hold, these days, since Cara died. He was seventy-three years old, and in the last twelve months, ten of his oldest and closest friends had died. People he had grown up with, worked with, laughed with and fought with . . . signposts, each of them, marking a different passage in his life. And one by one they were dying, the markers vanishing into memory, leaving his life somehow . . . uncorroborated. He had seen Cara a hundred times since her death, seen her every time he looked at the living-room couch on which the two of them used to sit, side by side, reading their separate books, content in each other's presence. He'd felt her every time he caught a scent of plumeria, so like the perfume she used to wear. Were these apparitions in the city so very different? Could Jacinda be right—was he just an old man, bereaved by the loss of family, friends, and now, a planet he had loved from afar?

He didn't know. He didn't want to think about it. Slowly, he felt himself drifting to sleep, dreaming of Cara, and a green bright Earth—

—and awoke, standing, on the bridge.

There was no sense of time transition; one minute he was drifting off to sleep, and the next—

The next, Bledsoe was wrestling with him, trying to grab something from Knowles's hands. Shocked and disoriented, Knowles staggered backward. "Bledsoe—what—"

"You son of a bitch!" Bledsoe was yelling. "*Give* me that—"

Knowles's arms dropped and he saw that he was holding a length of metal, a steel rod, like the support to a computer stand. Bledsoe snatched the rod away from him, hurled it across the bridge, where it landed clangorously. Before he could even begin to guess what was happening, Knowles found himself pinned from behind by the stocky crewman.

"For God's sake, man," he said, wincing, "what do you think you're *doing* . . . ?"

"Me?" Bledsoe seemed incredulous. "What the hell were *you* doing?"

Knowles looked up, then, and saw, directly in front of him, the main panel of the sensor web—or what was left of it. Someone had gone at it with a vengeance, destroying the controls and readouts, smashing the organic memory chips. Knowles lost his breath. He looked at the ruined sensors, at the length of the steel which only moments ago he had held in his hands . . . and he went pale with horror.

"Oh, my God," he said softly. "No."

The doors to the bridge hissed open, admitting Jacinda and Archer, both awakened by the sounds of the struggle. Jacinda's eyes widened as she took in the scene.

"What the hell is going on here?"

Bledsoe told her: how he'd been awakened by noise coming from the bridge; how he'd found Knowles, rod in hand, flailing away at the sensor web; how they'd struggled, moments before. Archer was already at the board, checking the damage; Jacinda looked at Knowles in disbelief. "Donald? Did you . . . do this?"

Knowles felt utterly helpless. "I . . . I don't remember,

Jacinda. I don't remember *any* of it. The last thing I recall is going to sleep in my cabin, and when I woke up, I . . ." He let the sentence hang; even incomplete, it was damning.

Jacinda looked betrayed. "Oh, Donald. How could you do this to"—she amended herself quickly—"how could you *do* this?"

"Jacinda, it wasn't me, it was *them!* Don't you see? It had to be *them.*"

"He's crazy," Bledsoe snapped, "I *told* you he was—"

"Mr. Bledsoe, kindly *shut up.*" Jacinda's tone was cold and terse. She folded her arms across her chest, faced with one of the most difficult decisions of her life; she shut her eyes, briefly, as she weighed her options, and when she opened them, fought to keep her voice calm and measured. "Mr. Archer? Damage to the web?"

"The backups are working fine, but some of the finer spectro functions are impaired. We'll need at least a day's layover at a repair facility, maybe two. Outpost Twelve is closest."

Jacinda nodded to herself. "Raise ReSource and tell them" —she hesitated only a moment—"tell them we're returning Dr. Knowles to Outpost Twelve. Medical emergency. Arrange for a shuttle to connect him with the next available commercial flight to Galthor."

She looked at Knowles sadly. "Donald . . . effective immediately, you're . . . confined to quarters. I'm sorry."

"Jacinda," Knowles said imploringly, "I swear to God, it wasn't *me.*"

But if Jacinda made any reply, Knowles did not hear it as Bledsoe hurried him through the door and off the bridge.

Angry, humiliated, Knowles kept silent as Bledsoe ushered him down the long corridor to his cabin; the crewman smiled an unpleasant little smile. "You know, Professor," he said suddenly, "I almost believe that *wasn't* you on the bridge."

Knowles looked at him, startled and hopeful.

"The look in your eyes when we were fighting?" Bledsoe said. "Like a sleepwalker. And how you kept at it, hardly feeling any pain. You may be telling the truth, at that. Except . . ." A nasty smile: ". . . I don't really care if you are."

Knowles's anger redoubled; he wrested free of Bledsoe's grip, stopped. "You son of a bitch."

"Look on the bright side," Bledsoe said cheerfully. "Another week and you'll be back in civilization, on a comfortable star liner, instead of spending the next month and a half on mining vessels and survey ships. You don't really belong out here, Professor."

Knowles started. Back to civilization . . . ?

Bledsoe took him by the arm again, trying to make him move on, but suddenly it all started to make sense. Back to civilization. Yes, of course. Damn them, of *course*. Knowles wrestled free of Bledsoe again and, oblivious to all else, began to move in the opposite direction, his face red with rage. "*Damn them*," he said to himself, "damn them to *hell* . . ."

Bledsoe rushed after. "God damn it, get back here!"

He grabbed Knowles; Knowles, in a fury—at him, at the apparitions, at the humiliation and hurt he had suffered—grabbed back. He dug his fingers into the fabric of Bledsoe's tunic, gave him a violent shove backward, into the wall. Bledsoe, unprepared for the attack, staggered back; Knowles pressed the advantage, grabbed him again, and deliberately slammed the back of Bledsoe's head into the hull. Bledsoe slumped to the floor, and within seconds, Knowles was on his way to the airlock.

He suited up, scrambled down the ladder that extended along one of the ship's tripod legs, and hurried out of the park, into the ruins of Manhattan. Even if Bledsoe recovered consciousness immediately, Knowles reasoned, he could lose himself amid the decaying buildings for hours, until, inevitably, they found him. No matter. If he didn't find what *he* was looking for in that time, he might as well be found.

He couldn't return to Penn Station—it would be the first place Jacinda would look—and instead sought out the music store in which he first saw Blaine and the other apparitions. That, of course, would be the *second* place Jacinda would look, so if they were not there, he'd best leave quickly.

After half an hour's hurried walk, he stood, breathing hard, outside the store on 53rd Street—enraged, shouting blindly into the sallow darkness: "Cowards! Liars! *Show* yourselves!"

Silence. Not even the sound of the wind, for even wind could not exist in an atmosphere at equilibrium.

"I *dare* you!" Knowles taunted his unseen audience. "I *dare* you to face me!"

The only movement in the sallow air came from Knowles's angry hand motions, and from the almost indetectable disturbance of gases made by the sounds from the old man's speaker-box. Frustration building to a high pitch, Knowles shouted at the top of his voice:

"God damn you, *show yourselves!*"

Slowly, the yellow air around him congealed . . . sculpted, as by some invisible hand, into the shell of a human being, blank at first, featureless, then refining itself into the face and form of a young man—Blaine. Knowles stepped back, both fascinated and frightened by the materialization.

Blaine just looked at Knowles, sadly. "Go back to your ship, Professor," he sighed. "You might as well."

"Because if I don't," Knowles said, his anger returning, "you'll just take over my body and *make* me go. Won't you?"

"That's right."

Knowles could not remember ever being so enraged. "You lied to me. You *wanted* me to make a fool of myself . . . *wanted* me to be shipped back to civilization! And you—you'd come *with* me, wouldn't you?"

Other specters began to appear on the empty street, drawing upon the inert gases for their physical substance. Blaine seemed almost apologetic. "Please understand, Professor. There's no other way. We can't travel through warpspace in this form, but in a host body—your body—that's a different matter. I can serve as a beacon for the others, showing them the way through normal space."

"And me?" Knowles said. "What happens to me, my body, when you're done with it?"

Blaine looked uncertain. "I'm . . . not sure. I have to sublimate your consciousness, completely, to weather the journey . . . I . . . I'll try to leave, once we've arrived, but—"

"But you don't know if you can?" He took Blaine's silence for affirmation. "Why now?" he demanded. "Why force me back now, when you could just wait until the operation is over and I return *then?*"

Blaine exchanged awkward, embarrassed looks with the other apparitions around him. "Part of what I told you is true," he said quietly. "This Earth, such as it is, is all we have left. We'd rather not be here, when it's being—dismantled."

Knowles just stared at him in disgust.

"Please," Blaine went on, softer still. "Just try to understand. We want to reclaim our future, that's all, our—"

"Your future!" Knowles shouted. "You don't *deserve* a future! *Any* of you!"

A murmur rose from the specters around him; Knowles spun round to face them, his voice ragged, accusing.

"*We* may have fled the Earth, once it became uninhabitable, but you—*you* were the ones who made it that way! You could've saved it, you could've *done* something, every one of you—but you didn't! *Did* you?"

The apparitions looked down, words striking uncomfortably close to home. "How many of you," Knowles accused, "thought *you'd* be on one of those ships, fleeing the dying Earth? How many of you thought *you'd* escape . . . but died before you could?"

A murmur of guilt and shame ran through the crowd. Blaine, alarmed, stepped up, took Knowles by the shoulders. "What you say may be true . . . but it's over and done with, long ago. There's nothing to be done about it now."

Knowles shook him off. "Isn't there?" he said. "You changed the air in that train station from methane to oxygen. From poisonous to breathable."

Blaine started. A few cries of agreement came from the crowd; Blaine, nervous, tried to quell the rising sentiment. "That was different! A small, controllable environment. We couldn't—"

"Why not? These . . . astral . . . forms of yours. They're energy, aren't they? Energy that once worked in synergy with biological mechanisms? If you *merge* those energies with the environment—"

"You're talking about a planetary scale!" Blaine shouted. "Even if we could do it, we might lose our awareness, our consciousness—"

Knowles stared him down.

"Like you propose to do to *me?*" he said.

Blaine was silent, as were the others. Knowles surveyed the crowd with contempt. "Cowards. You're still the same bloody cowards who let this planet die. Aren't you?"

He knew, then, that it was hopeless. He straightened, addressed them coolly, evenly, without fear or hesitation.

"All right," he said. "Go ahead. Take my body . . . my

life . . . to save yourselves. At least when my time comes, I'll know . . ." His voice wavered but did not break. "I'll know that I can die . . . with a hell of a lot more courage, and dignity, than any of *you*."

He turned and did not look back. He walked to the end of the block, turned the corner, and leaned up against the wall of a building for several moments, wondering if they would take control of him now; but of course they didn't. Why possess him now, then risk exposure should Blaine say the wrong thing, exhibit some uncharacteristic mannerism, while in control of Knowles's body? No; they would let him walk the last mile alone. He wasn't sure if he was grateful for that or not. He straightened, oriented himself, struck off down the street, and with slow, proud strides headed for Penn Station—where Jacinda and the others were doubtless waiting for him.

Knowles lay on his bunk, eyes shut, feeling strangely at peace. The ship's engines were vibrating subtly, in preparation for liftoff; he had lain awake here for hours, remembering all that he could of his life, his work, his friends, before that moment came when he would no longer be able to remember anything. His anger was spent; his only hope now was that when Blaine took over his body, his own spirit would fly free, free to be with his Cara again.

The door buzzed; Knowles opened his eyes. "Come in," he said. The door slid open, and Jacinda—looking awkward and pained—entered.

"I thought you should know," she said quietly. "I told ReSource you requested a . . . medical leave. Stress reaction to space travel; it's not uncommon." She paused, then added, "I haven't logged your actions last night."

Knowles sat up, touched by this. "I appreciate that," he said. "How will you explain the sensor board?"

Jacinda didn't respond to the question. "You're looking better," she said. "Rested."

Knowles smiled sardonically. "Yes. You might say I'm . . . expecting to be a new man, once we leave this planet." Then, in a soft voice: "Jacinda . . . if I should, by any chance, not . . . see you again, after this . . . I just want you to know how—how sorry I am, for all that's happened. I know I've disappointed you. I only hope I haven't betrayed you, as well."

"Donald—you don't—".

"And I want you to know," he went on, "that I'm grateful for the chance you gave me. And for your friendship. And for—"

A deep rumble interrupted him, and for a moment, Knowles thought that the engines were firing up; but it sounded different, somehow, and by the way Jacinda was rushing to the port, this was not, obviously, typical. "What was *that?*" she said, peering out a port.

Knowles suddenly identified the sound. "It sounded like . . . *thunder.*"

Jacinda turned away from the port. "Impossible. This atmosphere's at equilibrium—there can't be *any* meteorological activity at all, much less—"

There was a soft drumming on the hull of the spacecraft; Knowles looked up, listening to it increase in intensity, thinking suddenly of autumns spent with Cara in their cabin in the northwest, of falling to sleep with that selfsame drumming on the roof. Jacinda looked up too, recognizing the impossible, unmistakable sound of—

"Rain," Knowles said, wonderingly. "It's *raining* . . ."

Jacinda spun around to face the viewport again.

Outside, a yellow rain was pouring down onto the parched, dry Earth.

They rushed to the bridge, Knowles's confinement to

quarters suddenly forgotten, and burst in as a baffled Archer and Bledsoe sat, wide-eyed, before the sensors. Jacinda hurried up behind Archer, scanning the readouts with disbelief. "Is that really *rain?*" she said.

Archer nodded dully. "Not just water, either, but . . . amino acids. Nutrients, raining into the—"

"Good God." Jacinda, Knowles, and Archer turned to see a white-faced Bledsoe frantically checking and rechecking his instruments. "I . . . I'm getting *life-form* readings. In the oceans."

Knowles's heart skipped a beat. Jacinda elbowed Archer aside, taking over his instruments, shaking her head in disbelief. "This is impossible," she said, punching up readout after readout. "It takes thousands of years for even the simplest life-forms to develop—"

"It's as if something is . . . accelerating evolution, somehow," Archer said. "As if—"

"This can't be right," Bledsoe snapped. "Maybe the sensors are skewed after yesterday's—"

"They're *fine*, we ran three separate systems checks not half an hour a—"

Knowles stared at the viewscreen, at the downpour washing New York City in its first rainfall in a millennium, and a smile came to him slowly . . .

"My God," Jacinda whispered. She hesitated. "The oceans are *swarming* with . . . cyanobacteria."

Knowles rushed excitedly to Jacinda's side. "Are you sure?"

Bledsoe looked at them blankly. Knowles straightened, looked at Bledsoe, and allowed himself a satisfied smile.

"Cyanobacteria," he explained, "were the first complex organisms to evolve on the Earth. They led the way for all life-forms to come . . . including us."

Jacinda leaned back, stared at her instruments a long

moment . . . then looked up at Knowles and sighed. "I don't pretend to understand what's happening, but . . . there's obviously more going on on this planet than we suspected."

"Than *some* of us suspected," Knowles corrected.

Jacinda smiled apologetically. "Yes. Some of us." She swiveled in her seat, turning to her crew. "Mr. Archer, Mr. Bledsoe . . . log the data on the emerging life-forms and transmit them to ReSource. I have *no* idea what's going on here, but it would appear . . ." Her smile grew broader. ". . . that *we* are out of a job."

Knowles stood on one of the middle rungs of the ladder, staring up into a sky beginning to clear of dust and rust; the yellow light seemed paler, the horizon streaked with traces of green as the wounded atmosphere began to regain some semblance of its former health. The rain continued, running down the glass visor of Knowles's environment suit, washing the centuries from the ruined city even as it did the rest of the planet. It was raining everywhere on Earth, from the arctic to the tropics, from the steppes of Asia to the shores of South America; and Knowles suspected that it would not stop for a long time to come.

He looked into the lightening sky for many minutes, not knowing if those he sought were even capable of hearing him any longer. But they were, nevertheless, here. They were here in every drop of water, in every roll of thunder, in every flash of lightning and every tiny organism fighting for life in the reborn oceans. They would always be here. And no matter what strange new life-forms might emerge—carbon-based, silicon-based, whatever wondrous combination of molecules that might occur on this resurrected planet—Knowles knew one thing for certain.

"We'll be back," he promised, as another peal of thunder shook the city. "Someday. We'll be back . . ."

He climbed up the ladder and into the ship, and, soon after, the ship was gone. For the Earth, the long night was over; and if she knew what strange dawn was about to break, she kept her counsel, and remained silent; silent as the dead.

Her Pilgrim
Soul

1

A pillar of stars stood in the center of the room: a shaft of deep violet light, perhaps three feet in diameter, rising from floor to ceiling like a Roman column—sculpted not of marble, but of light, and steel. Kevin watched, frowning, as a spiral nebula—a dusky rose in color—rotated elegantly on its axis, each spiral arm sweeping across the starfield in arcs of a billion years, revolving at its own accelerated pace . . . like a dancer, arms outstretched, growing older with each pirouette. It was lovely to watch, and when the astrophysics department saw their theoretical model so beautifully rendered, they'd surely be delighted, but there was something in it that disturbed him, and with a distracted tap on the keyboard he brought the wheeling spray of stars to a halt, then wiped it completely from the image area. In the same motion he called up another program, and now a gas giant—the same dusky rose as the nebula, its banded atmosphere merely deeper tones of the same color—appeared in the display. It arced in its vast orbit, disappearing from the column of light as the pastel rings of Saturn swung briefly into view—they too vanishing as they made way for Jupiter, the asteroid belt, Mars, and finally Earth, growing larger and larger in the display. The cloud cover scattered like smoke on water, Kevin feeling as though he were plummeting from thirty thousand feet—gaining momentum as he plunged through a second layer of clouds and the vivid topography of continents, oceans, and mountain ranges was revealed; the Earth rotated below him as he fell, then the line of horizon was lost and he was diving toward the urban gridwork of Boston, veering over the Charles River, the Yards and Commons of Cambridge looming up—

The image dispersed, scattered, dissolving back into a starfield once more. It was perfect. Every nuance of orbit and rotation taken into account; every detail of the Earth's surface reproduced to exact scale. The program had taken all the variables, all the parameters, and coordinated them without a hitch. It was the third time he'd run it today, and each time it had performed flawlessly; he should have been jubilant, he should have been giddy with triumph at the thought of three years of exhaustive research and development this near to fruition.

So why, instead, did he feel so empty . . . so depressed . . . when he looked at it? This device, once merely an abstract construct in his own imagination, now fully realized? Why couldn't he seem to take any joy in its creation, much less its completion?

Kevin sighed, ran a hand through his hair, and switched off the system. The column of violet light winked out, leaving two steel-blue cinctures on floor and ceiling; the room looked suddenly incomplete. And only when he'd pulled himself from his immersion in the strange starlight he'd conjured up did he realize that the phone was ringing; that it had, in fact, been ringing for quite some time. He crossed the lab to answer, stealing a glance at the clock, and realized he was late for his 2:00 optics class. With one hand he started shuffling papers into his briefcase, with the other he snapped up the phone. "Drayton," he said, more brusquely than he'd intended.

"Kev? Good God, the phone must've rung thirty times. You forget to put the machine on?"

Awkwardly he stripped off his white labcoat and shrugged into a suede sports jacket, juggling the receiver from hand to hand. "Carol, I can't talk just now, I'm late for class—"

"Are you okay?"

"Of course I am," he said, a bit peevishly. "I was just working. Can I call you after—"

"This won't take long." Kevin detected a certain sharpness in her tone, in response to his own. "Are we still meeting at Wirth's, at six?"

Damn. He'd forgotten to make the reservations, but he wasn't about to let Carol know that. "Right," he said, his free hand grabbing the phone book, flipping the Yellow Pages open to the restaurants section, "six o'clock, give or take a little."

"Is everything all right over there?"

"Everything's fine. I'm just late. See you at six, okay?" But it wasn't just his 2:00 class that made him anxious to end the conversation, this or a dozen others in recent months. His father would've called it ants-in-the-pants, as when the young Kevin would fidget restlessly around the house on a dull Sunday afternoon; but at least then he knew *why* he was anxious—for the life of him, he could not say what it was that made him so uncomfortable, so impatient, these days, around his wife.

"Okay," she said uncertainly. "See you then." He hung up, made a fast call to Jacob Wirth's in Boston, leaving his name and request for reservations on their answering machine, then hurried out of the lab, sealing the room with the palm of his hand pressed against an optical scanner—a burst of light, briefly silhouetting his splayed fingers, and then the door slid shut and locked, the room accessible now only to Kevin, or his lab assistant, Daniel.

Kevin took the stairs two at a time (spatial imaging projects were headquartered in the basement of the Wiesner Building, relatively buffered from the vibrations of ground traffic) and hurried out of the flash and dazzle of the Media Lab, cutting across Ames Street and McDermott Court to building fifty-six, where his class, accustomed to his rather rococo sense of punctuality, would be indulgently waiting for him—at least for the customary fifteen minutes' grace period, after which, also according to custom, they would bolt, run, and scatter like a flock of horny geese.

He still enjoyed them, even after ten years, these students who watched as Kevin ambled down the aisle of the classroom, who laughed as he joked with them about his own tardiness before launching into a discussion of the effects of second- and third-order nonlinear susceptibility—he liked them, liked being among them. Up here, standing at a podium or enthusiastically scribbling a Fresnel equation on the chalkboard, he felt at home in a way he did nowhere else. And at class's end, he would spend perhaps fifteen minutes talking with individual students, wondering which of them might show the kind of promise Daniel had, back when he'd been a student in one of Kevin's graduate seminars. He was an assistant professor now, and in point of fact only a year or two younger than Kevin, but though friends, they were not intimates, or confidants; as proud as he was of Daniel's achievements, and as grateful as he was to him for his help with the holography research, they rarely talked of anything but work, or campus politics.

But after class, when he returned to the lab, Daniel, as ever, was waiting for him, running through the astrophysics program again, a pale rose galaxy rotating inside the shaft of violet light; he seemed never to tire of it.

"Hi, Doc." It was a mark of the careful distance between the two men that Daniel rarely called him by his first name. "Looking good, isn't she?"

Kevin felt another pang of emptiness as he looked at the whorl of stars. At first he'd chalked it up to the stress of spending half his time in intensive research and the other half grading papers on Gaussian beams and Fourier spectroscopy; but as winter drew to a close and the pressure of finals eased, that sense of detachment, of depression, had remained. He could no longer attribute it to overwork or divided attention; but neither could he determine its cause.

All he could do was try to ignore it. He shrugged back into his labcoat. "Yes," he agreed. "Very good."

"I ran a full systems check—we should be ready for the presentation in another week, I'd guess, maybe less—"

Kevin wasn't listening. His mood had darkened as he flipped the answering machine to playback, listening to the message from Wirth's informing him that they were very sorry but they were all booked up for that evening. *Damn.* He switched off the machine, punched the autodial for his home number, and in the calmest, most measured tones he could muster, told Carol he couldn't get the reservations.

"But I thought you said you'd already gotten them."

"I'm sorry. I forgot. I tried to get them, but they were full up."

"Why didn't you just tell me you'd forgotten in the first place?" she asked.

"Look," Kevin said, impatient again, "why don't we just go to Grendel's Den? I'll call now and make a—"

"That's not important, Kevin. What's important is why you felt you had to lie to me about it."

Kevin struggled to keep his anger in check. "Look, why is this such a big deal?"

"It's not. That's what I'm trying to—"

"I've got to go," Kevin said preemptorily. "I've got some tests to run. Why don't you call wherever you want to have dinner, make the reservation, and call me back, okay?"

There was a frustrated, confused silence at the other end of the line. "Kevin, I know you don't want to have this talk tonight, but—"

"Carol, I've got to go." At the far end of the room, Daniel pretended to be engrossed in his work. "I'll see you later, okay?" Kevin hung up as though the receiver had suddenly become electrified and he couldn't bear to hold it a moment longer. Jesus. Why did every conversation with Carol end this way, these days? He turned, about to apologize to Daniel for holding things up, implicitly for making him a reluctant observer of the dispute—

And, as he turned, his eyes widened in surprise and bewilderment.

"What the hell is *that?*" he asked.

Daniel looked up from his desk and followed Kevin's gaze. Floating in the middle of the pillar of violet light was no galaxy, no tapestry of stars, but what appeared to be—a human fetus. Suspended about three feet off the ground in a halo of pinkish light, rocking gently in some invisible womb, a ropy umbilical cord trailing up and out to the very edge of the image area, where it ended abruptly—but as it moved, as it shifted position, almost as though in amniotic fluid, one could see parts of the cord appear from "outside" the shaft of light—as if it continued, somehow, beyond the parameters of the display . . .

Kevin and Daniel walked slowly around the anomaly, examining it with a mixture of amazement and irritation. "I . . . I don't know," Daniel said finally. "It's not any program of *ours* . . ."

Kevin stared at the fetus, noting the embryonic heartbeat

inside its tiny chest, the way its not-fully-formed fingers moved, slightly, as a real fetus might stir in the womb. He fixed Daniel with a sober look. "If this is a joke," he said, "this would be a good time to let me in on it."

"If it's a joke, it's not mine." Daniel was already at the keyboard.

Kevin frowned. "Some clown in the Comp Sci lab is probably having fun with us. Just dump it and let's get on with our lives."

Daniel's hands moved across the keys . . . but the fetal image remained in the display. Several moments later, Daniel looked up and declared, flatly, "I can't."

"What?"

"I can't dump it."

"Then abort the program. Reset the system."

Daniel punched in the appropriate commands and the shaft of light winked out; seconds later he reactivated it, only to find the fetus still there, still suspended in midair. Worse yet, Kevin was becoming slowly aware of a dull, rhythmic beating sound coming now from the system's audio speakers . . .

Irritation turning to anger, Kevin took Daniel's place and began inputting commands into the computer—to no effect. After several minutes, Kevin finally turned and glared at the uninvited visitor to his lab.

"*Damn* it," he said softly. "That bastard Jacobi, in Life Sciences. This is just the sort of warped practical joke he'd pull." He considered his options, but only one seemed practical just now. "Okay," he sighed. "We'll have to clear the memory. Power it down and reload the system from the tape backups."

Daniel looked aghast. "It could take hours to bring it back up again."

Kevin raised an eyebrow. "You have a better suggestion?"

They powered it down. It did indeed take hours to bring the system up again, during which Kevin had the unpleasant task of calling Carol and telling her he'd be an hour or two later than planned; she accepted it with the tense silence of a woman who suspected she was being put off, and all of Kevin's protestations to the contrary couldn't convince her otherwise. After all, he *had* been putting her off, all week, about this dinner and this particular conversation; he could hardly expect her to believe him when a genuine crisis came up.

Finally, at a quarter to eight, Kevin sat at the keyboard, took a deep breath, and started punching keys. "Okay," he said. "Let's see where we are."

He keyed in the final sequence of numbers, looked up as the hologram display hummed into life—

A violet column of light, empty and clear of any images whatever, reappeared in the middle of the room. The two men let out their breaths almost simultaneously.

"Well," Kevin said, switching off the display once again. "That was interesting."

"Yeah, but where the hell did it come from?"

Kevin stood, stretched, shook off his labcoat. "Something that sophisticated has to leave tracks. If it *was* Jacobi, I'm going to nail his ass to the wall. Tomorrow. Tonight, I'm late for dinner."

Kevin was already in the doorway; Daniel lingered, staring back at the empty air in which, hours before, the image, the thing—the fetus—had floated in its dusky halo. "I don't know," he said quietly. "It almost seemed . . . *alive* . . ."

Kevin snapped off the lights, plunging the room into darkness.

"Probably was," he said. "Video of a real fetus, computer-enhanced. C'mon, Dan. Don't get weird on me."

Daniel made an uncertain, noncommittal sound and shrugged on his own jacket. The two men exited, the door sliding and locking behind them; for a full minute the lab was still and dark, the only light the faint blue nimbus of a computer readout. Then, all at once, a column of bright violet light erupted in the middle of the room—like a candle, inadequately snuffed out, flaming to life. And now, at the center of that flame, was the image not of a human fetus—but a newborn infant. An infant whose cries and squalls, reflected off walls of metal and glass, off instruments blind to its birth and indifferent to its discontent, echoed unnaturally in the empty lab; alone and afraid in its cradle of light.

They missed their dinner reservations, couldn't get into Boston in time, and so the conversation Kevin had been so dreading occurred instead in the bedroom of their co-op on Trowbridge Street. Carol Drayton was an attractive, dark-haired woman in her early thirties, with intense dark eyes and an air of reason and calm about her; that was what had first attracted Kevin to her, that assuredness, that inner serenity. You didn't find it in most artists, even commercial artists, but Carol was atypical; even now she struggled to retain that composure, trying to fathom this man who had, so suddenly it seemed, become so much a mystery to her.

"Kev, I don't understand. You knew when we got married that I wanted children. I thought you wanted them, too."

She was sitting up in bed, several pillows between her and the headboard; Kevin sat on the edge of the mattress, weighing his words carefully. "I do," he said, sounding unconvincing even to himself. "I just don't . . . feel ready yet, that's all. There's still too much to do at the lab, and—"

"To hell with the lab," she said with uncharacteristic

vehemence. "I barely see you anymore, and when I do, all you can talk about is the damn *lab*."

"It's three years of my life, Carol! I can't just throw that away, can I?"

Carol hesitated only a moment. "You've got four years invested in our marriage. You can't very well throw that away, either, can you?"

Kevin turned, saw the look of fear in her eyes—Good Lord, when had he ever seen Carol *afraid* of anything?—and in a gesture of conciliation put his hand on hers. "No," he said. "No, of course not . . ."

She moved over to his side of the bed, put a hand to his back, feeling the knot of tension in his neck, trying to knead it out. "Kev, what is it? What's bothering you?"

His muscles, if anything, seemed to grow tighter. "I've just been under a lot of pressure to get the project done. That's all."

"Kevin—please," she said, feeling his body belie his words. "It's not the work. You've been under job pressure before and things have never been this bad between us. What's wrong? Can't I help?"

Kevin stood, suddenly unable to bear the touch of her fingers, unable to accept either the gentle caress or the desire to understand that came with it. This whole conversation— children, babies—all seemed a mockery after what had happened today in the lab; but who could have known that they'd be discussing this tonight, who could be cruel enough to offer up such a black-humored joke? He'd told no one of the nature of his problems with Carol, not even Dan; how could anyone possibly have known enough to send that jape, that mockery, that *thing*, in the holo display?

"I'm sorry," he said, facing her, backing off. "I just can't handle this right now. I've got to be alone for a while. I'll sleep in the den; just for tonight. Okay?"

He started out, pausing in the doorway, wanting to say something but not knowing what; failing, he turned and left the room. Carol Drayton looked after—baffled, confused, frightened; worried that she was watching her husband drift slowly out of reach—and worse, not having the slightest idea why.

2.

Kevin left the house the next morning before his wife had even awakened, more out of avoidance than necessity. He was seeking the sanctuary and solace of his lab, a place he understood, an environment he could control; it was only as he put his palm to the image scanner at the door that he got his first intimation that that control was, in fact, illusory. As the scanner responded with a blast of white light, Kevin heard something inside the lab—something soft, and muffled, but sounding uncannily like the cries of a small child. The door slid open and the sound became louder, more distinct; Kevin rushed in, only to stop dead a few feet from the closing door.

A little girl, no more than five years old, sat hunched over in the center of the circle of violet light, hugging her knees, crying to herself. She was wearing a frilly, old-fashioned dress, a straw bonnet adorned with a band of flowers and secured by a ribbon gathered in a bow beneath her chin; like all images in the display, she was a pale rose monochrome, though parts of her—her hair, her eyes—were darker than others.

She seemed not to notice Kevin as he stood there, too

stunned to move; until he realized that of course she wouldn't notice him—she was just a video image, like the fetus, albeit far more sophisticated. Heartened by this realization, he took a step forward, more assuredly.

The little girl looked up at him and met his gaze.

With that one simple motion—that slight tilt of the head—Kevin's ordered, orderly world threatened to capsize. There were no video or audio inputs that allowed the computer to "see" or "hear" what went on in the room; it was impossible for anything inside the hologram to interact, therefore, with anything or anyone outside the display area.

Yet despite this, the girl suddenly sniffed back her tears and spoke up.

"They left me here," she announced, in a tone both wounded and affronted, "all night. All *alone.*"

She started crying again, the baffled cries of an abandoned child. Maybe, Kevin thought desperately, maybe it was just a coincidence that she'd looked in his direction; perhaps whoever had designed the program had simply made a good guess as to where he would enter the room. Yes. Of course. That had to be it; a lucky guess. Encouraged, he began crossing the lab to get a closer look.

The girl's eyes tracked him across the room.

He stopped, stunned and disbelieving. She continued to look straight at him. He took a few steps backward, and to the side; but each time, the girl's gaze followed.

Jesus God, Kevin thought. Any thoughts of artificial-intelligence programs, or outside access to the computer, were quickly forgotten. The girl in the hologram simply could not *do* what she was doing.

She kept on doing it, tears flowing from translucent eyes that shouldn't—by all reason, by all sanity—be able to see.

Even her cries, though they clearly emanated from the system's audio speakers, sounded uncomfortably real, and Kevin found himself wanting to still them, somehow. He took a few slow steps forward—instinctively lowering his voice, trying to sound calm and soothing, as he squatted down beside her. "Hey," he said. "It—it's okay. Everything's okay . . ."

For the moment, all he could think of was how to quiet her, how to comfort her. Grabbing the nearest keyboard, he began punching in coordinates, selecting programs—

In the violet light above the child, a rose-colored sphere, cone, and funnel began to take shape. "Look," Kevin said. "What's that?" As she looked up, Kevin manipulated the computer-generated forms, making them spin and dip in a playful ballet. The girl stared up, fascinated, at the dancing objects, her tears momentarily forgotten; then she took a jump up and tried to touch them, succeeding in hitting the sphere a glancing blow, making it spin all the faster.

Kevin punched in another command and the sphere took on the appearance of a banded rubber ball; he wiped the cone and funnel from the image area, then allowed the ball to drop into the girl's arms.

She caught it, bounced it once on the base of the display, caught it again and laughed delightedly, her fear and loneliness apparently fled. Kevin stood slowly, eyes wide as he watched it—her—play with the ball. He barely heard the hiss of the door behind him as Daniel entered, caught one glimpse of the image in the display, and stopped short, even as Kevin had. He cast a querulous look at Kevin, but before he could respond, the girl looked up, saw Daniel, and, with a big, happy smile, said, "Hi!"

Daniel looked about ready to drop through the floor.

"Say hi," Kevin prompted, amused despite himself.

Daniel cleared his throat, looked at the girl. "Uh . . . hi," he croaked out.

Daniel glanced at Kevin. "AI program?" he asked hopefully.

Kevin shook his head. "No program in the world can mimic spontaneous reaction to unexpected stimuli."

Daniel looked at the girl again. She waved at him. He waved back.

A wan smile frozen on his face, Daniel said in a low tone, "What the hell *is* she?"

Kevin stared at her as she bounced the ball, happily, on the floor of the holo display. Under the circumstances, he could think of only one reply.

"I don't know," he said, moving toward the display. "Let's ask."

The girl looked up at his approach. "Hi," he said, as casually as he could manage. "You . . . like the ball?"

She nodded. "Yeah. Thanks, mister."

"The name's Kevin. What's yours?"

"Nola," the girl replied.

By now Daniel had joined Kevin at the display, circling it slowly, carefully. "You . . . have a last name, honey?"

She glanced over at Daniel, her face screwing up in concentration. Finally, after several moments, she announced triumphantly, "Granville."

"Nola Granville," Daniel repeated. He cast a spooked look askance at Kevin. "Pretty name. Where do you . . . live, Nola?"

Nola thought a moment, then said, "I used to live in Wesschesser."

Kevin smiled. "You mean Westchester? In New York?"

"Yeah," Nola said. "In a big green house. Across from the sprained lake."

"The what?"

"Grassy Sprain Lake," explained Daniel, a Long Island native. "It's a big reservoir in upper Yonkers . . . near Hastings-on-Hudson."

Kevin squatted down again, wondering how best to couch his question. "Nola?" he said gently. "What are you doing in here, honey?"

Panic flared in her eyes, the pupils dilating with sudden fear, then quickly covered by a little-girl bravado. "Silly," she admonished them. "Isn't this where I'm *supposed* to be?"

Kevin looked at Daniel. Daniel looked at Kevin. Her *pupils* had actually *dilated*.

"Yeah . . . sure," Daniel said, at a loss for what else to say. "Of course it is, Nola. You're . . ." He glanced helplessly at Kevin, then back to Nola. "You're *home.*"

Nola broke into a wide, confident grin, bouncing the ball again, catching it with eager hands. Kevin sank into a chair and watched her. This promised to be a very long day. How long, he was scarcely able to guess.

She was aging, it seemed, at a rate of about five months every hour; ten years each day. At eight o'clock in the morning she had been a frightened, lonely five-year-old girl; by eight that evening, she was a more mature, outgoing ten-year-old. Kevin called in sick to the dean's office, had his classes suspended indefinitely, and over the next twelve hours watched as Nola literally grew up before his eyes. The degree of detail—as her hair grew longer, then shorter, then long again; as her body slowly but perceptibly elongated, at just the right rate of speed for a normal child's growth—was astonishing. The minutiae involved, from the subtle changes in weight distribution to the larger growth in bone structure, were staggering to contemplate

—they required thousands of different "processes" running at once; even her garments would change from hour to hour, from dress clothes to play, all of it still quite old-fashioned. Kevin spent all day listening carefully to this shy, beguiling apparition as it went from kindergarten to elementary school, from five to six to seven years old, speech becoming increasingly more sophisticated, reactions exactly appropriate for a girl of whatever age she was at that moment—by the time she reached six, she had outgrown the ball, so Kevin had fashioned a holographic doll for her; at seven, a jump-rope; and at eight, a set of jacks.

That evening, Daniel returned from Rotch Library with his research on the "big green house" Nola had described twelve hours—or was it five years?—earlier.

"There *is* a Granville family living in that area," Daniel said, sotto voce, as they watched Nola sitting cross-legged in the holo display, playing jacks. "The house she described . . . It's been in the family since the turn of the century. The current owners don't have a daughter named Nola, but . . ." He hesitated. "The woman I talked to *did* recall a great-aunt of hers by that name . . . something of a black sheep, apparently; the family never talked much about her."

Kevin put a hand to his mouth, restraining a manic laugh. This was becoming more baroque by the minute. "Does anybody know where this . . . 'great-aunt' *is?*"

Daniel hesitated again. "She died. Quite a while back; no one knew the exact date, and county records for the area don't reveal anything, either."

Kevin didn't reply. He got up from his work station, moved over to where Nola was playing with her jacks; there was a faraway look in her eyes, but as soon as she glimpsed Kevin, her face lit up with a wide smile. "Hi, Kevin." She had the shy, guileless look of a young girl with her first crush.

"Hi, Nola." Her smitten look was not lost on him. "You, uh, want me to make you some more toys? You must be getting tired of the jacks."

"That's okay," she said, standing. "I don't need any."

"Don't you get kind of . . . bored, Nola?" Daniel asked.

She shrugged lightly. "Sometimes. But when I do, I just . . . go somewhere else."

Kevin and Daniel exchanged puzzled looks.

"In my head," she explained. "Like just now, I was out by the sprained lake. Remembering the time Daddy took us out for a picnic, and I walked into the water up to my knees, and"—her face clouded over—"Daddy paddled me. Hard." She winced. "I didn't want to remember that part."

"So when you think about places . . . people . . . things . . . it's like you're almost there?" Kevin asked.

"Yeah," she said, then added, with a shy smile: "But I like being here, with you, better."

Kevin couldn't help but smile back. Daniel looked at him and thought: My God, he's actually blushing! "Nola?" he said, filling the awkward silence. "You remember when it was your Daddy took you to the lake? What year?"

Again that endearingly sober look as she concentrated. "I think it was . . . nineteen and—seventeen. Or maybe sixteen. Yeah," she said, more confidently, "that's right. Nineteen and sixteen."

Kevin and Daniel stared at each other, dumbfounded.

Later, in Kevin's private office adjacent to the lab, Daniel sat slumped in a chair as Kevin paced. "Maybe," Daniel suggested, "we should call in Hinerman, over in AI Alley."

"No," Kevin said quickly. "He'd turn this into a sideshow. And even if she *is* an AI program—which I don't believe for a minute—how does she *see* us? Hinerman would be as incapable of explaining that as we are."

Daniel shook his head. "She's totally aware of her surroundings—even her *form*—yet seems perfectly comfortable with them. As though it were the most natural thing in the world."

"Well, despite her memories of a . . . previous existence, she's spent all her life, subjectively, in that hologram. And the older she gets, the more she remembers. It's almost as though she's existing on two different levels of consciousness—one a remembered past that expands as she ages, the other her real-time presence here, with us."

Daniel hesitated. "Look," he said, tentatively, "I know this is going to sound pretty bizarre, but . . ." Daniel screwed up his nerve under Kevin's even gaze. "Do you suppose that somehow . . . in some way, a . . . a soul . . . a human *soul* . . . has been —reincarnated, inside that computer?"

Kevin sighed indulgently. "Daniel, I'm not even sure I believe in the human soul, much less in reincarnation."

"Why? Why is the idea of a soul any less believable than that of any of a dozen subatomic particles? We can't prove *they* exist, either."

"Yes, but that's *different*. We *can* posit their existence by the behavior of other, observable phenomena."

Daniel was silent a moment, then stood, went to the door, and opened it. He nodded in the direction of the lab. "There's your phenomenon in there, Doc," he said. "Go observe."

3.

Over the course of a single night, Kevin saw Nola grow from child to woman; he saw the passing of seasons in her face and in her body, observed the transit of years in her ever-changing clothes, and marveled at the flowering of what was becoming a quick and agile mind. She went from a shy ten-year-old to a studious twelve-year-old, and together they discussed the books she'd been reading (in that other place, on that other level of consciousness manifested here only as memory): *Silas Marner, Les Miserables, A Tale of Two Cities.* At fourteen she began avidly reading poetry—Browning, Blake, Keats, Marvell; Kevin, who'd barely had time to indulge his fondness for literature since his undergrad days, found himself racing to keep up with her. Her appetite for literature was enormous; she was as intelligent as she was beautiful.

And she was—was becoming—very beautiful indeed. It was the beauty of a soft, sensitive face, a quick wit, and the lingering traces of girlhood shyness in her smile. Every time she laughed, every time she smiled, it was warm, and open, and meant for him and him alone; with a dizzy sense of wonder and delight, Kevin was experiencing anew the excitement of *discovering* someone, exploring not simply shared tastes and common interests, but the delightful differences, as well—ideas and experiences he had never encountered, which made him think in new ways, consider other points of view. She was a young woman coming to maturity in the 1920s; he was a man who had reached his majority decades later, in the 1970s. They were separated by more than fifty years of progress and decline, undreamt-of war and uneasy peace; yet not only did they find common ground, they thrilled to the discovery of the other's world.

This, more than any scrutiny of data or processes, convinced him that this woman of light was just that—a woman. Not an artificial intelligence program, not a hoax or a joke. He had no idea what she was doing here, how any of this had come about, but after twelve sleepless hours, mesmerized by her intelligence, her humor, and, quite often, her pain—only intimated when she was a child, the unhappy home life which seemed to kindle her immersion in books—Kevin believed in her.

And yet *if* he believed in her, *if* she existed—there had to be a reason for her presence here. But whenever he tried broaching the subject, she just shrugged it off; this room, this place, it all seemed to be somewhere she was merely *visiting*, while living on another level . . . as though Kevin existed between the instants of her life. She did express curiosity as to what these odd machines were surrounding her, but when Kevin used the analogy of adding machines, that seemed to quell her interest: "I liked math up until trigonometry," she told him. "Does anybody really *understand* trigonometry?" He relied instead on more gentle probing—finding out about her life, her feelings, taking surreptitious notes during coffee breaks, anything that might provide raw data for Daniel to investigate.

But Kevin did not have to force himself to ask those questions. He enjoyed them; he enjoyed her.

"I remember one time," she said, a radiant twenty-year-old sitting cross-legged at the very edge of the column of light, "Daddy got hold of a book of poetry I was reading . . . William Butler Yeats? In one poem, Yeats uses the dread word, *copulate*, and Daddy—" She laughed. "—well, Daddy was neither amused nor enlightened." Kevin joined in her laughter. "I tried reading him the one that begins, 'I will arise and go now, and go to Innisfree/And a small cabin build there, of clay and wattles made—'"

Kevin picked up the rest: "'Nine bean-rows will I have there,'" he quoted, searching for the elusive lines, "'a hive for the honey-bee'—"

"'And live alone in the bee-loud glade,'" they finished

together. Nola laughed at their simultaneity; Kevin leaned forward on the backrest of his chair, finishing, a bit distantly, "'And I shall have some peace there . . .'"

There was a pleased smile on Nola's face. "You know Yeats."

"I know . . . *some* Yeats," Kevin allowed. "What about your father? Did he like the poem?"

Nola's face clouded over in much the same way it had as a child, recalling the picnic at the lake. "He didn't let me finish," she said quietly. "Took the book away from me, and . . . tossed it in the fire." She looked down. "'It's not a girl's place,' he'd say, 'to think about such things.' And whenever I'd ask questions . . . about politics, or history . . . he'd just smile a patronizing little smile, and tell me how beautiful I was."

"But it was the 1920s. Suffragettes. Flappers. Women getting the vote."

"Not in my home," Nola said flatly. "My father was holding on, desperately, to the world he knew. My mother would always take his side, do whatever he told her; and there I was, constantly questioning him, contradicting him . . ." Her voice trailed off; she shook off the bleak mood which seemed to have descended on her and looked up, trying for a gay smile. "But honestly—you must be bored silly by me and my stories," she said. "What about you? What's your life like? Tell me everything."

"Nothing much to tell, really," Kevin answered evasively. "About your parents—"

"Are you married, Kevin?"

Kevin hesitated, then reluctantly held up his ring finger. "Yes. I am."

Nola's face fell. "Oh," she said, then, quickly, to mask her disappointment: "What's her name?"

"Carol," Kevin said, and, finding the subject uncomfortable, tried again to return to Nola's life: "So how old were you when you—"

"What's she like?" Nola persisted. "Is she smart? She'd have to be, for you to marry her."

"Yes," Kevin admitted. "She's very smart. We . . . met in a night class, five years ago." He surrendered to the memory of that night, the crisp autumn breeze cutting through the auditorium during break, his first glimpse of Carol, a fan of dark shoulder-length hair whipped by the wind. "This woman, she just . . . sat down and started talking with me. Inside of five minutes we were chatting away like old friends. Inside of a week, I was in love. Not long after that, we were married." He smiled, shook his head. "I never thought it would happen that quickly, to me. I—"

He looked up and saw the feelings Nola was trying so hard to conceal. "Well. Anyway. Yes, she's a . . . very bright lady."

Nola smiled at him, and mixed with the disappointment there was a sincerity when she said, "That's . . . that's nice. I'm happy for you, Kevin." She looked at him with impossible longing. "She must be a very lucky girl."

Carol Drayton watched, unnerved and uncomprehending, as her husband finished packing a small suitcase with socks, shirts, and underwear. The entire scene felt unreal; he seemed to be moving in strobe-motion, every other moment a blank, and in those hidden moments, she knew, was the answer, the explanation for all that was occurring. She watched him take a pair of socks from the dresser drawer, and spoke to him as though to a ghost, as though he already belonged to the realm of memory.

"Kevin," she heard herself ask, as from a distance, "what do you expect me to say? You spend all night on campus, you don't call, I can't even get through to you on the phone—"

"I explained that." Kevin did not turn. "We had the phone

lines to the lab temporarily disconnected, for security reasons. And I forgot to call. I'm sorry."

"And now—" Carol got up from where she had been sitting on the bed, stood beside Kevin as he packed the last of his clothing. "What could possibly be so wrong with your project that you have to go sleep in the *lab?*"

Kevin turned to her, sighed, briefly considered the truth but quickly discarded the notion. "If I told you, you'd think I was crazy."

"We've lived this long with each other's craziness," she said gently. "I think I can stand a little more."

"For Christ's sake, Carol, it's just for—" He stopped, lowered his voice. "I don't know how long it's for. But it's only temporary. Until I can get this . . . sorted out."

Carol watched as her husband went into the bathroom to select some toiletries, his back to her. "Sorted out," she repeated. "You mean your project . . . or us?"

Kevin didn't reply. Didn't know how to reply. He returned to the suitcase, tossed the toiletries inside. Very quietly, Carol asked, "Are you leaving me, Kevin?"

The vehemence of his reply surprised him as much as it did her.

"I don't *know!*" he yelled, causing her to flinch, to shrink from him for the first time in their marriage. "I don't *know* anything anymore!"

He slammed shut the suitcase, snapped it up, and headed for the door. Carol did not turn. She refused to turn. Refused to let him see her face, the tears welling up in her eyes . . .

He paused in the doorway, looking back. He couldn't see her face, just the way her shoulders were hunched with tension. He wished he had an answer for her, something that would make sense, something she could accept; but the truth was, things had ceased making sense between them even before this business in the lab, and he could no more explain that to her than he could Nola.

"I'll call," he said lamely. "I promise."

He hurried out. Carol heard his footfalls on the steps, listened to the front door as it swung open, then slammed shut; heard the motor of their Volvo turn over as the ignition was keyed. She remained where she was, fighting the urge to go to the window and watch the car back out of her driveway, onto Trowbridge; knowing that she was losing him, that much was clear, but to whom, or to what, she had no inkling. Not an affair, that much she knew, that much she would be able to tell; but something else. Something she couldn't put a name to—and something, she knew instinctively, with which she could not compete . . .

4.

The big green house on Grassy Sprain Road, across from a sprawling golf course that Daniel doubted had existed in Nola's time, was much as she had described it; there had been a great many coats of paints applied in the last fifty years, another couple of bedrooms added on, but it was essentially the same rambling Victorian home the young girl claimed to have grown up in. At the door, Daniel was met by a blondish woman in her mid-twenties who introduced herself as Susan Granville; Daniel had spoken to her the day before, purporting to be involved in genealogical research at MIT. He felt guilty now as she ushered him cheerfully into the house—uneasy at the ruse which had gained him entry, but fascinated by what he saw around him.

He saw, as they moved through the house, a winding staircase fanning in a lazy curve down from a spacious second story; he remembered Nola telling of how she had tripped on that staircase when she was four, chipping her tooth on the banister. He saw two bedrooms on the upper floor, one with a view of a tall oak tree easily a hundred years old—the same tree Nola had described as being outside her own window. He saw, in that glimpse of the backyard, an old toolshed, many times restored, a toolshed in which Nola's father had repeatedly taken the strap to her, in an age long before the term "child abuse" had been coined.

"After you called," Susan was saying, "I started digging through some old trunks in the attic. Found a few family albums that might be useful. What exactly are you looking for?"

"Corroboration," Daniel answered truthfully. "We just need to confirm some birth dates, death dates, that sort of thing." He'd invented a mythical 17th-century Granville for whom, he told her, he was trying to establish a genealogical time line; he felt uncomfortable at the excitement this falsehood seemed to bring to her as she led the way up into a musty attic filled with cardboard boxes, discarded toys, overstuffed furniture, and a large steamer trunk.

"Here we go," she said, opening the trunk, taking a dozen photo albums from atop the heaped contents. She opened the oldest of the albums, carefully turning its brittle pages, eyes brightening as she came to one in particular. "Here she is," she said, as Daniel took a step forward to look; "this is Aunt Nola. When she was five years old."

It was an old sepia-toned photograph, flaking around the edges, only two of its gummed corners still in place. The background was faded but vaguely recognizable as the backyard of this very house; the girl in the picture was pretty but bashful-looking, wearing a straw bonnet gathered with a bow at her neck, a band of flowers decorating the hat.

It was, unmistakably, the same five-year-old girl who had appeared in the hologram two days before.

Jesus, Daniel thought, his discomfort ebbing as he scanned the page and Susan leafed slowly through the album. There she was, Nola at eight, at ten, at twelve . . . exactly as she had appeared, at various stages, hundreds of miles away. The sepia tones of the snapshots gave her the same ethereal quality as the dusky rose of the holo display; Daniel wasn't sure if he was awed or alarmed, filled with wonder or with fear.

"Her father—my great-great-uncle, Thomas—was a banker," Susan explained. "Snobbish, provincial old bastard . . . lost half his fortune in the stock market crash. Hated the fact that he'd been brought down to the level of the masses. They lived a comfortable life, better than most of the country during the Depression, but that wasn't enough; not for him."

As the years progressed there were fewer and fewer pictures of Nola; but those few corresponded exactly to the image of the twenty-year-old Nola Daniel had just left, hours before.

"I asked my mother about her—she says Nola and her father had some kind of falling out when she was in her twenties. That's when the family lost contact with her."

"A falling out?" Daniel asked. "Over what?"

Susan turned a page, and Daniel saw the last photograph of Nola in the album—a smiling woman in her mid-twenties sitting in the front seat of a '39 Plymouth, a man in a snap-brim hat and dark suit leaning into the picture beside her.

"Him." Susan nodded to the man. "Law student, tutoring at NYU. Her father threatened to disinherit her, but Nola didn't care; she'd always felt guilty about her family's wealth." She laughed. "Very little of which survives today. Myself, I wouldn't mind being a bit more guilty."

Daniel returned the laugh, distractedly, as he leaned in to study the man's face: angular, bespectacled, with dark, intelli-

gent eyes and an easy smile. "I think his name was . . . Robert,"
Susan ventured. "Robert—"

"—Goldman," Nola said. "He was nothing like the polo-
playing dunderheads I grew up with . . . he saw the sorry state
the world was in, wanted to *do* something about it . . ."

It was the evening of the fourth day of Nola's "life," and she
sat at the base of the column of light, looking like a frosted image
on amethyst crystal, but a moving, speaking, living image. She
was approximately thirty years old, her youthful beauty matured
and multiplied; she was wearing a V-neck dress, a string of pearls
which she fingered absently as she spoke, her hair upswept in
back, a high pompadour in front. Since county records had put
her actual birth at 1908, at the moment she was remembering up
to—but not yet beyond—1938.

"He was an attorney?" Kevin said.

She nodded. "And he *listened* to me, Kevin . . . just like
you do." She smiled, and Kevin returned it, feeling an odd mix of
satisfaction and guilt. He thought of Carol, told himself he was
merely gathering empirical evidence, but knew better.

"We talked about . . . *everything*. Politics, religion, literature, the law, every forbidden subject on my father's list of
Don'ts. Father didn't want me going to college in the first
place—kept bringing round the sons of old country-club friends
of his, hoping one of them would sweep me off my feet—but
after a few years he gave up, relented, and let me go to NYU, to
major in English. That was where I met Robert."

"This was when you were, what, twenty-three, twenty-
four?"

"Twenty-four, when I started. I met Robert in my senior
year—he was tutoring a classmate of mine, a pre-law student—
and we . . ." She hesitated, in a rather charming reticence that
was very much of her time and breeding, and Kevin found

himself fighting a stab of jealousy. ". . . we began seeing one another. By the time I'd graduated, we'd decided to get married; he wanted to move to Boston, set up a law practice for the disadvantaged, and I could get my master's in literature at Boston College."

The scientist in Kevin sparked at that last part, wondering if the connection could be geographical: If Nola had lived in Boston, could her spirit have become tied to this area somehow? Could that be why she was manifesting herself here, in this computer? But if so, why the rebirth, why the aging process? And why wasn't she conscious of *all* her life, as ghosts—Good God, he couldn't believe he was actually taking all this seriously—as ghosts usually, supposedly, were?

"So you moved to Boston?" he said, trying to keep the excitement from his tone.

She nodded. "South Boston, actually. A little apartment off West Broadway. Not the best section of town, but we made do."

"Couldn't your parents have helped out?"

Nola's face darkened; she shook her head. "No," she said tersely. There was a flush of anger and hurt in that otherwise calm and composed face, and Kevin felt suddenly wary in his questioning: "What *did* your parents think of all this? The move, the marriage, grad school—?"

Nola looked down, her eyes hooded.

"Father . . . didn't approve. Of any of it." She hesitated, then added, "Especially Robert."

"Why not? Because the guy wasn't rich?"

"That, too," Nola said tonelessly. "But mainly because he was Jewish."

Kevin started. "You're kidding." Bigotry against blacks, or Asians, that was the sort of prejudice Kevin had grown up around, but anti-Semitism? It seemed positively antediluvian. Then he thought of the year in which this was all taking place—1938—and of the events that would follow in a few short years, and he began to understand . . .

"He made it quite clear," Nola continued flatly. "If I married Robert, I'd be . . . cut off. From him . . . from Mother . . . from—" Her voice broke. "From everyone," she said softly. "The whole family."

Kevin instinctively reached out to comfort her.

"Nola, I'm sor—"

His hand, outstretched to take hers, instead passed right through it—as suddenly this woman who had seemed so vibrant and alive became, for a moment, discarnate, as Kevin was abruptly reminded of her tenuous existence, her fragile purchase on this world. He quickly drew back, but the damage had been done; Nola sat, looking down at her hand, which only moments before had actually shared the same physical space as Kevin's, and when she looked up Kevin saw for the first time the true distance between them, reflected in her face—itself only a refraction, a trick of light.

"Kevin . . ." Her tone was muted but frightened. He hadn't heard or seen fear in her since she was a child, only . . . three days ago? "Kevin, why am I here? Like this, with you?"

He stared into her eyes—what color *were* they, he wondered, in real life?—and sighed wearily. "I don't know, Nola," he admitted. "That's what I've been trying to figure out."

"Why you've been asking me about my life?"

"Yes."

She hesitated a long moment. "Am I . . . dead, Kevin? Is that it? Am I a—" She didn't finish. Kevin flinched. This was the moment he'd been expecting, the moment he thought himself prepared for, and now he was adrift, floundering for words:

"Daniel . . . found a record of your birth, but not—" He

hesitated, feeling as though nothing he could say would be the right thing. "We . . . don't know for sure."

But she knew. He looked at her, and he could tell: she knew. "What year is it, Kevin?" she asked.

After a moment's hesitation, he told her.

She shut her eyes briefly, then opened them again. "Then I must be dead," she said, tonelessly.

"Not necessarily," Kevin said. "Perhaps——"

"Perhaps what? Am I very old, my spirit drifting from my dying body, accidentally caught here, somehow? Or am I a . . ."

She still couldn't bring herself to say the word. She looked away; Kevin couldn't be sure, it might have been a variation in light, a fluctuation in wavelength, but there seemed to be tears in her eyes.

"I feel . . ." She looked back, and seemed as though she were trying to recall something, something urgent. "I feel like there's something I have to *do* . . . something I have to *accomplish* . . . but I can't seem to . . . remember . . ."

She held out her hands, palms up—half helplessness, half entreaty—in a gesture both touching and frustrating.

"Help me, Kevin? Help me to remember?"

Kevin hesitated—then, slowly, he reached back into the holo display, as he had minutes before . . . but this time, he placed his hands just under Nola's, as though cupping them in his. His hands were washed in rose and violet light, and for a moment, it appeared that that part of him might have been made of light, as well. Seeing what he was doing, Nola turned her own hands over, and, silently, pressed the palms close to his—their hands just barely meeting, almost overlapping; joining and not-joining. A defiant act of affirmation and union, to whatever gods had placed them here, together, like strands of a double helix: discrete yet united, entwined but never touching.

5.

He watched the seasons change in her world, as spring gave way to summer—a happy, dreaming time for her and Robert, a time of mutual discovery and pleasure, despite the gathering clouds of war over Europe. She told of going down to the Haymarket to buy the day's groceries, the smell of cod and halibut just in from Long Wharf, the feel of crisp vegetables freshly picked from farms in Deerfield or Agawam; even that was remarkable to Kevin, the idea of buying groceries, fresh, each day, in those days before adequate refrigeration. She told of frequent visits to the Old Corner Book Store in the long-vanished crescent of Cornhill Street, lost forever along with neighboring Brattle Street and Scollay Square, a procession of phantom roads, like narrow Change Avenue, existing only in the memory of those who walked their paths, decades ago—and now, with their balustrades and dormer windows, conjured up for a rapt Kevin. She spoke of riding the trolley to Franklin Park, of hearing the bells of King's Chapel ringing out on Sunday walks, of stealing a kiss in the shade of Adams Square Station during a warm summer rain; she spoke of long-dead authors as though they were bright new discoveries, as indeed they were, to her. e. e. cummings, Auden, and Eliot; James Hilton's *Random Harvest*, and Robert Nathan's *Portrait of Jennie*. Often she would read aloud at night, and depending on the author they would either fall asleep in each other's arms (Robert Frost) or spend half the night making love (D. H. Lawrence).

With Pearl Harbor, of course, that short summer was brought to a jarring close. Robert tried to enlist in the Army, but his astigmatism (evidenced by all the photographs Daniel had unearthed of this intense young man wearing thick, round glasses) ranked him 4-F. Within the year, however, he had found a niche: his storefront law office became a mecca, of sorts, for hundreds of immigrants, most of them Jewish, fleeing in Hitler's wake. Robert helped them wend their way through government bureaucracy, helped find them housing, jobs, and a sense of home in an unfamiliar land. When Nola spoke of them it was not as a mass but as a collection of individuals: more than one spent a night, or two, or three, on the floor of the Goldmans' cramped apartment. There was a look to their eyes, she said, even in the oldest men, of lost children wandered far from home; a distant glaze that spoke silently of family and friends who were not as lucky as they, left behind in a land stripped of sense and gentleness; a mixture of relief at having escaped, and guilt for those remaining.

It was 1943, that morning, to judge by Nola's bobbed hair and long cloth skirt; she had been talking about their apartment in South Boston, how they loved it but had outgrown it: "My books and Robert's law texts were the real occupants," she said, grinning. "We were just boarders. But when I finally became pregnant, we knew we'd have to—"

"Wait a minute," Kevin interrupted. "*Pregnant?* You never mentioned that before."

Nola thought for a moment, then laughed, wonderingly. "I just remembered it," she said, a distant glaze to her eyes. "In an odd sort of way, Kevin, when I sit here, remembering, it's . . . almost as though it's all happening for the first time." She shook her head as though to clear it. "Anyway," she went on, "the pregnancy came as quite a surprise. My obstetrician had said I had a slight malformation of the uterus . . . warned me it might be difficult to conceive a child, but—"

For the next hour, Kevin watched in awe and fascination as Nola's slim figure filled out with the onset of pregnancy, her eyes shining with something new, an anticipation and happiness only hinted at before. As Nola rattled on almost constantly about the baby-to-be—about clothes and cribs, possible names (Sarah if a girl, Jacob if a boy), all the usual obsessions of impending motherhood—Kevin saw, if not understood, that excitement in a way he never had before. The time compression at work—five months passing in just one hour—made for a vivid cameo of joy and anticipation, exhilaration and trepidation. He was no closer to understanding that parental pride and excitement than ever, but he found himself excited for Nola's sake—pleased that someone who'd known more cold than warmth in her life would have a share of some genuine happiness.

By noon she was seven months pregnant, and talking about a vacation she and Robert had decided to take, that month. "Robert had been working twelve hours a day, seven days a week, for a solid year," she said, "and we realized that if we didn't get away now, after the baby came there was no telling when we might have time for a holiday. Robert's law partner, John Ruskin, had a small cabin in the Berkshires that he let us use . . . it was a full day's drive from Boston, way out in the country, but it was beautiful, there was a small stream in the woods where Robert did some fishing, while inside I did a little writing. I remember thinking about Yeats's lake, at Innisfree, and how it couldn't have been more peaceful than this. And then—"

Her expression went from serene to troubled. "It . . . all went wrong," she said, looking confused, frightened, as the "new" memories flooded into her, unbidden and somehow now unwanted. "After a walk in the woods, I . . . I started having contractions. First an hour apart, then half an hour, then every ten minutes. I was going into . . . premature labor." Her voice wavered; Kevin, pouring a cup of coffee, stared at her, a feeling of dread claiming him. "There were no hospitals around," Nola went on, "just a local doctor. Robert rushed me into town . . . I remember the doctor's office, in the back of his house . . .

I remember him forcing my fingers open . . . I'd been writing a paper for the Poetry Review, and unconsciously I'd clutched it all the way from the cabin—"

Her left hand clenched into a fist, and as she stared at her suddenly trembling hand, her face twisted in discomfort. "He . . . he finally pried it loose as I was being lifted onto the operating—"

Nola suddenly cried out in pain. She fell to the floor, hands bracing her fall, as Kevin rushed to her side. *"Nola!* What *is* it, what's *wrong?"*

She was doubled over, clutching her stomach, her baby. "Oh, *God*, make it *stop!"* she screamed. "Make it *stop*, please, make it—"

Kevin dropped to his knees, helpless as though watching a fire on the moon. Something was horribly wrong, but whatever it was, it had happened over forty years ago; and as he knelt there, powerless to offer anything, even a hand in comfort, Kevin knew that he indeed *was* powerless—that whatever she was going through she had gone through decades before, and was merely reliving now. He wished he could jump into the hologram, become a thing of light and refraction himself—hold her, *help* her—but he couldn't; all he could do was stand by and watch her tortured face, listen to her terrible screams . . . screams so loud they brought Daniel rushing in from Kevin's office.

There were tears in her eyes now, eyes shut tight against the pain. "Kevin," she implored, aware of him for the first time in what seemed minutes, "Kevin, please, *do* something—"

Kevin's words sounded hollow and leaden. "Nola, I . . . I *can't*, I don't know *what* to—"

And then, as suddenly as it began, it stopped.

All at once, the pain in her face gave way to shock; the shock to astonishment; the astonishment to sorrow. Her cries stilled, Nola remained hunched over, continuing to clutch her stomach . . . a stomach no longer full with child, as empty as the look in her eyes, the vacant stare with which she gazed into space.

"Nola?" Kevin asked finally. "Are you—all right?"

At the sound of his voice, Nola turned, seeming to pull herself away from whatever bleak, lost place she had been, and when she looked up at him, when she spoke, there was immeasurable sorrow in her voice. "I . . . I lost it, Kevin," she said softly. "I lost the baby . . ."

Her eyes widened, and in that moment, it seemed to Kevin, there was a sudden maturity, a wisdom born of pain and grief, that had not been there before. "I remember now . . ."

Kevin felt her pain as his, felt almost as though he had lost a child of his own, and for the first time understood something of her need, her desire, her love for something yet unborn.

"I'm sorry, Nola," he said, just as softly. "I'm so sorry."

Nola nodded, but her gaze was once again remote, unfocused. "I have to . . . be by myself for a while, Kevin," she said distantly. "Just a little while. But I'll be back. I promise. I'll be back . . ."

Even as she spoke, her image turned from translucent to transparent, from dusky rose to glassy amethyst; and when she'd faded completely from the shaft of violet light, the display abruptly winked off—the system shutting down, seemingly of its own volition.

Daniel started. "I . . . didn't know she could do that."

"Neither did I." Kevin was less startled than in shock. Daniel looked at him—at his rumpled clothes, the unruly mop of hair, the dark circles under his eyes—and he felt a stab of fear, and concern. "Christ, you look awful. How much sleep are you getting?"

"Enough. Couple hours a night. I can't afford to squander my time with her, Dan."

Something in his tone disturbed Daniel even more than the way he continued to stare at the empty hologram display. Daniel tapped him, lightly, on the arm, trying to draw him out, draw him back from whatever far places he was living in, more and more, each day.

"C'mon," he said. "Let's get some air. I think we need to talk."

They crossed the sprawling green of MIT's Great Court as Kevin drank what Daniel estimated to be his twelfth cup of coffee that day, his hands still shaky as they held the styrofoam mug. Across Memorial Drive, up and down the Charles, white sails swept across the water like gulls; on the other side of the river, the Victorian houses of the Back Bay, though dwarfed by the gleaming towers of the John Hancock and Prudential buildings, seemed serenely comfortable with their modern neighbors, in that architectural repose of past and present so unique to Boston. It was a bright, almost preternaturally beautiful spring day, but if Kevin had any inkling of it, it didn't show in his hooded, brooding expression as he updated Daniel on events in the lab.

"Have you told her about the death certificate we found for Robert?" Daniel asked. "Does she know he died in 1953?"

Kevin hesitated. "Dan, you can't just tell someone that the man she loves, the man she still thinks of as *alive*, is long dead—*will* be dead, from her viewpoint."

Daniel felt alarmed once more. "Doc . . . this is information. We're scientists, we can't just . . . ignore relevant data because it may be too painful, or—"

"You still haven't turned up anything similar for Nola?" Kevin asked, turning the subject aside.

Daniel frowned, shook his head. "Bureau of Vital Statistics for Westchester County has a record of her birth, but not her death. Neither does Boston."

"What about the names she gave us? Robert's clients?"

Daniel took out a well-thumbed notepad, flipped it open. "Most of them were fairly well along in years when they emigrated to the U.S. Their sons and daughters, those I've contacted, may remember Robert's name, vaguely, but that's all."

"Damn it," Kevin muttered. "There must be someone still alive who knew them, someone who might be able to give us a clue—"

"It was a long time ago, Doc."

"No, it's not. It's happening now, across the street, in my lab, and I want to know *why*. She *needs* to know why."

"How can you figure *anything* out," Daniel said, "when you're so damn exhausted? Maybe I can spell you. Spend some time with her, while you grab a few hours' sleep."

Kevin looked almost jealous at the suggestion. He shook his head, reached into his pocket, and ripped a page from the small notebook he'd been keeping. "Not necessary, Dan. Besides, I think we may have a decent lead. Today she mentioned a partner in Robert's law firm—must've joined sometime between 1938 and 1943—named Ruskin, John Ruskin. See what you can turn up on him."

Daniel took the slip of paper reluctantly, an unvoiced concern in his eyes so plain that even Kevin, absorbed as he was, could see it. "Daniel, she's a very special person. She's as confused by all this as we are."

"Is she?"

Kevin's eyes remained hooded. "What's that supposed to mean?"

"We know she's controlling the computer. Ordering up the different processes needed to simulate her image . . ."

"Autonomous functions. She's no more conscious of doing it than we are of the way our heart pumps blood, or our blood assimilates oxygen . . ."

"She seemed awfully damned conscious of shutting down the system, just now."

"I can't explain that," Kevin said, feeling besieged and not a little helpless. "But she's not here for any . . . ill intent. I *know* it, Dan. I can *feel* it. My God, I've watched her grow *up*. I'd *know* if there were something wrong about her."

Daniel looked at him, then looked away, at the sailboats drifting up the Charles, then turned back to Kevin. "Look . . . Doc. You and I, we've never really had more than a . . . professional relationship, so maybe this is out of line, but—" No turning back now: "You're not getting yourself . . . involved . . . here, are you?"

"'Involved'?" Kevin tried, without much success, to sound incredulous. "With a . . . a *spirit*?"

Daniel shrugged. "Some would say, that's what we fall in love with, when we fall in love. A soul . . . a spirit." He saw the telltale wince on Kevin's face, knew that his words had struck home. Hating the necessity of it, he went on, as gently as he could: "She's aging ten years for every day. At this rate, she'll be . . . gone . . . in three or four days. What do you do then?"

Kevin had no answer. To anything.

6.

He waited all that day for Nola to return, but by evening the system remained shut down. Finally, he gave in to the temptation he'd been fighting all day and switched on the system himself. The display snapped on, the column of light shimmering from floor to ceiling; but it was empty. Kevin fought back his fear, telling himself that if Nola had had control enough to shut down the system, she had control enough not to manifest herself if she didn't want to; but he wasn't sure what he was afraid of, the possibility that Nola had been taken away against her will, removed for the same arbitrary reasons she had appeared, or perhaps that Daniel, in his cautions, was right, and that there was more to Nola than Kevin was allowing himself to see.

By evening his exhaustion at last claimed him; he rigged an alarm to go off once the display was reactivated, then lay down on the cot near the far wall for what he assumed—what he hoped—would be one or two hours' sleep. Within minutes his body had taken quick advantage of the opportunity.

Kevin had only one dream in that time, at least only one that he remembered, and it was of Carol. She was here, in the lab, with him—but *he* was inside the hologram. He saw her through a violet veil, and when he looked down at himself—at his hands, his legs—he saw that they were a pale, translucent rose. Carol sat outside, in his chair, weeping, but when he tried to reach out to comfort her, his hand was swallowed up as it reached the edge of the image area; and as he watched his fingers disappear, he lost all feeling in them, as well, all control, as though they had ceased to exist. Panicky, he jerked back his arm—his hand came back, and with it, his feeling and control. He flexed the fingers of one hand to prove to himself that he was real—that he had substance—

And then Carol got up, went to the control station, and turned him off.

The alarm sounded a little after eight the next morning, a high whistling tone that brought Kevin immediately awake. He was startled to find that nearly twelve hours had passed, but at least the numbing fatigue which had dogged him these past days had abated; he felt rested, refreshed. He looked up to find the system back on, the column of light in the center of the room—and, in *its* center, Nola sat on a holographic stool . . . a stool, he realized later, unlike any he had conjured up for her.

"Nola?" He hurried to her side, relieved to see her, but distressed at the pace of years evident in her appearance. She looked to be about forty-four, forty-five, still very lovely but with a new maturity to her, the beginnings of which he had only glimpsed before. The small lines around her mouth and eyes, the lighter hues in her hair which Kevin took for thin streaks of gray—they did not detract from her beauty; if anything they added to it, lending her the grace of time.

"Hello, Kevin," she said, with the trace of a small smile. Her eyes, which had shone so brightly just twenty-four hours ago, seemed melancholy now. "I'm sorry I stayed away so long. I just . . . needed some time. To think."

"Are you all right?" Kevin asked, wanting to reach out and touch her, knowing he could not.

Nola nodded slowly. "It was . . . a long time ago," she said, unwittingly echoing Daniel's words of the previous day. "He was a country doctor. Didn't have the facilities they'd have had in Boston. Maybe if we hadn't gone away, if we'd stayed in town . . . but maybe not. Robert blamed himself for it."

"But there was no way he could have known. You were two months from term."

"Intent didn't matter to him," she said quietly. "Only result. Cause and effect. He was a very logical man, a good lawyer; that was the way he thought. If we'd been in the city, it might not have happened; we weren't in the city because he'd taken a vacation; therefore, it was his fault." She was silent for several long moments; then, her eyes fixed at some point far from Kevin, she said, sadly and softly, "It was a little girl, Kevin. A beautiful little girl . . ."

What could he say? All the alternatives sounded lame, and clichéd. "I'm sorry, Nola," he said finally, as he had before. "I'm so sorry."

Nola drew a deep breath and sighed. "God, Kevin—I

wanted it so badly," she said wistfully. "The chance to give someone the kind of love I never had, growing up . . ."

Kevin heard in Nola's words and voice an unsettling echo of another woman, another place, a similar regret. Nola saw his disquiet, glanced at him. "Kevin? What is it?"

Kevin slowly sat down on his desk chair, poised backward as before, hands resting on the backrest.

"Carol's mother . . . my wife's mother . . . was an alcoholic," he said, staring past Nola into space. "I remember this time Carol said to me how she really wanted to have a baby . . . because she wanted to be the kind of mother *she* never had." He paused, then admitted, quietly, "I guess I never really understood what she meant . . . until now."

The tone of their discussions was different after that; it became less a chronology than a colloquy, less historical than philosophical—they spoke more and more of books they'd read, or doctrines they'd studied, favorite plays or books or movies. Kevin even created—at Nola's request—a holographic chessboard that floated, unsupported, above her lap; she moved her pieces by hand, while he used a keyboard in his lap to make the pieces rise, float across the board, and take their squares. When a piece was captured by either of them, it winked out of existence.

They talked sometimes of Robert, and the changes that came over him in the passing years—the enthusiastic young man she married turning slowly inward—but she spoke less and less of her life, presumably because she didn't wish to dwell on it, on the ways it had turned sour. Once Kevin asked if they had tried having another baby; Nola merely shook her head in a way that suggested it was no longer an option, and Kevin did not press the issue.

By the end of the day Nola was well into the autumn of her

years, hair almost completely gray—as gray as anything was in her monochrome image—and cut in a Fifties style. They were deep into their fourth chess match of the day, and as Nola moved a rook, Kevin nodded admiringly.

"You're a good player," he said.

"I had a good teacher. Robert loved chess."

"However . . ." He tapped at the keyboard, moving one of his own rooks. "Check."

Nola smiled. "You're no slouch at this yourself."

"She said, having won three games in a row."

Nola interposed a knight between Kevin's rook and her king; he'd expected it and had his next move ready. He felt a pang of guilt for enjoying this—the game, her company, her presence—when he knew he should be searching for the reasons for that presence. "Nola, are you sure you want to be . . . playing games, like this . . . instead of—" He hesitated. "I mean, what about your later years with Robert? Was there anything that happened between you that might account for—"

"Oh, Lord, Kevin, I'm so tired of talking about myself," she sighed. "Let's just enjoy the game, for now, all right?"

Kevin backed off. "All right," he said, relenting. He moved his bishop along the diagonal. "Check."

Nola studied the board a long moment, and studied Kevin for perhaps even longer. She moved a pawn forward to threaten the bishop, asking, offhandedly, "Have you spoken to your wife lately? To Carol?"

Kevin took her pawn with a rook, said, "Check," but nothing more.

Nola didn't touch the board. She looked soberly at Kevin, her tone quiet. "Do you really want to lose her, Kevin?"

Kevin looked up sharply, suddenly angry—the same anger, the same irritation, he felt with Carol. "Don't talk to me about *losing* things," he snapped. "All I know is, the minute you become truly happy in this life, that's when they pull the rug out from under you! *That's* when it's all taken away."

Nola nodded. "And if you never *know* happiness . . . you never know what it's like to *lose* it. Do you?"

Her words caught him unawares; it was an idea that somehow had never occurred to him, and he groped for some easy way to rebut it.

"No. No, I wouldn't put it like . . . I mean, that's . . . that's not what I—"

He trailed off—confused, uncertain, his anger replaced by doubt and a certain . . . embarrassment. He looked at Nola—at her knowing, understanding smile—and he laughed a small, awkward laugh.

"I . . . guess it is kind of a . . . foolish way to look at things," he admitted. Embarrassed and uncomfortable, he looked down at the board; Nola moved a pawn to capture his bishop, held the captured piece between two fingers and smiled teasingly.

But Kevin merely tapped at his keyboard and pushed his queen through a gap opened by her capture: "Checkmate."

Nola looked down at the board, and when she looked up again, it was, oddly, with pleasure, and satisfaction.

"Very good," she said, approvingly. "You're learning."

7.

The retirement home was just outside Brookline, in that area where Jamaica Plain and Forest Hills meet, near the Arnold Arboretum. The grounds were large and well kept, broad pathways shaded by wide beech trees; there was a scent of lilacs in the air. All in all, Daniel reflected, not a bad place to end one's days, and John Ruskin, despite everything, seemed to agree. A reedy, gentle man in his early seventies, Ruskin navigated the winding path expertly, and when Daniel offered his help rounding a bend, he just laughed quietly. "I know my way around," he assured him. He stopped at a rosebush, absently caressing the petals, assuredly avoiding the thorns; it was only in the way he held his head, free from having to look directly at someone with whom he was speaking, that one could tell he was blind.

"I appreciate your taking the time to talk with me, Mr. Ruskin," Daniel said, still a little off balance. When the Massachusetts Bar Association had given him Ruskin's current address, as well as his physical condition, Daniel had not expected to find such a spry old bird. "I haven't been having the best of luck tracking down most of Robert and Nola's friends. Most of them are—"

He caught himself, but Ruskin finished the sentence for him: "Most of them are dead?" he said with a trace of amusement.

"I'm sorry. I didn't mean to sound . . . tactless . . ."

Ruskin laughed softly. "I've spent the last fifteen years in darkness," he said, "and I've managed to enjoy life in spite of it. If it's darkness I have ahead of me, I think I can make the best of it."

Daniel began to feel more at ease. "You knew Robert and Nola for—how long?"

"Ever since Robert opened his law practice. I had the office across from his, and after two or three years, we decided to set up shop together . . . about the time the Second World War broke out. They were lovely people—Robert with his passion for justice, Nola and her love of poetry . . . she published quite a few papers, did you know that?"

"Yes. I did."

Ruskin reached out and brought down a lilac blossom to his face, breathed in its distinctive aroma, and smiled. "These must be beautiful," he said.

"Yes," Daniel agreed. "They are." He hesitated. "Did either of them . . . Robert or Nola . . . ever attend MIT, at some time in their lives?"

Ruskin seemed baffled by the question. "Not that I know of. They both graduated NYU, as I recall, but only Nola went on for further studies, and that was at—Boston College, I believe."

"Did they ever live anywhere in Cambridge?"

Ruskin laughed. "Good Lord, no. You couldn't get Robert very far from his office, or his clients."

"Did either of them"—Daniel groped to express the inexpressible—"did either of them leave behind any kind of . . . 'unfinished business'? Some goal, some dream, they never fulfilled?"

"Well, yes, of course," Ruskin said, seeming almost to regard Daniel's question as a little dense. "When someone leaves as suddenly as Nola did, there's bound to be unfinished business. He blamed himself; lost so much of that passion of his in later years." He shook his head sadly. "She was taken from him so early, you know. I don't think he ever really recovered from that."

Daniel stopped dead in his tracks, though Ruskin kept ambling along the shaded path. "Excuse me," Daniel said, trying to regain his balance, "but . . . exactly *when* did Nola die?"

Ruskin could obviously tell from Daniel's voice that the younger man had stopped, so he too paused. "In March, I believe," he said thoughtfully. "March of . . . 1943. She was only thirty-five." Ruskin shook his head ruefully. "What a waste. What a terrible waste . . ."

Daniel stood there, stunned, beginning to realize just why Nola's death certificate might never have found its way to Boston.

"*How*—did she die?"

Ruskin turned and faced him for the first time.

"I thought you knew," he said, surprised. "She died in childbirth."

The phone rang a little after nine a.m.; Carol ran downstairs, hoping to God it wasn't a wrong number or a phone solicitation, and snapped it up on the third ring. "Hello?"

To her relief, the voice at the other end was Kevin's. "Carol? It's Kevin. I'm at the lab."

"Kev?" She tried to keep the fear, the uncertainty, from her tone. "Are you all right?"

"I'm fine. And I've missed you."

"I . . . I've missed you, too," she said, voice wavering only a little, her heart suddenly racing as she heard her husband say: "I'm ready to come home. Think you can swing by and give a guy a lift?"

Carol smiled. "Yeah,' she said, tears welling up in her eyes. "I think I can manage that."

"See you in a while," came the reply. "I love you."

There was a click, and then a dial tone, and Carol Drayton hurriedly put the receiver back into its cradle, grabbing her coat and crying tears of relief that whatever had happened—whatever had gone wrong—was over . . .

At the lab, the autodial on the telephone hung up the call even as the speech synthesizer switched itself off. Kevin lay sleeping on his cot, as, nearby, Nola stood in the center of the hologram—a grandmotherly, white-haired woman in her early sixties. A part of her consciousness reached out into the speech synthesis program and deleted the exact modulations of tone and pitch which she had earlier painstakingly matched to Kevin's voice. She looked down at the sleeping Kevin with a pleased, protective smile, then bent down until she was kneeling on the floor of the holo display, and said gently: "Kevin? Kevin, it's time to wake up."

Kevin stirred, not remembering when he'd fallen asleep, but certainly not prepared for what he saw as he sat up, groggily, and looked at Nola. Good God—how long had he been asleep? Her hair was a halo of pale rose light surrounding a lined and aged face; her hands, braced on her knees for support, were thin and wrinkled. And yet—

She was still beautiful, to him; still Nola. He saw in her smile the same shy affection he had seen in the ten-year-old she had once been; saw in her eyes the enthusiasm, the curiosity, the intelligence, of the twenty-year-old lover of Yeats and Byron and Browning; read, in the lines around her eyes and mouth, the sadness of past grief and disappointments, none of which had dimmed the things he'd come to love about her. For some, age became a shriven reminder of bitterness and decay; for others— for Nola—it merely confirmed that the body was but a shell to the soul, a testament of flesh to spirit.

Kevin got shakily to his feet as Nola announced, calmly, "It's time for me to go now, Kevin."

His heart pounded; he felt as though he were falling. "*No*," he said, as though by sheer force of will he might keep her here.

"I'm afraid so," Nola said. "I accomplished what I had to, and now . . . now it's time to leave."

Kevin started; the purpose, the meaning which he had labored so to discover this past week, was now starkly evident in her tone. *She* knew, even if he did not. "What?" he demanded. "*What* did you accomplish? Why were you *here*?"

Nola laughed a small, easy laugh. "I was here for you, Kevin," she said, as though it should have been apparent all along.

"For *me*?" Kevin took a deep breath; tried to keep calm. "Look," he said, trying desperately to buy some time, "I . . . I don't understand what you're saying, but if what you say is true . . . please. Don't leave . . ."

"My time is up, Kevin," she said sadly. "I'm sorry."

Suddenly angry, Kevin snapped, "You can't! Not *yet.*"

"I have no *choice.*"

"*No!*" Kevin yelled. "Damn it, Nola, I can't lose you again!"

Nola said gently, "Like you lost me before?"

"Yes!" Kevin said. "Like before! Like—"

He stopped, suddenly aware of what he was saying. Part of him tried to deny what he was slowly coming to realize, while another part, a deeper part, knew the truth; had always known the truth. Nola smiled at him with love and sorrow.

"I left you too soon, my darling," she said, softly. "I didn't mean to, but I did."

Kevin shook his head; his voice was a hoarse whisper. "No . . . no, this isn't . . . *possible* . . ."

"But it is," Nola said. "You carried the grief with you all your life . . . and into the next."

Kevin was ashen; disbelieving.

"But I don't . . . I don't *remember* . . ."

"You remembered enough to be afraid," she said. "Afraid of love . . . afraid of losing it. I had to live out a life with you . . . to make up for the one we never had a chance to share . . . so the fear would go away."

Kevin's hands were trembling. "You knew?" he said, a trace of betrayal in his tone. "From the start?"

"No," Nola said quickly. "Only after I . . . lost the baby." She hesitated, her eyes glazed with the memory of that moment. "I wasn't just remembering my pain, Kevin . . . I was remembering my death."

Kevin shut his eyes, which he found were filled with tears. He knew, now. He may not have remembered, but he *knew.*

"After that," Nola said tonelessly, "it all became clear . . ."

Kevin put his hands to his head, holding his throbbing

temples, letting the tears flow. "I don't know if I . . . can believe *any* of this . . . ."

Nola nodded. "Perhaps that's just as well. You have a life to get back to." She fixed him with a sober gaze. "Don't let it slip *by*. Not *again*."

She stood, slowly, as Kevin took his hands away and stared up at her. "I have to leave now," she said again.

"No," Kevin said, and this time it wasn't an angry entreaty but a simple, respectful request; "wait. Just a minute more?"

He held up a hand, and Nola nodded her assent. Quickly he turned, went into his office, rummaged under a pile of books on his desk until he found the one he sought, as Nola watched with an amused, affectionate smile.

He came back into the room, one hand clutching the leatherbound book. He smiled. "Yeats, again," he said with a small laugh. "Do you remember the one called . . . 'When You Are Old'?"

The old woman with the child's smile nodded in recognition. "'When you are old and grey and full of sleep—'"

"Yes," Kevin said, flipping through the book, searching for the right page. "There's this one line . . ."

He found the page, looked up at Nola, and read:

"'How many loved your moments of glad grace,

"'And loved your beauty with love false or true—'"

His eyes shone; his voice was clear and strong.

"'But one man loved the pilgrim soul in you,

"'And loved the sorrows of your changing face . . .'"

Nola smiled a soft, gentle, happy smile.

"Goodbye—Robert," she said softly. "I love you."

Her figure turned from rose to amethyst, from frosted glass to clear crystal; Kevin watched, strangely without sadness, as the last trace of her faded from the display, leaving behind a vacant shaft of violet light, a shaft that would always seem empty to him, no matter what universes might fill it in the future. And yet for the first time he felt pride in its creation, in its completion—for the first time he felt happy, and unworried that that happiness might be taken away from him.

His reverie was interrupted by the sound of the phone; still clutching the small book of poetry in his hands, he picked up the receiver, only half conscious of what he was saying. "Yes?"

"Dr. Drayton, this is security. There's a woman here; says she's your wife. Should we let her in?"

Puzzled but not displeased, Kevin told them yes, by all means, send her in. He put aside the book, feeling an unaccustomed sense of anticipation and excitement at the thought of Carol; finding himself hurrying, in fact, to the door, pressing his palmprint against the scanner, counting the seconds it took for the burst of light to register his print and disarm the lock—

The door slid open, and Carol stood there, nervous but happy, a small anxious smile on her lips.

"You called for a taxi, mister?" she said lightly.

Kevin didn't understand, but discovered that he didn't care; all that mattered was that she was here, and she was real, and he could touch her. He embraced her, held her with a longing he had not felt in many months; he kissed her tenderly, and she eagerly returned it. He stroked the side of her face, brushing aside a strand of long brown hair, and they laughed shyly at one another, like teenagers on a first date. He took her in his arms again, let his mouth find hers, then let her rest her head on his shoulder while he stroked her back with his hands. And he marveled at the happiness he felt, at the absence of the stress and uneasiness that had separated them these many long months.

Carol rested her chin on his shoulder, his muscles so relaxed, the tension vanished; she put a hand to his other shoulder, stroked it gently, opened her eyes—

And blinked at what she saw in front of her.

"Kevin?" she said wonderingly. "What's that?"

They separated, and Kevin turned to find, floating in the middle of the hologram display, a sphere . . . a striped ball, identical to the one he had created to calm the five-year-old Nola. Slowly, he and Carol made their way to it as it danced a tuneless dance, moving to a melody they could not hear; they squatted down to study it, and Kevin thought again of Yeats, of the poem composed by a spurned and angry young man, which Kevin—once so angry himself—had oddly interpreted as a thank-you, and farewell:

And bending down beside the glowing bars,
Murmur, a little sadly, how Love fled—

Fled but not forgotten; never forgotten. It was all right to love her, even now, because he would never love anyone else in the same way he had loved *her*—just as he would never love anyone in exactly the same way he loved Carol. He would love them both, each in their own ways, one in life and one in memory.

—And paced upon the mountains overhead—

The ball suddenly dropped out of its floating dance, bounced off the floor of the display—and for the briefest of moments, its image seemed to spring *out* of the column of light, so real, so immediate, that Carol brought her hands up to catch it—but by the time she had, the afterimage had faded, like a retinal blur, a shadow at twilight—

And hid Her face amid a crowd of stars.

In the middle of the hologram display, a spiral nebula appeared once more, starry arms revolving in calm repose, and Kevin no longer felt afraid.

—for Asha